THE SECRET DETECTIVES

ELLA RISBRIDGER

Louise
    McCullagh
P6 Leith Walk

    nosy Primary
    crowschool.

First published in the UK in 2021 by Nosy Crow Ltd
The Crow's Nest, 14 Baden Place,
Crosby Row, London SE1 1YW

Nosy Crow and associated logos are trademarks and/or registered
trademarks of Nosy Crow Ltd

ISBN: 978 1 78800 600 2

A CIP catalogue record for this book is available from the British Library

Printed and bound in Great Britain by Clays Ltd, Elcograf S.p.A.
Typeset by Tiger Media

Papers used by Nosy Crow are made from wood grown in sustainable
forests.

1 3 5 7 9 10 8 6 4 2

www.nosycrow.com

for Leila
&
for Lettie

– E.R.

"*[She] made the long voyage to England under the care of an officer's wife, who was taking her children to leave them in a boarding school. She was very much absorbed with her own little boy and girl, and was rather glad to hand the child over to the woman … sent to meet her in London.*"

– *The Secret Garden*, Frances Hodgson Burnett

Chapter One: A Funny Little Thing

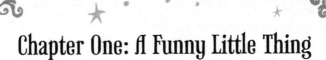

Week 1

*Calcutta, the Bay of Bengal; the Laccadive Sea,
the Arabian Sea*

Isobel disliked Letitia from the very start.

This was not because Letitia disliked *Isobel*, although she probably did.

Everybody disliked Isobel, perhaps because she herself disliked almost everybody.

People seemed to Isobel to be almost another species. They followed rules that Isobel had never been taught; as if they all knew the steps to a dance for which Isobel had never even heard the tune. They looked at each other for too long. They told lies for no reason. They all knew how to *be* with each other in ways Isobel did not, and she disliked them all. All the ones she knew, anyway – although it *was* true that she had never known many people, and very few people of her own age. There had been very few people at Steel's Way.

Steel's Way was the house outside Calcutta where Isobel had lived in the time before.

"You're Isobel Petty," Letitia had said, the first time they met. "And *I* am Miss Letitia Hartington-Davis." She said it as if Isobel ought to recognise her.

Her name sounded a little bit like a sneeze, thought Isobel: *le-TISH-ah, ah-TISH-oo, we all fall down.*

They had been standing on the dock at Calcutta, waiting to go aboard. "I'm ten years old. You're the same age as me."

"I'm actually eleven," said Isobel. This should, she felt, have given her superiority – but it was hard to feel superior to Letitia. Letitia had a great deal of self-possession; she was tall for ten, and very capable, and she knew it. She was also – even Isobel could see – a likeable sort of child. Grown-ups liked her, and this was one reason why Isobel did not. Isobel was not the kind of child grown-ups liked. She knew it perfectly well. Isobel was all wrong, in all the ways: she was untidy and sharp-faced and her cheeks were not pink or gold or brown but whitish yellow, like she had been growing under a log instead of in good Indian sunshine.

Her face was wrong, and her manners were wrong, and her clothes were wrong too. Her black dress, which should have been decent, was somehow both too tight and too loose. The fabric had been chosen carelessly from the end of a roll that had been sitting in the sun, so that in places (where it had been in shade) it was properly black, and in others (where the light had faded it) it was sort of brownish. Combined with her features – eyes a little too big and round for her face; nose and chin a little too sharp – it lent her something of the appearance of a house crow. And Isobel knew it.

It had not been so bad in the lawyer's office, but it had been pretty awful at the clergyman's house where she had been staying, and worse *again* the instant she met the Hartington-Davises. Mrs Colonel Hartington-Davis was a smart woman, and she liked her children to be smart, too. The little boy – Horace – was wearing a blue sailor suit for the voyage.

And Letitia, of course, was properly dressed too. She had been wearing a white muslin dress with blue bows on the bodice, and a large, wide-brimmed, white straw hat. The hat had blue bows on it, too, and so did Letitia's shoes and the end of her long, fair plait.

Letitia's hair, Isobel knew, was considered to be very beautiful. Mrs Colonel Hartington-Davis brushed it with one hundred strokes every morning with two shining silver hairbrushes. Isobel brushed her own hair, but hers was dark and very thin and tangled easily.

Isobel's mother had had hair like that. Isobel's mother had been exceptionally beautiful: she had worn gowns full of lace, and had enormous blue eyes, and Isobel had barely seen her at all. Isobel had lived in one part of the house at Steel's Way, and her mother and father in the other. The house at Steel's Way had been big and white, all on one level, and all around, the hills had been very green with tea and snakes.

Isobel had lived with her ayah. She had not loved her ayah – she had had six or seven different nannies by the time she was ten – but then again, she didn't really love anybody. Her mother and father had lived quite separately from her, in a world full of candlelight and wine glasses and dancing. Isobel had loved – when she was little – to slip away from her ayah, and hide and watch, and her mother had seemed to her then like a kind of fairy: a fairy princess with diamonds at her wrists and throat.

"Funny that the child should be so dark when you're so fair, Mrs Petty," someone had said to Isobel's mother once, a long time ago, in another life. Isobel had been hiding under the dining-room table. Isobel's mother had said distantly, "Well, she's rather a funny little thing altogether." And the man and Isobel's mother had both laughed, and gone away into the garden to look at the hibiscus flowers. *I am a funny little thing*, thought Isobel to herself, *I am a funny little thing*. And she could tell that her mother had not meant it in a nice way. But Isobel's mother was dead now. So was her father.

They had died, and Isobel had been left all alone in the bungalow in the hills, and she did not especially like to think about it. There had been a snake – small and brown and curious – and she had liked the snake. She missed the snake.

In any event, someone had come for her eventually, and brought her to Calcutta, and now she was here aboard ship with the Hartington-Davises.

This was because there had simply not been anyone else to see her to England. That was what the lawyer had told her. She had *almost* liked the lawyer. He had seemed to Isobel to be a person who told the truth. Her parents were dead; there was nobody to take care of her in India any more. There was in England a person who could take care of her; therefore she would go to England. There was nobody to take care of her on the boat to England; therefore she would have to go in the charge of some responsible lady with children of her own; therefore, Mrs Colonel Hartington-Davis. He had told Isobel all of this in exactly this way: one sentence after the other, very neat and obvious. She would be sent like a parcel: to the English address on the front, from the Indian address on the back. She would be labelled, equally neatly and obviously, and sent from one place to another. Isobel had approved of this, too.

That is to say, she had approved of the lawyer being straightforward. She had not approved of the plan, particularly. She had certainly not approved of Mrs Colonel Hartington-Davis.

Mrs Colonel Hartington-Davis would have been pretty, except for the crying. Her clothes were very smart, and she, like Letitia, had fair hair that shone from brushing, but her face was perpetually blotchy, and her hair often a little dishevelled from running her hands through it so often. She ran her hands through it whenever she had a headache. She often had headaches. This was because she missed her husband – *the* Colonel Hartington-Davis himself – who was staying in India without her, and without the children. She was taking the children to boarding school.

"Do you want to go to boarding school?" Isobel asked Letitia. "I wouldn't want to go to *school*." But Letitia just put her nose in the air and said that it was probably actually better to go to boarding school than to go to where Isobel was going.

Isobel was going to live with her uncle, if they ever got to England. Isobel had never been to England, and it was a long way off yet. Three weeks at least, even if they made good time. Part of Isobel hoped they would not make good time. England sounded very cold and unpleasant, and her uncle, worse.

England, the uncle and the rain. A new life. That was what the lawyer said, and Mrs Colonel Hartington-Davis too.

The first life – the ayah, the hills – had been one kind of life; and the next life – the uncle, the rain – would be another. And in between there was this: three weeks of the ship *Marianna*. Three weeks of the Hartington-Davises. And three weeks of the ocean: boundless, infinite and touching the sky in all directions.

There was almost nothing to do on board the ship. This was not something Isobel minded: she was used to not having things to do. There had never been very much to do at home in Steel's Way.

Once, long ago, she had had an ayah who told her stories. She had liked that then. But that ayah had gone away when she was quite a little girl of five, and the next ayah didn't tell any stories at all. Isobel liked stories about things that really happened. She liked to know everything that really happened, and that was the

7

reason for the notebook.

She carried the notebook everywhere, and she wrote everything in it. She wrote down everything that happened, and everything that she saw. Isobel was a very noticing kind of child: she was good at seeing people, and she was even better at taking notes on what she had seen. She liked looking at things and naming them; she liked seeing what people were doing, and putting it into words. She liked matching what people did to the word for it, like playing Snap, between the world and the describing of the world: it made it all easier to understand.

She was keeping the notebook tucked into the top of her knickers for now, underneath her frock. It seemed safer that way, at least until she was sure what kind of people the Hartington-Davises were. In fact, she thought, until she was sure what kind of people were aboard the ship at all. Nobody had cared much at Steel's Way, but they might care on the *Marianna*. What she really wanted was to go off on her own and write everything down about the *Marianna* right away, but it struck her at once that this was going to be rather more difficult on board ship.

"Why don't you girls go off and play?" said Mrs Colonel Hartington-Davis, the first morning.

"I don't *play*," said Isobel.

"All children play," said Mrs Colonel Hartington-Davis.

"Not me," said Isobel. They were in the cabin: a *stateroom*, Mrs Colonel Hartington-Davis called it. There was a porthole, and there were two bunks – one for Letitia and one for Isobel – and a door going off it to Mrs Colonel Hartington-Davis's room, which she was sharing with Horace.

Mrs Colonel Hartington-Davis had been crying in the night – Isobel had heard her – and this morning she already had a headache, which meant they couldn't go up to the dining room for breakfast.

They had not eaten in the dining room the night before, either. It was very irritating. How was Isobel supposed to find out who was on board if they never went to the dining room? The night before, they had only managed to get on board and eat a little supper in their cabin, and immediately after that Mrs Colonel Hartington-Davis had told them to get into nightgowns and into bed.

It had been an awful bother getting all the buttons on the new frock undone by herself, and a worse bother getting them done up again in the morning, but she had managed. She was rather proud of herself.

"Letitia plays, don't you, Lettie?" Mrs Colonel Hartington-Davis, who had no intention of dropping the subject, was finishing Letitia's plait.

"Why do you do her hair?" said Isobel.

"I'm sorry, dear?" Mrs Colonel Hartington-Davis wasn't really listening to Isobel.

"Why doesn't her ayah do her hair?"

"What's an ayah?" said Horace, from the floor.

"It's the person who does your hair," said Isobel to Horace. "The person who looks after you."

"Mummy looks after me," said Letitia, smugly.

"And me," said Horace.

"Lettie doesn't have an ayah," said Mrs Colonel Hartington-Davis.

"Nor do I, now," said Isobel. "She died too."

Mrs Colonel Hartington-Davis shot her an alarmed glance. *She thinks I'm a funny little thing*, thought Isobel. *Or something worse.*

"*Passed on*, I think," Mrs Colonel Hartington-Davis said to Isobel.

"Passed on?" said Isobel.

"The ayah passed on," said Mrs Colonel Hartington-Davis, firmly.

"Passed on where?" said Isobel.

"Isobel," said Mrs Colonel Hartington-Davis.

"Please don't be impertinent."

"I'm not," said Isobel. "She didn't pass on anywhere. She just died."

"It's not very polite to say *died*," said Letitia.

"Don't listen to her, Letitia," said Mrs Colonel Hartington-Davis. "Don't listen to her, please."

"I can't help listening," said Letitia, reasonably.

"Died like the chicks died when the snake got them?" said Horace, suddenly, from the floor.

"If she died," said Isobel, "why can't I *say* died?"

"Children," said Mrs Colonel Hartington-Davis. She finished tying Letitia's bow and put her hands to her forehead. She looked, Isobel thought, as if she might cry again. "Children. I am getting one of my headaches. Will you all please go and play? Girls, take Horace with you."

Almost everything gave Mrs Colonel Hartington-Davis headaches. Reading. Arguing. Perfume. The sun.

"I told you that I don't play," said Isobel. "I simply don't."

"I'm not playing with girls," Horace said.

But Letitia said, "Leave them with *me*, Mummy. I'll take them both out on to the deck."

"I don't need taking anywhere," said Isobel, but Mrs

Colonel Hartington-Davis was already lying back on Letitia's bunk with her hand over her eyes.

Letitia took Horace's hand and led him out of the stateroom. He went with her willingly enough, and Isobel followed, dragging her feet. Her legs were hot, and her stockings had wrinkled around her ankles in a way that was already uncomfortable.

"Mummy gets headaches," said Letitia knowledgeably. "It's because she misses Daddy. I miss Daddy too, but we'll see him again soon." She said it like she was copying something somebody had said to her.

"I won't see mine again," said Isobel. "He's dead too." She wanted Letitia to feel bad about this, but Letitia barely seemed to notice.

"Is everyone you know dead?" asked Horace.

"I don't know many people," said Isobel.

"But are the ones you know all dead?"

"Probably," said Isobel. "Except you."

"Have you ever been on a ship before?" said Letitia. She was changing the subject, Isobel knew, and that was like a grown-up person also.

Isobel said nothing.

"I've been on ships four times," said Letitia. "Including this one. I've been to England twice, counting the time I was born there. You weren't."

"I don't care," said Isobel. She did, a bit, but she didn't really know why.

"You've never even been to England even once, to be born," said Letitia. "How *extraordinary*." She made the last word very long.

"I haven't been to England," said Horace.

"But *you're* English," said Letitia. "Because you're my brother and I was born in England, which makes me English and that makes you English because you can't have a brother and a sister that are different. But *she* isn't."

"I don't want to be English," said Isobel, fiercely.

"What are you then?" said Letitia. "Are you a *native*?" There was suddenly something unpleasant about Letitia's voice: something hard and brittle, like sugar cooked too long. It sounded not like Letitia's ordinary voice at all. It was, Isobel thought again, like she was copying something she'd heard someone else say.

Isobel flushed. The colour looked peculiar in her sallow cheeks and gave her suddenly an appearance of liveliness that she did not otherwise possess. "I'm not a *native*."

"Servants are natives," said Letitia. "Perhaps you're a sort of servant."

"I'm not," said Isobel, hotly.

13

She could feel herself getting crosser. She had always had a temper, but she was starting to think her temper might not dent Letitia at all. She had never had to argue with a person her own age before. And Letitia might be a special case. Besides, she was not entirely sure about this argument.

She *had* only met natives – Indians – who were servants: that part was true. It was also true, of course, that she had not met many people. The bungalow in the hills where she had grown up was very far from anywhere, and nobody brought their children to play with her.

But her mother and her father had only white friends; the officers and officers' wives who came for the dinner and the candles and the dancing were all white people. Isobel was quite certain that she, herself, was a white person too. And it was true that the native servants had to salaam to her and bow to her and do everything she said. That was simply the way it was. It had never occurred to Isobel to question any of it before, but when Letitia said it, it started to sound rather unpleasant. It started to sound – even to Isobel – rather unfair.

But Isobel did not know anything different: that was the trouble. It had always been this way, and this was the way all the grown-ups had made the world, and it had never occurred to Isobel to question it for one minute until Letitia had started calling her – Isobel! – a native herself. She did not want to be a native. She did not want to be a servant. But it struck her suddenly that perhaps not even natives *wanted* to be servants, and it gave her a peculiar feeling deep down in her stomach. It made her feel rather sick. She thought it might be the movement of the ship.

Letitia started up the stairs again, Horace trailing behind her like a blanket, and then turned back suddenly. "If you're not a native and you're not English, what *are* you?"

Isobel said nothing.

"You have to be something," said Letitia. "You have to be something. One thing. You have to choose. And you're not English, so what can you be?"

"What can you *be*?" Horace echoed.

"I can be what I want," said Isobel, but she felt it was rather a weak answer.

"Nobody gets to be what they *want*," said Letitia, scornfully, just like a grown-up, and she and Horace went up the stairs through a heavy metal door, out on to the deck, and outside the sun was very bright indeed.

Isobel looked after them, and then looked to the

left and to the right. There was nobody else about, and Letitia and Horace were not looking back. And so Isobel slipped away, down the long forking corridors, into the belly of the ship.

Chapter Two: And All Who Sail In Her

Week 1, Day 7
The Arabian Sea

They were seven days – eight nights – in when Isobel saw it.

She had discovered on the fourth night that it was possible to get out on deck without being seen. There were two corridors of cabins – Row A and Row B – and their cabin was on Row A. This was much better, Isobel thought, because Row A had the stairs and the door to the deck.

To get out on to the deck, the inhabitants of Row B had to walk all along the corridor and through the heavy fire door that led to Row A before they even got a sniff of salty air. The door between the corridors was propped open in the day, but at night it was latched shut in case of fire, and it was so heavy that it took the strongest steward to open it in the mornings.

But Row A could slip out on deck any time they liked.

Isobel had by now a reasonably good grasp of the geography of the ship. This meant, in practice, their part of the ship, because it was impossible to get anywhere else.

It was a mail ship, really: much smaller than the ordinary ships, or so Letitia said. They were going by mail ship because there had not been any places on the proper ship.

There were two parts to the ship: a part for the crew, and a part for the passengers like Isobel. She had tried hard to get into the crew part, just to see, but a burly sailor turned her round and sent her back up to her own deck.

"You don't belong down here," he said, and it was true: all the crew were big men, and she was a small girl. Even if he hadn't seen her, she thought, grimly, there was no way of getting through. There was no way for a sailor to get on to the passenger deck, and no way for a passenger to get on to the sailors' deck. Only the captain and the purser could go between the two, and they went through the captain's own rooms to do it, and the captain's rooms were locked at all times. Isobel was a resourceful child, but even she had to admit defeat.

It might have been just as well, though, because there were a lot of people to watch on the ship without counting sailors too. *Thirty*, she thought on the first morning, and then, on the second day – when she had counted all the labels on the stateroom doors – *twenty-seven*. Twenty-seven people to watch, including her own party, and two ugly little babies who were the twin offspring of a widowed major from Colombo. Twenty-seven was a lot of people, and for some children that might have made watching them all at once rather difficult. But not for Isobel. She was good at this, and she enjoyed it: it was *like* playing, she supposed, but better. It was *like* a story, but real.

Isobel had by now matched almost all the names on the stateroom doors to the people she had seen on deck. She was missing only two people called Khan, whose name was on the cabin door next to theirs. They did not seem to come to meals, and Isobel wrote this down in her notebook as suspicious.

There did not seem to be anybody else suspicious in the passenger cabins. A pair of Russian sisters, one thin, one huge. A very wealthy American lady – Mrs Caroline Drake – who had been born in New York, and who wore diamonds round her neck and pinned to her silk turban (a selection of which she had in all the colours of the rainbow), and whose husband was dead. Isobel despised Mrs Drake because she had said to Isobel on the first day, in her high silly voice, "You're an orphan? I'm an orphan too, dear, so I *understand*." Isobel had glared at her and run away. Nobody with so many diamonds could understand anything. And it was different for adults to be orphans.

A French family comprised mainly of heiresses; a thin, bald Swede who did not like the sea at all. "God bless her and all who sail in her," said the Swede, patting the side of the ship as they pulled away from the dock, and that was the last cheerful thing anyone had heard him say. He had looked rather green ever since. Then there was an English lord famous for stargazing, who had a twirly moustache and mop of golden curls to rival even Letitia's; his Indian valet, who fussed about on deck and wore his black hair slicked forward across his forehead like it had been drawn on with paint; then the mysterious Khans on one side of their cabin; and a German doctor – Doktor Weiss – on the other. Their cabin, thought Isobel crossly, was quite the least interesting of all. There was nothing *to* Letitia; she was the most infuriating girl Isobel had ever met. She would have been the most infuriating girl Isobel

20

had ever met even if Isobel had met hundreds of girls. It wasn't just the shiny hair and the clean frocks; it was that she was always exactly where Isobel wanted to be.

It couldn't be that Letitia was a noticer – nobody who looked like Letitia could be a noticer – but somehow, *somehow*, she always seemed to see exactly when Isobel was hoping to slip off by herself.

Letitia was always asking meaningfully, "And where are *you* going, Isobel?" or saying, slyly, "Actually, I think I'll come with *you*, Isobel," or simply *following* Isobel about like a spy and asking endless questions about what she was doing and where she was going and what she was writing in her notebook.

Isobel had tried to hide the notebook, but Letitia saw it anyway. At least she knew that Letitia had not looked inside the notebook. Isobel kept it under her pillow when she was asleep, and the rest of the time tucked safely between layers of clothes. That was some comfort, Isobel supposed, but not much. She wished Letitia hadn't seen the notebook at all. She hadn't thought Letitia would have even been *interested*, but then, Letitia asked questions about everything. Letitia asked people questions about the dullest things Isobel could imagine, twinkling her big blue eyes at the purser and asking him about his own little girl onshore, as if anybody cared about people who weren't even there.

The only time Isobel could be sure Letitia wasn't going to start asking questions was when Letitia was asleep, which did not exactly leave Isobel much choice.

Isobel disliked Letitia more than she could remember disliking anyone, and since Isobel had never liked anybody in her life, that was saying a lot. But it was because of Letitia, really, that Isobel saw it at all.

It was quite late at night, on the eighth night of their voyage, and Isobel had slipped out of the stateroom up on to the deck.

She thought it might be a bit dangerous, but she wasn't sure she minded. She thought she might quite like danger: it was exciting.

In any case, because their stateroom was in Row A, it was not difficult to get out on deck. She could get back quite easily if something went wrong. And she had done this already once before, three nights ago – and it seemed to her to be the best possible adventure on board ship. It had been *wonderful*.

There had been nobody about. On the floor below – on the crew deck – she had seen a sailor moving steadily about on watch, and if she craned her neck round the corner she could see the captain's cabin with the light on and the dark figure of the captain silhouetted. But nobody else. It had been entirely deserted.

You could get to the deck two ways: the stairs at the end of Row A, or a narrow ladder at the other side up to the captain's cabin. There was a iron railing all around it, painted white, that came up a little higher than a grown-up's waist.

The first-class deck was shaped sort of like a big fat L. The long part was long enough to have a really good run (or would have been, if she had been a running-about sort of child) and the short part was deep and wide, and set all over with deckchairs.

The ladder was in the middle of the long part of the L, and the door from Row A opened up on the end of the short part of the L.

On the short part of the L – at a right angle to the door – there was a little jutting-out part, like a platform. The platform part was directly over the sea. This was so that you could stand and look down at the water far below without having to look at the crew deck underneath. This was very important to the passengers: Letitia said so. It was Letitia who had explained to Isobel why the platform part was there. It stuck out above the ocean, and by the edge was a brass telescope fixed to the railing so that anyone who wanted could see how the ocean stretched boundless and far, a world without end.

Isobel had marked out in her plan the places where everybody ordinarily seemed to like to sit: the French heiresses liked to sit at the end of the short part of the L, for example, because the wall in which the door was set sheltered their elaborate hair from the sea breeze. The Russian sisters, the Misses Karamazova, liked to stand by the railings on the corner of the L clutching each other and counting down the time until their next cup of tea. Next to them stood the German doctor, complaining to anyone who would listen that the light from his window woke him in the morning. He looked very tired. The thin Swede liked to stand briefly in the Row A doorway before retreating to the comfortable lounge to drink hot chocolate. It seemed far too warm to Isobel for hot chocolate, but he drank cups and cups of it. (Perhaps that was why he was so green.) And Isobel wrote it all down.

She had only been on the short part of the L so far by herself at night. She wanted, tonight, to go all over the deck: to listen to the waves without everybody's voices getting in the way; to look at the faint lights of the ship reflecting in the dark sea; to look at the white

24

crests of waves against the side of the ship.

And she was determined to get out tonight. So she did. It was late. She had heard Mrs Colonel Hartington-Davis go to bed; heard the creak of bedsprings all along the corridor. The German doctor said something to the steward, and then there was the sound of people going down the corridor and the big door closing. Probably fetching one of his horrible hot salt waters. Isobel made a mental note to write it down once she had her notebook.

She waited until she was sure Letitia was sound asleep – that irritating snuffly breathing – and slid noiselessly out of bed. Getting dressed would be too much trouble. Instead she put a shawl round the shoulders of her nightgown and put her feet into her bedroom slippers. She picked up her notebook and quietly, quietly let herself out into the corridor.

As soon as she had stood up she'd wondered whether she had made a mistake. The waves were much rougher than when she had gone to bed. The boat pitched and rolled rather alarmingly. As she went up the stairs and heaved open the heavy door that led to the deck, she saw already that the floor was slippery with spray. The sound of the waves was very loud; as loud as the engine, or louder.

The lamps were all extinguished on the deck, except one on the corner. It was dark, and the air was thick and wet. It was much less good than it had been the first time; much more tricky. But she had made up her mind.

Isobel went along cautiously, one arm against the wall. She would go along by the wall, away from the door, until she was opposite the platform. And then cross the deck quickly to get to the railing. Yes, that was all right. She could keep her grip up here. She wanted to see through the telescope.

She sidled along, looking mostly at her own feet. But as she turned her face to the platform and stepped away from the wall, something stopped her in her tracks.

There was somebody already there.

Two somebodies. Two dark figures. Two dark figures on the platform by the telescope. One of them had a lantern – a bright, flickering yellow light. Even by that light she could see neither of their faces.

They were saying something Isobel couldn't hear over the waves.

She held her breath.

She heard, clearly between a gap in the waves, one say to the other, "No, what?"

The other said, "It won't do, you know!"

And then the ship pitched. One figure stooped, and suddenly, as Isobel watched, this first figure tipped the other over the railing, and into the darkness of the endless sea.

They seemed to fall for a long time. There was no splash, or if there was it was lost in the waves. Isobel was frozen to the spot for a moment – and then her common sense caught up with her, and she stepped back quickly into the shadows.

And to her horror her elbow bumped against something – something warm – something warm and soft and alive – and she heard a sharp intake of breath. She was not alone. There was somebody else in the shadows, too.

"Shhh," hissed the somebody else, through gritted teeth, and Isobel realised it was a boy of about her own height. He put his hand on her arm. "Stay still and we might just—"

But the figure at the railings was turning towards them, lantern in hand. There was no time to think. They had no time to wait. Any second he would see them. There was no way of getting back to the door in time, and besides, he could easily follow them down into the corridor – and then there would be nowhere else to run but their own cabins. There was nothing they could do

– they were stuck – but then they had a stroke of luck. A huge wave crashed up and on to the deck, wetting them all with salt spray; the figure turned back to the railing; and Isobel saw their chance and took it.

"Run!" she whispered. And they ran.

Chapter Three: Holmes And Watson

Still Week 1, Day 7, very late
Still the Arabian Sea

They ran. They couldn't stop to see if the figure had seen or heard them. Isobel hoped the waves had drowned out their footsteps, but she couldn't be sure. They ran, all across the deck, rounding the prow of the ship, gripping the railing that ran along the inside wall of the deck as if their lives depended on it. Their lives *did* depend on it, Isobel thought.

She thought suddenly of the dizzying drop down to the waves – that body falling almost noiselessly over the rails – and felt terribly, suddenly sick.

They were both soaked with sea spray, and Isobel was already tired, and then the boy ducked suddenly under an upturned lifeboat. Isobel, without thinking too much about it, followed behind. The boy slid into one end and Isobel into the other. They sat silently for a little while. The sound of the waves went on and the boat dipped and pitched. She felt better for sitting down. There were no footsteps following them that Isobel could hear, but she was frightened nonetheless.

"Did you *see* that?" she said, when she thought it was safe, and when they had both got enough breath to speak. She was whispering.

The boy nodded.

"It's a *crime*," said Isobel.

"It's an actual crime," whispered the boy, distinctly. In the lifeboat it was hard to see him properly; he looked about twelve, with a mass of dark hair that seemed to grow out in all directions. He was wearing pyjamas: striped ones. His face was all in shadow. "Like in books."

"I don't like books," said Isobel.

"Don't you?" The boy sounded rather shocked. "Why don't you like books?"

"I don't especially like anything," said Isobel, truthfully, and once she'd said it she saw that it sounded rather sad.

"Gosh," said the boy.

"I like some things," said Isobel.

"What things?"

"I like finding things out."

"Well, exactly." The boy nodded his head vigorously

in the direction they had come from. "*Exactly*. That's the point. That's what we're talking about. Finding things out. Finding out what happened out there. We know what it was, of course, but not why. And not who. An actual crime! Like in Sherlock Holmes."

"I know about Sherlock Holmes," said Isobel. She did, a bit. She had seen some of it in a paper once.

"Well, that's something," said the boy. "Anyway it's a crime, and we saw it. Didn't we?"

Isobel nodded.

"We saw it, and we can find out who did it, and why. Then we'll be in the papers. We'll be Holmes and Watson."

"I'm Holmes," Isobel said, quickly, before he could.

"I'm Holmes," said the boy. "You can't be Holmes. You're a girl."

"I can't be Watson either then."

"It matters less about Watson," said the boy. "Anyway I've got the pipe." He took a pipe out of the pocket of his pyjamas. It was very old, Isobel saw, and he had chewed the end of it until the stem was bent out of shape.

"It's a horrible pipe," said Isobel.

"It is not." He stuck it back in his mouth and drew in a great bubbly gasp of air through it. "It's a Holmes pipe. A genuine Holmes pipe."

"I don't believe you," said Isobel.

"I don't care," said the boy. "What's your name?"

"Sherlock Holmes," said Isobel.

The boy wrinkled his nose at her. "Your real name."

"Why should I tell you?"

He shrugged. "I'll tell you mine."

"Go on, then."

"You first."

They looked at each other, considering.

Then Isobel, to her surprise, found herself saying, "My name is Isobel Petty."

"Petty by name, petty by nature?"

"What?"

"It's a joke," said the boy. "You know what petty means, don't you? Sort of small and quarrel-ish. Petty is your name, so you must *be* petty."

Isobel frowned at him. "That isn't how it works," she said. "Now you."

The boy hesitated. "Sherlock Holmes," he said, gesturing with his pipe.

"Play fair," said Isobel.

"Fine," said the boy. He ran his free hand through his dark hair so that it stood on end the other way instead. "It's Sam. Sameer Khan."

"Khan!" said Isobel before she could stop herself. "You're in the cabin next to ours. You don't come to dinner."

The boy wrinkled his nose. "No. The food isn't very good."

"I think it's perfectly acceptable," said Isobel stiffly.

"Well, it isn't." said the boy. He was very firm. "As I say, anyway, I'm Sameer Khan. But you can call me Sam."

"*You* can call *me* Miss Petty," said Isobel, and the boy – Sam – started to laugh.

"You see what I mean?" he said, but Isobel didn't. "Miss Petty suits you," he added.

"No it doesn't," said Isobel.

"Miss Petty. You could be Miss Quarrel. Or Miss Cross. Or Miss Argumentative."

"I'm not argumentative," said Isobel.

"You are," Sam said, and added, thoughtfully, "I am, too."

"Are you?"

"Mostly. It's not one of my better qualities."

"What *are* your better qualities?" Isobel said.

"That's an extremely personal question," said Sam. He drew his knees up to his chin and sucked on his pipe again.

"That's a disgusting sound," said Isobel. It was, too.

"Sorry. It helps me think," he said, but he put the pipe down on the floor beside him, and Isobel looked around the lifeboat for the first time. The deck beneath them had been covered with a thick, scratchy blanket. There were books everywhere, and beside Isobel a stack of tins: some empty, and some unopened. "Condensed milk", she read on one label, and on another, "Sardines".

"Where are we?"

Sam looked pleased. "Welcome to my office," he said, solemnly, and Isobel felt an astonishing urge to laugh. She was not a laughing child, as a rule; there had been very few things in her life so far that had ever struck her as funny.

"This is a lifeboat," said Isobel, when she had stopped wanting to laugh. It had become clear to her quite suddenly that Sam would be upset if she laughed, and it had become equally clear to her equally suddenly that she did not want Sam to be upset. She did not normally mind upsetting anybody. "This is a lifeboat, not an office."

"It's hard to have an office on a ship," said Sam, patiently. "I have to share a cabin with my father, and he takes up all the available desk space with his work. He doesn't support me particularly, you know. He doesn't appreciate that I need an office too. I don't think he appreciates the seriousness of my ambition."

"Oh," said Isobel. She, herself, had never had any particular ambition to anything.

"I need an office for my journalism," said Sam.

"What's journalism?"

"Newspapers," said Sam. "I mean to keep several. I mean to be a proprietor. That means a person who owns newspapers. If you have a newspaper, you can do anything. You can decide what people think. You can run investigations. You can solve crimes. I mean to be a kind of Sherlock Holmes, except extremely rich. Of course, Holmes is rich, but only…" He paused. "Sporadically rich. Do you know what 'sporadically' means?"

Isobel shook her head.

"Don't feel bad about it," he said, kindly. "I know a lot of words. A prodigious quantity. 'Prodigious' means 'a lot', by the way. I'm in training for when I'm a proprietor. 'Sporadically' means 'only sometimes'. Sherlock Holmes is only rich when he has a rich client, which is only sometimes, and I mean to be rich every day."

"That's sensible," said Isobel. It did sound sensible.

"I mean to be exceedingly rich and have several

newspapers of my own and write for them all. You can write in them too."

"Thank you," said Isobel. He had a way of talking, she thought, which made you like him. He had a way of saying things that made you believe them.

"This will be our first investigation," said Sam. "We'll work as partners. Holmes (me) and Watson (you). Petty and Khan. We'll find it out, which is what you like, and then we'll write it down." He stopped, and nodded at her notebook. "*Do* you write things down?"

Isobel hesitated. She did not particularly want to talk about the things she liked to write.

"Stories? Poems?"

"Absolutely not," said Isobel, with feeling. "Absolutely none of that."

"But you do write things?" said Sam.

She nodded.

"I knew you did," said Sam, smugly. "I knew it. You were out on deck just so you could write it down, weren't you?"

Isobel said nothing.

"You were," said Sam. "And so was I. That's when I knew we were going to be friends."

"Are we friends?" said Isobel, astonished.

"Not yet," said Sam. "Not yet. But we will be. We'll

have to be, if we're going to be business partners. You do *want* to, don't you?"

And she found herself inexplicably saying yes.

Sam stretched out his legs in front of him and tipped his head back so that it touched the side of the lifeboat. He yawned, and Isobel found herself yawning too. She wondered what time it was, and as if he'd read her mind, Sam pulled out a large silver fob watch from the pocket of his striped pyjamas. Her eyes were getting used to the dark, and it glinted in the dim half-light, but still, she wondered how he could see the face.

"We'd better cut along to bed," he said, ruefully. "It's nearly three."

She wondered what time it had been when she got up; she seemed to have lost all sense of how long any of it had taken. Surely it could only have been a moment or two, but it felt like forever. Forever since she'd crept out of the stateroom; forever since she'd pushed open the door; forever since the man had … fallen.

Forever since she'd found the lifeboat. Forever since she'd found Sam.

"We'll investigate in the morning," he said, briskly, interrupting her thoughts. "I'll come to breakfast. Don't forget."

"As if I could *forget*," Isobel said, scornfully.

37

He looked at her strangely, thoughtfully. "No. I don't think you're an absent-minded sort of person."

"No." She nodded. "I won't forget."

Just then the boat tipped and a thick patter of spray landed on the deck and the canvas roof above them. It was cosy in the lifeboat, and made cosier by the sound of the water; the way it's even nicer to be indoors when you know it's bad outdoors, the way a lit window is more magic at night than in the day.

"Will you bring your notebook to breakfast?"

"I bring it everywhere."

It was his turn to nod. "I thought you did. Will you write this down in it?"

"Letitia will be asleep when I get back and I don't want to wake her up. She's the girl in my stateroom."

"Is she your sister?"

Isobel made a face. "Not likely. She's my companion's daughter." Then she added, somewhat against her will, "I don't like her."

Sam said, "Is she the girl with the blonde hair?"

He sounded sort of admiring, and Isobel decided all at once that she hated him, too. Her damp nightgown was drying off in the heat of the night, and clinging to her legs, and she felt particularly spindly.

She nodded.

"I've seen her."

"Did you see me?"

"I saw both of you. And the little boy. What's his name?"

"Horace," said Isobel.

"Like the poet," said Sam.

"What?"

"The *Roman* poet," said Sam.

Isobel shrugged. She was not, in point of fact, exactly sure who the Romans were either.

"There's a famous Roman called Horace. He was a poet. Do you not do Latin at your school?"

"I don't go to school," said Isobel, and it sounded funny even to her.

But Sam didn't seem surprised. "I suppose you do lessons at home. Girls do. But you'd think you'd know about Latin things, even if you are a girl."

"I can do anything you can do," said Isobel, even though she wasn't sure it was true. "Girls can do anything boys can do."

Sam looked scornful at first, and then when she said nothing more, merely thoughtful. "I don't really know any," he said, after a minute. "Girls, I mean. I'm an only child."

"So am I," said Isobel. Then she added, "And I haven't

any friends."

"You've got me," said Sam, cheerfully. "You're the first girl I've ever decided to be friends with since I was quite young. I suppose, speaking purely pragmatically, it's because there aren't any boys on the boat. Pragmatic means practical," he added, as an afterthought.

"Aren't there?"

"Aren't there what?"

"Any boys on the boat?"

"Well, have you seen any?"

"No," said Isobel. "But then I hadn't seen you, either."

"True, o King!" He brought the pipe to his mouth again, caught sight of Isobel's face in the half-light and put it down. "Anyway, we're friends – you and I, I mean – because we're in this together. The investigation." He added, magnanimously, "In any case, I don't know many boys who would have come out on deck in a storm to record the facts of the matter. So perhaps I'd have been friends with you even if there were lots of boys on board."

He stopped and looked at her. "Yes, I think so. I think you're interesting."

Isobel was not easily surprised, but it was turning out, one way or another, to be a very surprising sort of evening.

She said, carefully, "Why do you think I'm interesting?"

In the darkness she saw him shrug. "Well, you came on deck. That's one thing. You knew it was a crime. That's another thing. You didn't go inside to get a grown-up. That's a third thing. You didn't make a fuss about my office. That's a fourth thing. You've got a notebook. That's a fifth thing. You don't go to school and you don't like books. That's another two things. You don't like anything, which is interesting in and of itself. And you say things I don't exactly expect."

Isobel did not know what to say. She settled for "Goodness," and regretted it immediately. It didn't seem to convey any of the things she meant – but then, she wasn't exactly sure either what she *did* mean. It seemed to her suddenly that nobody had ever looked at her before; that nobody had ever noticed things about her in the way that Sam noticed everything about her. What if Sam were to write about her the way she wrote about everyone else? She shook her head, quickly.

"What?" Sam was looking at her in the dark; she could see the shine of his eyes.

Then he yawned again, and the spell was broken. "We'd better trot off to bed, like I say. Or we'll be useless tomorrow. And tomorrow we'll be the only witnesses."

"Witnesses?"

He looked at her like she was stupid.

"To the crime."

"Of course, the *crime*," said Isobel, scornfully in her turn. "It was murder."

He nodded. "Murder. Gosh. You spend all your life hoping to see one, and then it comes along when you least expect it."

"Have you spent your life hoping to see one?" Isobel asked.

He sounded astonished. "Of course. Haven't you? And we saw it. Everyone will want to ask us what we saw when they find out someone is missing."

"Did you see who it was?"

"Not really," Sam admitted. "No. But I saw it happen, of course, which the murderer wasn't counting on. And we'll know who is missing tomorrow because there will be a big hue and cry about it. A hue and cry," he explained, "is when everyone gets flustered and starts shouting."

"I wonder who it was," Isobel said, thoughtfully. "It looked like a man who went overboard. And like another man who pushed him."

"Most murderers are," said Sam. "Not all, but most. Do you know who's aboard?" Then he yawned again, and shook his head regretfully. "No, not now. I'm rather tired and I won't do my best detecting when I'm tired. Even Holmes has to rest."

"You're *not* Holmes," said Isobel, automatically. "Stop saying you're Holmes. You're Sameer Khan."

"He's not the only detective," Sam said. "There are lots. Do you know Wilkie Collins?"

Isobel tried to look as if she knew exactly what he was talking about. Then she said, "I've been making a list of passengers. To write down what they do."

"Oh, *excellent* egg!" Sam was pleased, and this – unexpectedly – made Isobel pleased, too. She felt her cheeks go pink and was glad it was dark. "Jolly good work, detective. It's more like a journalist than ever if you've already written down what people do. Can I look at your list in the morning?"

Isobel hesitated. "I don't like people to look at my notebook."

"But I'm not *people*," he said easily. "I'm Sam Khan, and I'm the Holmes to your Watson. Or the other way round, if you like. I'm not fussy. Say I can look."

And once again, to her own amazement, though not at all to his, she found herself saying yes.

They slipped out of the lifeboat and made their way along the wet deck, holding on to the rail, and through the lit door of the row of cabins.

The corridors were lit with a low gas jet at night and everything seemed very soft. Suddenly Sam stooped down and picked something up.

"Look!" he whispered. "It could be a clue!"

"What is it?"

It was a lump of pinkish stuff, dusted with white.

"What is it?" Sam stared. "It's Turkish delight. It's sweets."

"Sweets aren't clues," said Isobel, scornfully.

"Probably not," said Sam. "It's quite clean, though. It can't have been here very long. Do you want some? I'll share."

"Share?" said Isobel. "But you found it."

"Go on, Holmes," said Sam. He broke it in half and Isobel took it. "That's a pact," he said. "We've broken bread together now. That's in the Bible. Once you've broken bread together, you're friends."

"Friends?" said Isobel.

"Friends," said Sam. The Turkish delight was powdery and floral, and she wasn't sure she liked it very much. But she ate it anyway.

"Friends. Goodnight, Miss Petty," whispered Sam, and Isobel whispered, "Goodnight, Watson."

Chapter Four: Impossible Things Before Breakfast
Week 2, Day 1
Even further across the Arabian Sea

Isobel was dreaming, and she was afraid.

She was not used to being afraid. She did not have the imagination, for one thing, and she was not prone to nightmares. But she was frightened now.

Something about salt spray, and stacks of tins, and secret study rooms inside sailing boats, and among it all some slippery figure like a vast silver fish sliding just out of her grasp, sliding, slipping, falling, and the ground was shaking, and as she reached out to snatch the figure from the air and cram it back into one of the tins she saw that she, too, was falling, but perhaps she could catch it in mid-air...

But somebody was saying her name, and then she was awake.

"Isobel! Isobel, wake up!"

"I nearly caught him," she said, indistinctly, and then she remembered it all in a rush: a queer cold feeling that went completely through her, because the dream was partly a dream and partly it was true. Somebody was dead; and she had been out in the night; and she had met Sam; and there had been a crime; and somebody was dead; and she, Isobel, had seen it. She had seen it all.

"You were shouting," Letitia said. She was sitting on the edge of the bed, watching her. Her hair had not yet been brushed out, but her plaits had come undone and her golden hair stood out around her head like a halo.

"I wasn't shouting," said Isobel. She thought she might have been.

"You were. You said 'Stop!' and then you shouted something else."

"What did I say?"

"I don't know. Something. You weren't being very clear."

"I was asleep," said Isobel, aggrieved. "You can't hold people responsible for what they say when they're asleep."

"You've been asleep for ages."

"I can sleep as long as I like," said Isobel quickly. Then she asked, "What time is it?" She did not want to have missed breakfast.

Letitia was looking at her in a funny sort of way, as if she were about to say something else. But she only said, "I think it's just past eight. Because the decks are dry, but not all the way dry."

"What?"

"The decks are dry. They have to have the decks swabbed before eight. It's in the handbook in our bedside drawers." She looked at Isobel in some surprise. "Didn't you even know *that*?"

Isobel said, tartly (because she was appalled at herself for having failed to spot the handbook in the first place), "I know everything I need to know."

Letitia shrugged. "Suit yourself. Mummy's coming in a minute to brush my hair."

"It needs it," Isobel said, but Letitia merely said, "I know," and shook her head so that light ran through the fair curls in ripples, like a river, and Isobel felt her heart squeeze tight inside her for her own thin dark hair that had never once been plaited.

They went up to breakfast together, once they were dressed. Letitia was slow this morning, and took her time putting on her stockings. It would be *this* morning, Isobel thought. This *would* be her morning to be slow.

Mrs Colonel Hartington-Davis walked with Horace.

47

It would have been better, Isobel thought, if she had had one of her headaches. It would be harder to talk to Sam if Mrs Colonel Hartington-Davis was there.

"What a *breeze*," said Mrs Colonel Hartington-Davis, shuddering. "Has somebody opened the door?" She glared at the English lord's valet with the shiny hair, who was just coming in from the deck. He wore a very white shirt and he ducked his head apologetically at Mrs Colonel Hartington-Davis.

Isobel wondered when they would all realise that someone was missing. It would almost certainly be breakfast, she thought, and it gave her a queer sick feeling in the pit of her stomach: a little bit excited, and a little bit afraid, and a little bit something else she couldn't exactly parse.

The dining room was almost empty when they got there: it was, after all, only a little past eight, and the tables were laid beautifully. On a great long sideboard there were silver platters covered by silver domes, and under them all the kind of breakfast things that Isobel most disliked: kippers, kedgeree, and other yellowish foods from which a strong and fishy smell arose the moment someone lifted the lid. She wasn't particularly hungry in any case.

There were two busy tables besides theirs.

One was taken by the complaining German doctor. He was arguing with the steward in English. "You must bring me the salt," he said. "And the hot water. And I together will mix. This? This is poison to me. I must mix the salt and water myself." He sipped his hot salt water with evident distaste. "I find this not very good, and this morning when you bring this to me in bed it is the same. I have had a disturbed night." Actually, Isobel thought, he looked less tired than he had on previous mornings.

Opposite him, at the same table, was the bald Swede with the toothbrush moustache, who had both his hands cupped around a mug of cocoa and his eyes fixed on the horizon through the porthole. He looked rather green, pale and drawn – and well he might, thought Isobel: the strong smell of kedgeree and kippers was mingling with an equally strong smell of vinegar coming from the other occupied table, and the two together were rather overpowering.

For the last occupants of the dining room were the two Russian sisters. They had a jar between them, wrapped in a dirty old newspaper, and from it the thin one was spearing spheres of pickled beetroot with a small sharp silver knife. She was slicing the pickled beetroots into very, very little pieces with her small sharp silver knife; and the enormous one was eating the little pieces of beetroot with a large and rusty spoon and every sense of passionate satisfaction.

Isobel caught herself staring, but not before the enormous sister did.

The enormous sister tilted her chin towards Isobel.

"Rust is good for the blood," she said, crisply, in a thick Russian accent, and she sucked the vinegary spoon with an audible slurp.

Isobel turned her face away quickly and realised Mrs Colonel Hartington-Davis had been speaking to her.

She nodded and let Mrs Colonel Hartington-Davis pour her a cup of tea. She liked the teacups on board ship, which were so thin you could see the shadow of your fingers through the sides, and had the Royal Mail crest on one side in gold, and "SS *Marianna*" painted on the other, in gold as well.

The steward put the toast rack down on the table and Letitia helped herself to two slices of thick white toast. She buttered them conscientiously, right to the corners, and ate them slowly and neatly, bite by bite.

Isobel picked at hers, like a bird, and Horace said, "Mummy, why doesn't Isobel *eat* properly?" Mrs Colonel Hartington-Davis tutted a little, and Isobel wanted to bite them both.

Just then the door to the dining room opened and the French family came in. They sat in their usual places and ordered coffee, talking quietly among themselves. They, at least, seemed no different – and none of them were missing. Isobel would have liked to consult her notebook, but she couldn't risk it being seen. Regretfully, she made a mental note to write all this down later. As soon as she could get away. But where was Sam? The Khans' table was still empty, of course – but it had always been empty. It was laid every day (the stewards knew their business) but it had never been touched.

She couldn't go to his cabin, could she? What if Mr Khan spoke to her? What on earth would she say?

The door opened again and her heart leapt, but it was only the English lord coming in. He went straight for the kippers, scooped three on to his plate, and marched to his place.

"Don't you think he's very handsome?" whispered Letitia, and Mrs Colonel Hartington-Davis said, "Lettie, darling!" but she didn't sound at all cross really.

"He's a viscount," said Mrs Colonel Hartington-Davis. "A very important man. Although you'd think he'd be able to have the pick of the valets, with a *title*. You'd think he'd have his own man from England. Someone who could look after him properly. He's

51

barely shaved."

She cast a critical eye over the English lord. "Unmarried, too!" she said to Letitia, quietly. "And him so handsome!"

Isobel did not think he was handsome. He was tall and blond, with a swoop of hair curled on his forehead and eyes set deep into his face behind little gold spectacles. He was very tanned, from being in the sun. But Mrs Colonel Hartington-Davis was right: he hadn't shaved properly today, under his moustache, and there was a smudge of something dark above the rim of his little gold glasses. He seemed unkempt, and Isobel did not like that. He was much less handsome than the boys who had come to dance with her mother, she thought, and then she decided not to think about that any further. She mostly did not like to think about her mother, and especially not in front of other people. She was afraid that by thinking of her mother too much she would stop being able to picture her, like when you found a particularly beautiful bougainvillea blossom, and held it in your hand to keep it specially safe when you made a garden, and then when you were finally ready to put it in pride of place you found the heat of your hand had made it fall away into almost nothing, raggy and transparent and marked with your fingerprints. "No, thank you," she said out loud.

"Were you offered anything?" said Letitia, smugly, and Isobel made a face at her while Mrs Colonel Hartington-Davis wasn't looking.

Letitia, to Isobel's surprise, made a face back, so Isobel made another, and it was as she was making this second face that into the dining room came Sam and a tall, serious-faced and bearded man who must be his father. She was so surprised that she forgot to stop making the face, and Sam saw her and made one back and they both laughed. So did Letitia, and Isobel stopped at once. She didn't want to share Sam with anyone.

"Do you know that boy?" Letitia asked her, and Isobel shook her head, and again that funny look came over Letitia's face as if she was about to say something more, but again she did not.

"I've never heard you laugh before, Isobel," Mrs Colonel Hartington-Davis remarked, and Isobel pressed her lips together very hard to make sure she wouldn't ever laugh again. "Why, that's Dr Khan! I had heard he was going to be on this voyage. And that must be his little boy. I've not seen them at breakfast, have you, Letitia?" Without waiting for an answer she went on: "He's a very eminent man, too. It's said he knows the Queen herself. Despite being – well – an Indian."

There was something very nasty about the way Mrs Colonel Hartington-Davis said "Indian". Like the way that so many people, now Isobel came to think of it, talked about India. It was very strange, because they must like India enough to want to live there, and to live in low white houses in the green hills and busy bright cities where most of the people were Indians. When you came to think of it, it made no sense at all.

What was even more strange was that Mrs Colonel Hartington-Davis said "Indian" in that voice and then leapt up to greet Sam's father as if they were old friends.

She said, "My husband is a great admirer of yours, Dr Khan."

But Dr Khan merely twitched his lips, inclined his head a little and said, very courteously, "Good morning, madam," before going back to his newspaper.

"I am Mrs Colonel Hartington-Davis," said Mrs Colonel Hartington-Davis, and Isobel saw that the dining room was watching to see what the mysterious Dr Khan would do. "It is a very great pleasure to meet you, sir."

And yet Dr Khan said nothing more; he merely raised his eyebrows a little. Mrs Colonel Hartington-Davis, Isobel knew, was accustomed to getting her own way, by prettiness if nothing else. But apparently Sam's father was immune to her charms.

"Have you heard of my husband?" went on Mrs Colonel Hartington-Davis, a little desperately, and Sam's father said, briskly, "I concern myself chiefly with my work, madam, in which I must now immerse myself."

And then he actually turned his back on Mrs Colonel Hartington-Davis! Isobel wanted to cheer, but – to her horror – found herself feeling a little sorry for Mrs Colonel Hartington-Davis. People were very complicated. She looked at Sam, and Sam shrugged and brought his hands down flat on the white tabletop in a gesture of resignation. This, evidently, was how his father *was*, and she saw now that a father like that might not pay particular attention to his only son's chief ambition.

But Sam was doing something peculiar with his hands. He seemed to be stretching, but his arms were in very odd positions, and he was winking – actually winking – at Isobel. What on earth was he doing? She stared at him.

And then another astonishing thing happened. Letitia actually grasped Isobel's shoulder and whispered into her ear, "That boy is *talking* to you!"

Isobel stared at her too. "He's not saying anything."

"You should have read the handbook," Letitia said. "I did. It was in our bedside table."

"You said that this morning," said Isobel, bewildered. And then Letitia, too, started to stretch.

"Lettie, darling!" said Mrs Colonel Hartington-Davis, and Letitia put her hands demurely back down, but not before Isobel saw Sam grin broadly at her, and Letitia return it.

"I said we will find him by the captain's cabin," Letitia whispered, and Isobel whispered back, "*What?*"

"By the captain's cabin," Letitia said again. "*Starboard deck, first-class, captain.* That means captain's cabin."

"What are you *talking* about?" said Isobel.

"You really didn't read the book at all, did you? Eight days on this boat and you haven't even read the book!" said Letitia, and Isobel hated her double, triple, more than ever.

"I don't read *books*," said Isobel.

"You should," said Letitia. She pushed her plait back over her shoulder and beamed at Sam again across the room. "It's very useful. There's three pages in the back of sailor's code. So they don't have to shout."

"Sailor's code?"

"Like semaphore," said Letitia, but Isobel didn't

know what that was. She tried to look as if she did, but Letitia said, "It's where you make letters with flags instead of with a pen. In this one you have different hand signals for different parts of the boat. It's probably actually very useful if you'd bothered to actually look at it."

"I don't care," said Isobel, but she did.

"Well, it's lucky for you I bothered. Otherwise you'd never know what your boyfriend was saying."

"He isn't my friend," said Isobel, and felt disloyal.

"I think he's nice," said Letitia. "He's got a nice face. What does he want to see you about? How do you know him?"

"I'm not telling you," Isobel said.

"I'll ask him myself," said Letitia. "When I see him. After breakfast, by the captain's cabin."

"I'm going on my own," said Isobel.

"Not likely," said Letitia. She scrunched up her face, like she was thinking. "Really," she said. "What a lot of impossible things before breakfast, like in the book about Alice. Can we go and play now, Mummy?"

"Take Horace," said Mrs Colonel Hartington-Davis. "Is Isobel learning to play?" She said it in a silly, high voice as if talking to a baby or a little dog. She peered right into Isobel's face, and once again Isobel felt the urge to bite her. She resisted heroically.

Isobel looked at Letitia, who looked at her, and then they both looked at Horace, who was covered in egg.

"Could we play by ourselves today, Mummy? Me and Isobel? Because we're both girls. And you don't have a headache."

"It *is* nice that you two are getting along," said Mrs Colonel Hartington-Davis. "I like to see little girls playing together. All this whispering at breakfast has to stop, but I do like to see little girls playing together." Privately she believed that Lettie's dainty ways might rub off on this grubby scrap of an orphan, but she did not hold out much hope.

She thought for a minute, and nodded. "You'll play with Horace after lunch, won't you? And you might have the morning to yourselves."

Horace made a horrible face. Through the egg it was even more horrible.

Better Letitia than Letitia *and* Horace, Isobel thought, and together they went out of the dining room and along the stateroom corridors to the deck.

Chapter Five: Miss Holmes, Mr Watson and Miss Letitia Hartington-Davis
Still Week 2, Day 1
Even even further across the Arabian Sea

They hadn't been waiting long when Sam came up on to the deck, half running.

"I *knew* you knew," he said to Letitia. "I hoped Miss Petty here would grasp the meaning of my wild signalling, but when she looked so blank I thought the jig was up for a minute. And then there you were, like an angel."

"Come round the corner," said Isobel, hastily. "So nobody sees us talking."

"Hullo," said Sam. He grinned at Isobel. "You look nicer in your nightgown. That dress is horrible."

"I know," said Isobel.

"It's very yellow," said Sam, critically. "But I don't suppose it will matter." Then he turned to Letitia. "And you're Miss Petty's friend."

"You can call her Isobel," said Letitia swiftly.

"I like calling her Miss Petty," said Sam. "I think it suits her."

"I'm Miss Letitia Hartington-Davis," said Letitia.

"I'm Sam," said Sam. He put out his hand, exactly as if Letitia were a man and so was he. "Nice to meet you, Lettie."

"Aren't you going to call me Miss Hartington-Davis?" said Letitia.

"I don't expect so," said Sam. Letitia looked at him, and he looked at Letitia, and they shook hands like gentlemen.

"It's just a lot of name," he said, apologetically. "It would take a long while to say every time. And you seem like a Lettie."

"I can be Lettie," Letitia said, and dimpled at him.

Isobel glared at her and Sam laughed. He reached out an arm and ruffled her unbrushed hair. "Don't mind Lettie, Miss Petty. Petty, Lettie and Khan: detectives for hire. It's got a ring to it."

"Are we detectives?" said Letitia, at the same time that Isobel said, "We're not for hire."

"Both those statements," said Sam, "are simultaneously true. I was being extremely flippant. We are detectives, Lettie, because last night Miss Petty and I saw a terrible crime. Murder, to be exact."

"Murder!" said Letitia. She didn't say it. She shrieked it, and Isobel without thinking clamped a hand over her mouth.

"Shut up, Lettie," Sam said crisply.

Lettie shut up, her cheeks a little pink, and Isobel took her hand away.

"Do you want to tell what happened, Petty, or will I?"

"You can," said Isobel, and so Sam did, with Isobel putting bits in when it seemed necessary. He was a good storyteller, she thought, even if he had a tendency to think in headlines.

"Gosh," said Letitia when they had finished. They were all three sitting on the deck now, with their backs to the wall and their faces turned to the horizon and the great glittering sea stretched all the way from the edge of the world. It was very blue and very still today, and it seemed like a different ocean to the wild world of the night before. "Gosh, gosh, goodness, gosh."

She looked at Sam. "Really true?"

"Really true," said Sam.

"Not a game? Or pretend?"

"Not a game or pretend."

"Gosh," said Letitia. "Gosh, gosh, gosh."

Isobel looked at Letitia. She seemed almost on the

verge of saying "gosh" again. She was, Isobel thought, very pleasingly surprised.

Sam said, "Isobel's been writing things down in a notebook."

"She keeps it in her petticoat," Letitia said. Isobel looked at her in amazement.

"You're not the only person who notices things," said Letitia, smugly, and Isobel wanted to hit her again.

"Anyway, I suppose you've noticed the main problem," Sam said to Isobel.

Isobel nodded, although she hadn't.

"The main problem we have now," said Sam, "is that *nobody seems to be missing.* Everyone was in the dining room for breakfast as usual."

"Not everyone," said Isobel.

"Well, no. But there's been no fuss."

"Perhaps they just haven't noticed yet. Not everyone comes to breakfast. You didn't for ages. Nor did we on the first day," said Isobel.

"That's true." Sam looked thoughtful. "But then, that's why you're so useful. Because of your notebook."

Isobel was pleased. "I write down everything."

"Exactly. So you will have noticed who was there usually, and who isn't here today, and then we can go and tell the purser to look for them, and then we can be witnesses. The purser," said Sam, "is the man who is in charge of things. Not the captain. The purser knows things, like a matron at school. Oh, I forgot, you don't go to school."

"I'm going to school," said Letitia, unexpectedly. "That's why I'm going to England."

"Me too," said Sam.

"I don't want to go to school," said Isobel.

"Well, nobody's making you. Anyway, school is somewhat beside the point when we're detecting, isn't it? There's bigger things at stake here. It's going to be jolly difficult to detect until we know who the victim is."

"Impossible," said Letitia, thoughtfully. "I suppose we just have to wait until they start making a fuss."

"Wait?" said Sam. His eyes sparkled. "We don't wait, do we, Petty?"

Isobel stared. "What else can we do?"

"We can make a list," he said. "We can make a list of everyone on board ship who should be here, and everyone who isn't. Everyone we've seen, and everyone we haven't. Get the jump on them."

"Get the jump on them?" said Letitia. She looked faintly bemused.

"Get ahead of them. Find out who's missing before

even they do. Find out who's missing, and anything suspicious about them. Easy. Petty's already got her notebook, so we're already one up. Holmes, Watson and—" He stopped and looked at Letitia. "You can be Lestrade. He's the policeman."

"Can't I be a girl?" said Letitia.

Sam shrugged. "It doesn't really matter. There just aren't very many in Sherlock Holmes."

"That's not my fault," said Letitia. "I'll just be Lettie, then. You can just put a girl in if there isn't one I can be. Just put me in as *me*."

"You can't just put people you know in books," said Isobel, and Sam shot her a look.

"You don't read books anyway, Petty, so it doesn't really matter. She can be what she wants. Get your list."

Isobel wriggled her notebook out of her knickers, reluctantly.

"Go through in order, Petty, and I'll tell you what I've noticed about them."

"And I will," said Letitia.

"You won't have noticed anything I haven't noticed," said Isobel, and Letitia and Sam exchanged looks.

"Shall I say in order of the cabins?"

Sam nodded.

"There are twenty-seven passengers on this boat,"

Isobel said, rather grandly, "and three of them are us, and two of them are babies, and one is Horace. Which makes twenty-one people to watch."

"One of them is Mummy," said Letitia, primly. "I won't watch Mummy. We know Mummy isn't murdered."

"Your *Mummy* might have been the murderer," said Isobel, and Letitia shrieked again.

"It was too big to be a lady," said Sam. "I think, anyway."

Letitia looked smugly at Isobel, and Isobel looked crossly at the sea.

"Well, that's twenty to watch. Plus the crew, of course," added Sam.

"It didn't sound like crew."

Sam spun round to look at her. "Did you hear them talking?"

"Didn't you?"

"No! Think, Petty, what did they say?"

"One of them said 'no', I think," said Isobel. "And then the other one said it wouldn't do. Then it happened and then the waves were too loud for anything more."

"Men?"

"I don't know. They were sort of hissing."

"Were they English?"

"I think so," said Isobel.

"Which doesn't narrow it down much. Start your list, go on."

"Well," said Isobel. She opened her notebook.

"You've written *masses*," said Sam, admiringly. "The soul of a real journalist lives in you. I'll give you a job when I'm a proprietor."

"Or I'll give *you* a job," said Isobel. She glared at him. He grinned back.

Letitia said, "It's funny that nobody seems worried even now, isn't it?"

Other people were coming on to the deck now and taking up their usual places. Letitia was right: nobody seemed very worried.

"You'd think they might have noticed that someone was missing. Someone should have noticed by now. The last bell I heard said it was half past ten, and nobody could still be in bed at half past ten."

"It's very odd," said Sam. "It's all very odd."

"There are two rows of cabins," said Isobel. Sam and Letitia both nodded. "There's our row, and then there's the other row. Our has the door on to the deck." They nodded again.

"On our row there's you and your father, Sam, and next to us there's the German doctor. Doktor Weiss."

"He looks exactly like a fly," Sam said. "His beard sticks out like a proboscis. That's the nose-bit flies have to look for things with. And he looks like he's always looking for something over the top of his glasses."

"He drinks salt water. And he hates his cabin because the sun wakes him in the morning. And he had a disturbed night, probably because of it," said Isobel. "I'll write that down."

"Very good, Petty." Sam saluted. "Who else?"

"On the other side of you there's Mrs Drake. She's the American lady. The rich one. With all the diamonds."

"She's pretty," said Sam, and Isobel and Letitia both looked at him sharply.

"Her husband is dead," said Letitia. "It's very sad. I heard her telling Mummy about it."

"Then there's Major Bourne," said Isobel. "Major Ellams Bourne, it says on his door. He's the widow from Colombo with the two babies. His wife died."

"Diamonds Mrs Drake should marry Major Bourne," said Letitia. "She could look after the babies."

"Perhaps she doesn't want to look after the babies."

"Babies are lovely," said Letitia.

"Babies are awful," said Isobel.

"We can strike off the babies, anyhow," said Sam. "The doctor was there at breakfast. He ate some kedgeree and got yellow on his chin. Did you see both of them this morning? The Major and Diamonds Mrs Drake?"

Isobel shook her head, but Letitia nodded. "Diamonds Mrs Drake was going downstairs as we were leaving. I thought you said you noticed everything?" Isobel hated her more than ever.

"And there's the major now." Letitia inclined her head in the direction of the major. He was pacing up and down the deck. He looked tired, Isobel thought, and said so.

"As if he'd been up in the night?" said Sam, hopefully.

"Exactly," said Isobel. Behind him a girl in a white sun bonnet was trailing with an infant in each arm. She was about twenty.

"That's Clara," said Isobel. "His maid. The nanny for the babies."

"Fine. Tick them off as all being still on board. Very good work, Petty."

"Then there's Lord Trimlingham," said Isobel. "His is the last cabin in our row."

"The Discount Viscount," said Letitia, unexpectedly. "That's what they call him, because even though it doesn't rhyme you spell it the same. Dis-count vis-count, instead of vye-count. They didn't think he was going to get all the money, because of a will thingy, but it turned out to be all right in the end. He's terribly rich. And he's got a valet, who doesn't eat in the dining room because he's Indi—" She stopped and flushed.

"Because he's Indian, was what you were going to say," said Sam, evenly.

Letitia looked at Sam and then out to sea. She bit her lip.

"I'm Indian," said Sam. "And I can eat where I want."

Letitia didn't say anything.

"Properly Indian?" she said, after a minute.

"Properly, absolutely Indian," said Sam. "And properly, absolutely English. I can be both."

"Nobody can be both," said Letitia, in something like the voice she had used to Isobel that first day.

"I am," said Sam, and he looked so fierce that even Letitia didn't dare to say anything back. "I'm both completely. And if you don't like that then you can – you can just leave us alone."

"I don't mind it," said Letitia, uncertainly, but Sam still looked fierce.

"I don't want you not to *mind*," he said. "It's not something for you to *mind*. It's just the truth. I'm completely both. So if you're going to be irritating about it, you can leave now, and we can get on with our investigation. Go on about the Discount

Viscount, Petty." He turned away from Letitia as if the conversation was over.

"I won't be irritating," said Letitia, quietly, and Sam nodded, but he didn't look at her.

"He's got a valet," said Isobel. "An Indian valet who doesn't eat in the dining room."

"Nor do any other servants," said Sam. "Even the English ones. So you can put *that* in your pipe and smoke it." This last was to Letitia, who was bright pink.

"I didn't mean to upset you," she said, in a very small voice.

Sam looked at her and softened a little. "I know you didn't," he said. "People mostly don't. But they go on saying unfair things anyway. And being unfair altogether. And a person can get tired of it. I, myself, am exceedingly tired of it."

"I'm sorry you're tired of it," said Letitia. Isobel couldn't think of a single thing to say.

"So am I," said Sam, simply. "It's tedious in the extreme. Tedious means boring. And I am bored by it and of it and with it. People just need to think more before they speak. So if you can do that, we can be friends. I think. Friends?"

"Friends," said Letitia. "Please. And I *am* sorry." She

70

held out her hand to Sam, just as she had earlier, and they shook.

Isobel felt a familiar spike of jealousy in her stomach. She hadn't liked it when Sam was upset, exactly, but she didn't want Letitia to be his friend too.

Sam said, as if shaking off snow from his shoulders, "Have you seen the valet this morning?"

Isobel pointed. "He's there." The valet was preparing a deckchair, presumably for Lord Trimlingham, delicately plumping up cushions and fussily peering over a large stack of heavy books in a basket beside the chair.

"Tick him off, then. And the lord was eating kippers at breakfast. So tick him off too. Jolly good work, Petty."

"You've missed off the Russian ladies," said Letitia.

"I have *not*," said Isobel, crossly. She indicated the Misses Karamazova on the list. "I was just coming to them. They are in Row A, and we know they are still on board because they're there. Look. There's the thin one who drinks the tea, and there's the enormous one who exercises."

They both glanced across the deck to where the Russian sisters were. The thin one – "Miss Olga," said Isobel, thinking of the cabin labels – was clutching the rail with one hand and had a small silver stopwatch in the other. Her face was very pale, and she was watching her sister with a kind of awe.

Her sister, the enormous one – "Miss Natasha," said Letitia – was doing press-ups in a serge bathing suit. She wore the keys to her cabin round her neck on a tight chain, which sparkled in the sun, and a large, wide-brimmed canvas hat that tied under her chin with elastic, to keep it from flying off in the breeze.

"Hup!" Miss Olga was saying, in her reedy little voice. "Hup! Hup! Hup!" She was timing Miss Natasha and tutting.

Miss Natasha was very strong, and her press-ups were very fast, and they watched her in admiration for a moment.

Then Letitia said, "I didn't even mean them."

Isobel looked at her. "There aren't any other Russian ladies."

"There are," said Letitia. "There's the mother. Their mother, I mean. And their maid. She's in the cabin next to theirs. She's terribly seasick and doesn't come out on deck, and so is the maid. I saw her being sick on the second day and saying to the steward that she would take supper for herself and Madam Karamazova on a tray in their room. See? You had missed them off, hadn't you? Put a circle round them, because we haven't

72

seen them. Possible victims."

Isobel made a face, but she wrote it down, and put a circle round their names.

"Excellent thinking, Lettie," Sam said, crisply. "Excellent. That's exactly the sort of thing we need to be really considering. People we might not otherwise have seen, you know."

"Like you, you mean," said Isobel. She did not like it when Sam praised Letitia, she did not like it at all. Isobel felt distinctly snippish. "You stayed in your cabin for four days. And you've only come out now because of the murder."

"I did not," said Sam, with dignity. "I've been in my office. Perhaps you're just unobservant."

Isobel started to say something cross, but Sam relented all at once. He said, "No, you're not unobservant. I'm just particularly good at keeping a low profile. I am acutely talented at concealment. I've had a lot of practice."

"Who were you hiding from?" asked Letitia, but a shadow crossed Sam's face and he turned away.

"It's not terribly important just now," he said. "I propose we continue with the list of passengers. So after the Misses Karamazova, the Mrs Karamazova and their maid, who next?"

"The funny thin Swede who drinks the cocoa," said

73

Isobel. "And that French family."

"There's quite a lot of them," said Letitia.

"Six sisters," said Isobel.

"Six!" said Letitia. "I counted four."

"There's absolutely six," said Isobel firmly.

"Have you seen them all together?"

"Yes."

"Definitely?"

Isobel thought. "I think so," she said, which wasn't like her: she was a very certain sort of person.

"There's a murder at stake," said Sam. "Thinking isn't going to get us anywhere."

"There's six of them."

"Including the parents?"

"Six sisters."

"I still think there's only four," said Letitia. "Look."

They looked over to where the French sisters were coming out on deck: four of them, with their father and mother, their hair all coiled up elaborately on top and their four muslin dresses in lilac and violet and hyacinth and heliotrope.

"There can't be any more shades of purple than that," said Sam. "Maybe it is only four."

"I still think it's six," said Isobel. "They've got three cabins. Why would you have three cabins for four

74

people? That wouldn't make sense at all."

"What if there were supposed to be six, and not all of them came on board?" Letitia saw a weakness and jumped for it. "We can only actually write down what we actually see."

Then something awful happened. Unforgivable, Isobel thought, absolutely unforgivable: Letitia leaned over and took Isobel's pen and Isobel's notebook and drew a circle around the French family. Isobel held her breath. She hated anyone to touch her things. She hated anyone to know about the notebook. She felt the crossness bubbling through her, white-hot, like a kettleful of water tipped on to a poison ants' nest.

And then Letitia put the pen back in Isobel's hand cheerfully. "That's better. Now, who's next?"

"Don't touch my things," said Isobel, dangerously. The water was steaming; the ants were scurrying up her throat.

"It's the notebook of the investigation, isn't it?"

"It's not the notebook of the investigation. It's my notebook." Poison ants, poison ants, all over Letitia. She clamped her lips shut to stop them.

"Well, it's got the investigation notes in it. It's got the list in it."

"Don't touch my things," said Isobel again. "Don't

touch my things."

"Don't be such a *baby*," said Letitia. "You sound like Horace. It's just a silly notebook." She shook her head so that her blonde hair bounced contemptuously.

Isobel opened her mouth to say something – as vicious and terrible a thing as she could muster; a thousand poison ants crawling into Letitia's long hair and the collar of her sailor dress, stripping the flesh from her *bones*, even—

And then Sam said instead, lazily and firmly, "Lettie, don't take Petty's notebook, it's rather important to her. Petty, she didn't know about your notebook and she won't do it again. Will you, Lettie?"

He had, Isobel thought again, a way of saying things that made you want to agree with him. And Letitia did.

"No." Letitia looked at Isobel. "I'm sorry I said you were a baby."

"Are you sorry you took my notebook?"

"Isobel," said Sam, warningly.

"I'm sorry I took your notebook," said Letitia.

"Don't touch it again," said Isobel, but the poison ants were fading.

Sam looked at her. "You could say thank you, you know."

"What for?"

"She said sorry."

"She had to say sorry."

"Actually," said Sam. "She didn't. She made an honest mistake. She's being rather decent to say sorry. So say thank you."

And somehow – much to her surprise – Isobel did.

"Can we get on with the work, please?" said Sam.

"The Karamazovas, the cocoa man, the German doctor, the lord and his servant, the French family – six or eight of them. Who else?"

"Us, four of us. You and your papa. That's six."

"The major, Mrs Drake with the diamonds, the major's maid, the babies," said Sam.

"And that's everybody," said Isobel. "Somebody on this list is a murder victim, and somebody on this list is a murderer."

They looked around them, and down at their list, and then, once again, around the deck. The sun was warm and bright, high in the sky and nearly noon, and the sea was calm and lovely. Miss Olga was mopping Miss Natasha's brow with a towel; Miss Natasha was drinking beetroot juice through a thick metal straw; the French sisters were gently bickering at the rail. It was all exceptionally ordinary, and it did not look – even to the detectives – like a likely place for a murderer to be.

Still less did it look like a place where somebody had just been murdered.

"But we saw it," said Isobel. Nobody had said anything, but they all three knew what she meant. "We saw it, and it happened, and it was real."

They sat in silence for a while.

"We're going to have to talk to the captain," said Sam, after a moment. "We're going to have to go and see what's going on."

Isobel could have told them both how it was going to go from the beginning. She knew – as neither Letitia nor Sam seemed to – that there was nothing to be gained from speaking to grown-ups about anything that mattered; she knew – as neither Letitia nor Sam seemed to – all the ways grown-ups only let you down.

They made their way along the deck and indoors – past Miss Olga, sponging Miss Natasha's face from a big iron bucket; past the English lord in his deckchair, reading a large book about the moon; past the thin Swede cupping his cocoa in his hands and still looking distinctly greenish; and past the German doctor, writing something in a heavy black book.

They passed Mrs Drake on the stairs.

"Did you see that?" hissed Letitia.

"What?" Sam, in front, hadn't seen anything, but

Isobel had seen at once that Mrs Drake had been crying. Her perfect make-up was a little smudged, and there were blurry greyish marks under her eyes where her lash-black had run.

"Suspicious," whispered Isobel.

"Very," whispered Letitia.

When they passed their own cabin Letitia stopped. "Don't you think we ought to wash our hands and faces before we see the captain?"

"Not on your life," said Sam, with feeling. "I washed this morning."

"Well…" Letitia hesitated, but Mrs Colonel Hartington-Davis's training won out. "I'm going to. I think you should too, Isobel."

"Don't tell me what to do," said Isobel.

Letitia shrugged. "I'm going to."

"Go on then," said Isobel.

When she went in, while they waited, Sam leaned closer to Isobel. "I think," Sam said quietly, "that it would be better if Lettie stayed out in the corridor when we go in, to keep watch. Don't you? I just have a sort of feeling I'd rather not get her mixed up in this bit."

"What?" said Isobel.

"She's just so… Well, you know."

"Oh, I know," said Isobel, eagerly.

But Sam said, "She's just a very nice girl, isn't she? I think the chivalrous thing to do is keep her out of it if I can. Chivalrous means like a knight, you know. Gentlemanly. But politer. The chivalrous thing to do is to keep her out of it."

"But … what about me?" said Isobel.

"What about you?" said Sam, astonished.

"Do you not mind if I get mixed up in things?"

"But you're already mixed up in everything," Sam said. "It's your investigation. It's *our* investigation. Chivalry hasn't anything to do with *us*." He grinned at her. And she grinned back.

Just then Letitia came back. She had put a new ribbon in her hair, Isobel saw.

The captain's study was down another flight of stairs, and Isobel was worried that the steward would banish her back up again, as he had last time. But nobody saw them at all.

"Perhaps they're all investigating the crime," said Letitia.

"Perhaps," said Sam.

They settled Letitia on to the step. She didn't want to keep watch but Sam smiled at her and she gave way instantly.

As they were going down the hall they saw the captain, talking to the English lord about the mail times.

"It's all in the handbook," said Sam to Isobel. "Why doesn't anybody except me and Lettie read the handbook?"

"Books are boring," said Isobel automatically, and Sam grinned at her.

"You're reading the wrong books," he said. "And anyway, it's useful. Sir!" he called to the English lord. "The mail times are all in the handbook!"

The lord looked round and laughed. "A helpful child, what! If I did need the mail times," he said, grinning, "I'll be sure to find the handbook. Just a simple matter of some lost property, that's all. Are you here to see the captain?" He meant it as a joke, but Sam nodded.

"Well, goodness. We mustn't keep you waiting, then!"

"We must not!" said the captain, jovially. He shook the lord's hand, and the lord went off down the corridor. "Children! What can I do for you?"

They went into his office together, and came out ten minutes later together looking thoroughly dejected.

"It's always that way with grown-ups," said Isobel, rather smugly. They were back in Sam's lifeboat office. It was cramped with three of them, but it was secret. And they were talking in whispers, so as not to be overheard.

"He didn't believe us at all," said Sam. "He wasn't even a bit worried."

"He *laughed*," said Isobel. Even though she had been expecting this it was still disappointing. "He laughed. I don't think he believes anyone is missing at all. Grown-ups are awful. And," she said, suddenly remembering, "you know what else? That lord wasn't talking about lost property, he was talking about letters. *He* just lied for no reason. They lie and they don't do what they say they will and they don't ever, ever *listen*."

"The captain didn't seem even a little bit alarmed," said Sam. "He wouldn't even tell us who was aboard. And he said we read too many books."

"Which isn't true," said Isobel. "I don't read at all."

"I only read sensational crimes," admitted Sam. "Which doesn't help our case. But we did see it."

"We did," said Isobel.

They were quiet for a minute. The waves below made a kind of shushing sound, and the air smelled like salt and seaweed and thick paint peeling, which smells quite different to wet paint: tinny and sharp and hot.

"If nobody is missing," said Letitia, carefully, "are we … are we completely sure it happened?"

"It happened," said Isobel. "Just because you didn't

see it."

"Somebody went overboard," said Sam. "Petty and I saw it. Didn't we, Petty?"

"Don't call me that," said Isobel automatically.

"I'm jolly glad you saw it too, actually. Otherwise I'd think I'd gone off my head. That means to go loopy," he explained. "Round the bend. Imagining things. You know?"

"I know," said Isobel. "But I saw it. But nobody else seems to know it's happened. And nobody else saw anything."

Lettie looked for a minute as if she were about to say something important, but she said, only, "Well, this is *hopeless*."

"The main thing to remember," said Sam, determinedly, "is that it is really astounding to have stumbled into something like this. That's what comes of our being so jolly independent-minded and being awake in the night. Imagine! A murder where we need to find the victim, not the murderer. We're a brand-new kind of detective. There's never been a case like this. We'll be in all the papers."

"Maybe," said Letitia.

"We will, actually," said Isobel, but she didn't sound sure. And the sun went on shining, climbing higher and higher into the sky, and then dropping a little lower, and lower again. And then the bell rang for lunch, and then even when it was well into the afternoon, nobody on board the SS *Marianna* seemed to notice that they were talking and eating and laughing and drinking in a world where somebody had died. Nobody, that is, except three secret detectives.

Chapter Six: Lettie's Idea

Still Week 2, Day 1
Even even even further across the Arabian Sea

And at dinner there was still no fuss.

The tables were full, as usual, and everyone talked, as usual, and nothing was different at all.

"Nothing is different at *all*," whispered Letitia, and Isobel kicked her under the table to make her be quiet in case Mrs Colonel Hartington-Davis should hear.

Nobody even *looked* different. The purser, a white cloth over one arm, moving about the room pouring wine. The Russian sisters, Miss Natasha's face scrubbed pink after her exercises, sipping tea and pecking at their fried fish. The English lord, reading with one hand the same enormous book with a picture of the moon on the cover, and with the other hand absently conveying his own fried fish to his lips. The ship's captain, sitting with the major and Diamonds Mrs Drake. The German doctor and the moustached Swede talking earnestly; and the French family, bickering in French.

"*Mais non!*" one of them said, more loudly than was really reasonable indoors, and dropped her little reticule firmly on the table so that it clattered. "*Absolument pas du tout!*"

Isobel did not speak French, but she knew bickering when she heard it. Only four sisters, she thought. Which might be people missing, or it might not, although she didn't want to admit this to Letitia. She could have counted wrong. She *might* have done. She *might* have counted wrong, or seen wrong, and that seemed like a tricky sort of premise on which to begin an investigation. If only there were some way to check her list, she thought. That would make her feel better. For the French sisters did not seem quieter than usual, and there were no empty chairs.

No Sam or his father, of course, but everyone who ought to be there appeared to be present. Everyone who was usually at supper was at supper, and nobody seemed to be missing, and nobody seemed to be worried at all.

The purser poured Mrs Colonel Hartington-Davis a glass of wine and smiled at Isobel, who frowned at him. She did not approve of smiling for no reason. "Lovely day," he said to Horace. "Much better after a storm. Always is."

"I liked the stormy bit best," said Horace. "Waves crashing about."

"You'll be a sailor yet," said the purser, and went on about the room. But Isobel was thinking about the storm again. *I did see it*, she thought. *I did, I did, I did.* But the room was so ordinary, the gas lamps so soft and warm, the purser so entirely calm, and suddenly that scared her, too. The ordinariness scared her. *Why doesn't anybody see?* she thought. *Why doesn't anybody* see?

And then Isobel looked at Letitia, and saw, at once, that Letitia *saw*. There was an expression on Letitia's face that she did not expect: a sort of curious mixture of horror and surprise and pleased-ness. This was not a very usual expression, but Isobel understood it very clearly. It was an expression that she herself wore very often. It was the expression of a person who had just thought of something. It was the expression of a person who had just seen something. It was the expression, in short, of a *noticer*.

Isobel had never thought she would see that expression on Letitia's face. She had never, ever thought that she would feel better to see that expression on Letitia's face. But she was, all the same.

"After dinner," whispered Letitia to Isobel, and Isobel knew exactly what she meant without having to say anything else at all.

They were very well behaved at dinner, and Mrs Colonel Hartington-Davis thought that perhaps cross little Isobel Petty might have some hope of becoming a nice child after all.

"What is it?" said Isobel, the minute they were back in their cabin with the door shut. They were supposed to be getting ready for bed.

"It's the purser," said Letitia.

"The purser?" Isobel stared. "What about him?"

"Two things," said Letitia. She sat down on her bed, drew her knees up to her chin, and shook her hair out in a way that was deliberately charming. "Shall I tell you?"

"Go on then," said Isobel. She was too interested to be really cross about the charmingness. "What about the purser?"

"The first thing is that we didn't put the crew on the list. The purser can't get up on deck at night but there's the captain, and the night steward."

"But last night the captain would have had to be steering the ship, because of the storm," said Isobel, but Letitia held up one finger exactly like a grown-up.

Why was she always trying to be a grown-up?

"Yes. And the night steward—"

"His name is Edwards," said Isobel.

"Just let me say what I was going to say," said Letitia, frowning at Isobel. She looked much more human when she frowned.

She went on. "But Edwards was ill last night. He told Mummy, when she rang for her headache. He had a cold and he said he was sorry that they would have to leave the cabins unattended until the morning unless it was a dire emergency. And Mummy said it was outrageous. And Edwards said he knew, but that he was jolly ill. And she said it was a disgrace. And Edwards said he knew. And Mummy said she would tell the captain. And Edwards said that this was the trouble with coming by mail ship. And Mummy said it was disgraceful that Edwards would speak to her in this way. And he did look truly, truly sickly. So you see, it can't have been Edwards. Or the captain, because of the storm. And they can't be missing or the ship would have to stop."

"So the crew don't matter at all," said Isobel. "We're exactly where we started."

"Not exactly," said Letitia. "Because when I was thinking about that, I was thinking about the list. How we didn't even put the captain or the steward on to rule them off. How we can't check the list against anything."

"I was thinking that too," admitted Isobel.

"But then I had another thought," said Letitia. "And what I thought was, the purser has to keep lists of everyone on board the ship. He has to keep a list of everyone who bought a ticket and everyone who boarded and all their papers. They checked everyone for cholera before they boarded, so the doctor had to see everyone who came up the gangplank, and tick them off on the list. A list of passengers, absolutely certified as being on board, because the doctor had to examine everybody. And then I thought, what if we had that list?"

"They would never give it to us," said Isobel. She was cross, somewhere deep down, that she hadn't thought of this herself, but the crossness was buried under a rising tide of excitement. "They wouldn't give it to us. They wouldn't let us into the offices, even."

And then there was a knock at the door. They both jumped.

"Who is it?" called Letitia. Her voice was not quite ordinary, but nobody would have noticed who wasn't listening for it.

"It's me," said Sam, and they both jumped up together

to answer the door.

"What if someone sees you coming in?" said Letitia.

"Nobody saw me," said Sam. "And I'll hide under the bunk if anyone comes in here. Which reminds me, actually. We do have to bear in mind the possibility of stowaways."

"Stowaways!"

"Well, that might explain it. If a stowaway had been hiding on the ship, and *then* they got tipped overboard…"

He sat down on the floor with his back to the door, and Isobel sat down too.

"I hadn't even thought of stowaways," she admitted.

"Ugh." Letitia crumpled up her face. "That makes it impossible."

"Oh, not impossible," said Sam. "Merely another hurdle. But it might be that, you see, because you would have told me as soon as I opened the door if anyone had been missing at dinner from our list."

Then he added, "I have been a mite concerned, you know, about that list. We all remember different people coming on board, and we all three saw different things. What if there just happened to be someone we didn't see? What if there are four or six French sisters? It's things like that that worry me."

Isobel sat forward and pulled at his sleeve. "No, Sam, but listen. Listen to what Letitia's thought of."

He looked at her in some surprise, and then at Letitia. "Go on, Lettie," he said.

Lettie explained about the list: the list with the names, and the documents, and the papers.

"Which would also rule out the stowaway," said Sam. "Because nobody came up the gangplank without being checked. Because of the cholera. Oh, Lettie! I could kiss you!"

"You can," said Letitia. She blushed faintly, and Isobel wanted to kick her.

"I shan't," said Sam. "Not professional. But I could, just for joy. Clever Lettie."

"He'll never give it to us," said Isobel. "Not now."

Sam's shoulders dropped a little. "No. And the door is locked. The captain locks it all the time and keeps the key on him."

They thought for a minute, and Isobel wished she hadn't said anything. She felt suddenly rather dejected, because Sam felt dejected, and the little room was full of glumness and despair. She did not like this; this was why it was better mostly to be by yourself. She didn't like people – she knew that – and how strange to feel sad because someone else felt sad, and how strange to want something she couldn't have.

Letitia had been sitting quietly with her knees drawn up to her chin. Now she spoke.

"What if," she said slowly. "What if we took it?"

They gaped at her.

"Stole it, you mean?" said Sam, who was the first to get his voice back.

"Stole it," said Letitia.

Sam pretended to mop his brow. "Whew! Lettie!" he said, in a pretend American accent. "Burglary!"

"You think we should *steal* the list?" said Isobel.

"Oh no," said Lettie, calmly. "Not at all. I think *I* should steal the list. Nobody would ever think to suspect *me*."

They looked at her, and her fair hair shone gold in the gentle glow of the gas lamp. "Nobody ever suspects *me* of anything," said Lettie, and then she told them her plan.

It seemed to Isobel that it had not been much of a plan at all. It had seemed so simple, so obviously, easily, foolishly simple that surely nothing so obvious and easy and foolish could ever work. If she – Isobel – had done it, it would never have worked. Sam could not have done it. This, she knew, was why she had not thought of it. It was a Lettie plan: a plan that relied on

Lettie's golden hair, and Lettie's lovely manners, and Lettie's aura of sleek, well-fed goodness. And – much worse – Lettie knowing things that Isobel did not.

They had been lost for words again, the second time in as many minutes.

"Walk in and *take* it?" Isobel said.

"Just *take* it?" That was Sam.

"You can't just *take* it." Isobel again.

"You don't even know where it is."

"How would you know where to find it?"

"They would notice you."

"They'd see you."

"They'd see you take it."

"They'd want to know what you were doing."

"They'd be able to tell you were friends with us."

"We're not friends," said Isobel quickly. "This isn't about friends."

"Oh, but it is," said Lettie. They both looked at her, and she was smiling. "You see," she said gently. "I'm friends with the purser."

"Friends?" said Isobel.

"The purser?" said Sam.

"You remember," she said to Sam. "The man who runs the ship." She allowed herself a very small smirk, but Isobel saw it all the same. "*She* told me to shut up about him. Earlier. Isobel said he wasn't important."

"Well, how is he important?" Isobel said, rudely.

"You didn't see the list of passengers on the captain's desk," said Lettie. "Because the captain doesn't think about the people so much. He thinks about the sea, and the waves, and the ship."

"Of course the captain thinks about his passengers," said Isobel, loftily. "He's our captain."

"Captains think about sailing, and pursers think about people," said Lettie. "That's just how it works. I know," she added to Isobel, but without looking at her, "because I've been to sea before. Actually, captains think about sailing, and sometimes about eating dinner; and pursers think about how much they are spending on dinner, and how many people are going to eat it, and how much the cook had to be paid and whether the cook is going on holiday soon and all the things like that. Pursers think about people, and doctor's certificates are about people. That's just one of the things I know about sailing."

"You're not a sailor," said Isobel.

"I never said I was," said Lettie, with dignity.

"You must admit, Miss Petty, that she knows things we don't know about ships," said Sam.

Isobel was silent. It was true, but she would rather

not have admitted it.

"So you're *friends* with the purser, are you?" she said, eventually.

"He absolutely *loves* me," said Lettie, frankly. She wasn't even boasting. She made Isobel sick. "He loves me, and he even loves Horace. We remind him of his own little girl and boy. I know. I asked him. People love being asked things. And then they tell you things."

"Did you just go and *ask* him if he had a little girl?" Isobel said. She didn't mean to ask it. She just needed to know. It seemed to her completely extraordinary.

"I was asking him about all sorts of things," said Lettie. "Aren't you interested in people?" She looked, Isobel thought, genuinely interested as she asked it.

"I am," she said. "But not like that. I don't like talking to them. I don't like them."

"You don't like people?"

"She likes us," said Sam. "She likes people now."

"I do not," Isobel started to say, and stopped. Instead she said, "I don't like *most* people, Sam Khan."

Sam beamed, and so, to Isobel's surprise, did Lettie.

"People are always interesting," said Lettie. "They think such interesting things. And sometimes when you ask them things, they tell you things, and then you know. And what I know is, the purser misses his own little girl, and if I go in and ask him if I can do some drawing at his desk he won't mind at all. More than won't mind – he'll be pleased. And then I can gather up my drawings, and get the passenger list too, and then we'll have it. And he'll like me even more than he does now."

"I'm very likeable," she added, as an afterthought. "Everyone says so. It's partly because I'm pretty, but partly because I'm nice."

"But you're *awful*," said Isobel.

"No worse than you," said Lettie. "I just hide it better. Any objections?"

"It's a good plan," Sam said, before they could start again. "Let's do it."

"You can't just *take* it," said Isobel.

"You just *watch* me," said Lettie.

And they did.

Chapter Seven: Lettie's Heist

Week 2, Day 2

A little bit more than halfway across the Arabian Sea

It was as easy as Lettie said it would be. This took Isobel by surprise. She still, she told herself firmly, did not like Lettie at all. *It's Letitia, not Lettie*, she said to herself crisply, but it didn't stick. Lettie suited Lettie, and Lettie (it transpired) was good at heists.

"A heist," Sam said, "is a theft. A burglary. A heist is where you take something of great value with a plan that is orchestrated in advance and to perfection. And that is what Lettie has done. So it's a heist."

It was the next morning, after breakfast. They were sitting on deck, with their backs against the lifeboat HQ, looking at the people. The sun was shining on the water, which sparkled a deep navy blue, with white score-lines on it where the boat cut through like someone cutting a pane of glass with a diamond ring.

It was, Isobel conceded, pretty. She was not especially interested in the prettiness of it, though, for she had a crime to solve. She looked hard at the people going by. The German doctor who looked like a fly was standing by the telescope. ("Scene of the crime," Sam said. "Does that look like the same shape of a man?" But Isobel couldn't tell.)

The Russian sisters were looking through a large folder of papers and explaining something to the Swede with the spindly moustache. "We go to compete for the Madame Hercules Cup," Miss Natasha was saying. "It is most famous strongwoman contest in three continents."

"She must to beat reigning champion Wendy Sledge," said Miss Olga, and as she said it she spat very delicately (but with fury) over the railing. "Pah! That is what I think of Wendy Sledge!"

"It is very difficult contest," said Miss Natasha. "Lucky I am very strong." She nodded, and the shiny keys bounced at her throat.

The English lord with his large stack of star books winked at Isobel as he went by, and she did not even stick her tongue out at him. She didn't even think of it in time, and this worried her, too. The Isobel who had come on board this ship would have known exactly what kind of face to pull at a person who smiled at her. Who was she becoming? She didn't like it. First Lettie; now this. She resolved to say something unkind to someone, but the only person speaking to her currently was Sam. And she didn't want to be unkind to Sam. So she said nothing and looked at her shoes. There were salt marks on them, white wavy lines on the brown leather, left by the ocean spray lifted up to the deck by the breeze. No, not a breeze now: this was a real sea wind, brisk and high, and the waves were brisk and high too against the prow of the ship. They had had no storms since the night of the murder, but you could tell they were leaving India behind them. It was a little colder, maybe, and the air was somehow drier, as if you could taste the red sand of the desert in it, coming to them on that same breeze. For far away in the distance they could see the coast of Africa. It had been nine days since they had been on land.

Soon they would be at Suez, where the canal was. Suez was a port on the coast of Africa, where the ship would stop for an hour or two, and then pass through the Suez Canal that cut through Egypt and out into the Mediterranean. There was a map on the back page of the steamer handbook. This worried Isobel. She did not exactly know why.

"If we get to Suez before we find out who is missing," Sam said, echoing her thoughts in a most curious way, "whoever did it could slip away. Get off the ship and go."

"That's it," Isobel said. "That's the problem. Two days. And we still don't even have a list of suspects."

"She's getting it," said Sam. "You know she is."

"I don't even know if we can trust her."

"We can trust her," said Sam. He grinned. "Come on, Petty. You know we can trust her. She's in it now. She worked out the signalling code before you even knew there was a handbook."

"You like her more than me," said Isobel. She didn't mean to say it. It just came out. She looked at her shoes again, so she wouldn't look at him. It was quiet for a moment.

Then Sam said, briskly, "What an absolutely *ridiculous* notion. You don't have to like people more or less. You can just like them differently. I think she's jolly. And I've never met anyone like you. I've never met anyone like either of you, come to that. Girls, you know. But then again, people are all quite different, aren't they? So you have to like them all quite differently."

"If you had to pick one of us—" Isobel started, but Sam interrupted her.

"I don't," he said. "So I won't. Don't be a little goose. We're a team. And she's doing a heist for us right now."

Isobel felt rather shaken. She had never thought of any of these things. Part of her wanted to fling her arms round Sam's neck. But she would never do a thing like that. She didn't like to be touched, and she did not like to touch other people. "If she isn't back soon," said Isobel instead, in her best and steadiest voice, "it will be lunchtime."

"She'll be back," said Sam, and as he said it they both heard the door from the cabins swing open and bang against the wall with a hollow metal noise. "That's her," he said, as if he had summoned her, and just like magic Lettie came round the corner, trying very hard not to run and not quite managing it. Her cheeks were very pink, and her fair hair had come loose from its plait and was tumbling over her shoulders like strands and waves and folds of copper and bronze and gold, and she was beaming. Tucked under one arm was a manila folder.

"Got it," she called, breathlessly, and just as she said it a shadow fell across her, and Mrs Colonel Hartington-Davis rose from her deckchair and clapped a hand on Lettie's shoulder.

"Letitia, your hair, darling!" she said. "And where *have* you been? It's lunchtime and Horace has barely seen you today. And is that little Isobel over there, with the Khan boy?"

"Sorry, Mummy," Lettie said, in a voice quite unlike her ordinary voice. It was soft and lisping, and, just like the face she pulled when she spoke to grown-ups, it set Isobel's teeth on edge. "Isobel!" she called. "Is-o-bel! Is-o-bel! Mummy wants you to come for lunch."

Isobel made a quick face at Sam and got to her feet. "I'd better go," she said.

"The folder?" he said. They both looked at Lettie, but the folder was nowhere to be seen.

"Magic?" said Sam.

"Petticoats, I bet," said Isobel. "I really had better go."

"You'd better. Meet back here after."

"Of course."

Mrs Colonel Hartington-Davis cast a disparaging glance over Isobel's person. "Is that pinafore quite *clean*, Isobel?" she said. Isobel shrugged. "I'm astonished I didn't notice at breakfast. It's got marks all down the front. Don't you want a clean pinafore like my Lettie?"

Lettie smirked. Mrs Colonel Hartington-Davis saw her and said, more severely than usual, "Letitia, your hair warrants some attention. How on earth has it come out of its plait like this?"

She deftly replaited Lettie's hair, Lettie smiling all

the time in that ingratiating way, while Isobel stood and waited.

Horace was looking at Isobel. "You're all *dirty*," he said. "Because you were crawling about under the lifeboat. I *saw* you."

Lettie and Isobel shot each other twin glances of horror and alarm.

"What?" Mrs Colonel Hartington-Davis turned to Horace and pulled Lettie's hair a little in the process. Lettie yelped, a little more loudly than she needed to, and the moment passed.

"We must talk to Horace," Lettie whispered to Isobel, as they were walking into the dining room.

"He mustn't tell about the lifeboat," Isobel whispered back.

"He'll do as I say," Lettie said confidently, but Isobel thought of Horace's sly little face and wasn't so sure.

There was no time to talk at lunch; there never was. Lettie put her hand to her ribs, just where a manila folder tucked into a petticoat might be, and winked at Isobel, who winked at Sam over Lettie's shoulder. "After lunch," she mouthed, and Sam nodded. He was standing by the window, not eating. Dr Khan was nowhere to be seen.

It was just as lunch was finishing that something

dreadful happened; something that put the kibosh on any investigating for the whole afternoon.

"We're just going to go and play," Lettie told her mother, and then it happened. Horace, who had been silently devouring not only his lunch, but Lettie's lunch, and Isobel's too, let out a high-pitched wail. "You're leaving me behind *again*," he whined. "You left me all morning, Letitia! Why won't you play with *me*?"

"We're busy," said Isobel. Mrs Colonel Hartington-Davis shot her a look, and the looking made her clasp her hand to her forehead. It was one of her headaches, Isobel guessed, brought on by the high pitch of Horace's yell.

"Why can't *I* come and be busy?" Horace gripped Isobel's skinny wrist in his pudgy hands. They were very hot and sticky.

"No," said Lettie. "We've things to do."

"Won't you play with Horace?" said Mrs Colonel Hartington-Davis, and Lettie looked stubborn. Isobel had never seen Lettie look stubborn before, and she liked it. It made her look much less horrible.

"I don't know if I like this, Letitia," said Mrs Colonel Hartington-Davis, and she gave Isobel a hard stare.

"I want to play with Let-it-ia," Horace wailed. He cried like a baby, Isobel thought, not at all like a person of six. When she was six she was sure she had never cried at all.

The purser, walking through the cabin, heard Horace crying. "Hullo-ullo!" he said. "What's this? Trouble in paradise?"

"I want to play under the—"

"He wants to play with us," Isobel said swiftly. "He wants to play with us."

"You should let him," said the purser. He gave Isobel a quick, thorough glance, and she could tell at once that he thought the same as Mrs Colonel Hartington-Davis. He thought it was Isobel who was being a bad influence on Lettie, and it made Isobel furious. "Miss Lettie, you'll play with your brother, won't you?" he said. "I like to see a little girl playing with her little brother. My Betty always plays with my Jimmy." He looked a little bit misty-eyed, like he might cry.

"I want to play under the—" Horace wailed, and this time it was Lettie who cut him off before the purser could hear.

"Mr Purser," she said, in the lispiest lispy voice that Isobel hated. "You're right, I would normally play with my little brother, but—"

"Under where now?" said Mrs Colonel Hartington-Davis suddenly. "I wish you children would behave.

Oh, dear, you'll give me a headache."

I knew it, Isobel thought.

"He can come with us," said Isobel. She said it very crisply.

Lettie looked at her in amazement. Isobel tried to think "so he can't *tell*" at her and hoped Lettie might be able to read her mind. It was possible, she knew, for people to read minds sometimes.

Miraculously, Lettie seemed to understand. She prised Horace's sticky hand from Isobel's and took it in her own. "Let's go outside," she said, and Mrs Colonel Hartington-Davis smiled weakly at them all. The purser beamed at Lettie.

"What a nice little girl you are," he said. Isobel thought crossly, *It was me!* But it didn't really matter. It made no difference. Not really. It was just frustrating, that was the word.

"I'm going for a lie-down," said Mrs Colonel Hartington-Davis. "Be safe, and don't mess about with anything you shouldn't, do you hear me?"

"It's not *messing*," Isobel started to say, but Lettie grabbed her hand too, and pulled her away.

"I'll look after them both, Mummy," she said, just as she had that first day, but this time it was different; this time Isobel knew it was pretend, and just to keep

Mrs Colonel Hartington-Davis off their track. It was astonishing, honestly, Isobel thought, that one person could pretend to be so hateful. It was even more astonishing that she thought she might be starting to like Letitia Hartington-Davis.

Chapter Eight: The Thin Swede With The Toothbrush Moustache
Still Week 2, Day 2
Quite a long way past the middle of the Arabian Sea

It wasn't until they were washing their hands for supper that Lettie and Isobel managed to speak at all, and even then it was only for a moment.

"You got it?" said Isobel quickly, as she poured the jug of water into the basin and over Lettie's hands.

"Of course," said Lettie. She sounded a little bit smug, but for once Isobel thought it might be justified.

"The purser's list?"

"The purser's list, with everyone signed off by the doctor as they came on board. Crew too, though we can discount them." Lettie dried her hands on the front of her pinafore and pulled the manila envelope out of the top of her petticoat. "I was absolutely sure it was going to fall out when we were playing."

"It was good that you didn't drop it," said Isobel. It

was very nearly a compliment. "Let me look."

"There isn't time," said Lettie, and as she said it there was another knock at the door. "That'll be Mummy. Quick!" She passed Isobel the folder. "Put it in your notebook. Keep it all together."

Isobel folded it and put it in her notebook. She put the notebook back in her petticoat and wiped her own hands on her pinafore.

"You didn't wash them," said Lettie, and Isobel tried to rise above it. The Khans were at dinner for once, but Sam didn't look up when they came in. It was so ordinary, just like the night before. Why did nobody notice? Why did nobody do anything at all?

"They really don't know, do they?" whispered Lettie, over the blancmange. And then Isobel felt very cold all over, and she whispered back, "*Somebody* here knows…"

The purser, moving gently among the tables as usual, was clearing the plates, and the captain was setting up the wind-up gramophone for the dancing after dinner. There was always dancing after dinner. It was one of the lucky few ships with a gramophone, and three different records, which was supposed to make it better that you were going by mail ship instead of real ship.

"Imagine if this was a real ship," said Isobel to Lettie, very quietly. "Hundreds and hundreds of people. What an idiotic thing, to do a murder on a mail ship."

"Perhaps they didn't have a choice," said Lettie. "We didn't. We had to get back in time for school. Your parents passed awa— died," she corrected herself. "You had to leave. We had to leave. Lord Trimlingham has to get back because he's selling his house, he told Mummy. Sam's father has to talk to the Prime Minister about hygiene. Didn't you know that? That's what he does. He's extremely famous about hygiene. That's why Mummy is impressed by him."

Isobel shook her head. "I don't know anyone," she said.

"I know everyone who is anyone," Lettie said, smugly, and Isobel wanted to kick her.

Now the thin Swedish man was waltzing with the French sister in lilac, and Major Bourne was dancing with the one in heliotrope, and the other pair of French sisters were having to waltz together. ("Still two missing," said Lettie. "Or maybe not. We do need to look at those lists.") The French mother and father were dancing. The Karamazovas did not dance, and nor did Sam's father. Mrs Colonel Hartington-Davis was dancing, unexpectedly, with Lord Trimlingham. Trimlingham had a glass of wine in one hand, and was holding Mrs Colonel Hartington-Davis with the other. It was very deft. He was, Isobel thought, a very good dancer.

The ship's captain was dancing with Diamonds Mrs Drake; and then, at a twiddly bit in the music, he exchanged partners with Major Bourne. Diamonds Mrs Drake looked pleased. Outside, night had fallen over the ocean, and the portholes showed dim reflections of the dancers so it seemed that the moving bodies went on forever. Lettie and Isobel and Horace were sitting at the table. They had been given a pack of cards to play Snap, but Horace was counting his grubby little pocket treasures – a tarry bit of rope, two rupees, a scrap of paper he said had a good stamp on, and a disgusting bit of some blackish stuff that he said was paint but looked much worse – and the girls were trying to talk so that he wouldn't hear.

They were both rather tired. To keep Horace quiet they had had to play with him all afternoon – baby games like hopscotch (which, Isobel had had to concede, were more fun than they seemed and more fun when you had someone else to play with) and boy games like war (and these, too, were much more fun than Isobel had thought they might be, with lots of running and jumping and hiding). It had not been a horrible afternoon, really, except – she thought, glumly

– that they were one afternoon closer to Suez, and one more afternoon of a murderer among them, with nobody knowing anything about it except for them.

She said this to Lettie, and just as she said it, a shadow fell over them both. It was the thin Swede with the toothbrush moustache.

"Hello, children," he said. He looked very frightening, close to: his head was the same shape and colour as a ping-pong ball. *Murderer*, thought Isobel. So many people had secrets on this ship, and so many people did not want them found out. What was the Swede's secret? Lettie gripped Isobel's hand under the table, and Isobel gripped back.

"Why do you drink so much cocoa?" said Horace. Isobel was very glad he had spoken first.

"I do not drink tea," said the Swede. "And the mail ship coffee is abominable. And one must drink something. I have come, if you will permit me, to talk to these young ladies."

"What about?" said Isobel, fast.

"I have," said the Swede, "some information that may be interesting to you." He had a very soft voice, and his English was extremely perfect and correct. His accent was not like any that Isobel had ever heard.

"Information?" said Lettie. She looked at Isobel in

alarm, and Isobel in turn looked across the drawing room to try to catch Sam's gaze. But Sam was sitting with his father, and she saw his face; he was trying his best to be exactly the kind of boy Dr Khan wanted and was copying down a map of the sewers of London with every appearance of enjoyment. Dr Khan put his hand on Sam's head, gently, and Isobel felt a kind of feeling she wasn't exactly sure how to name: nobody, she thought, had ever put their hand on her head in this way. Nobody ever would.

"Young lady?" The Swedish man was looking at her expectantly, and she realised he had been waiting for her to say something. So had Lettie. So had Horace.

"Perhaps I should better say – advice. Advice that I have seen something that may, I think, be important to your investigation."

"Investigation!" Lettie and Isobel spoke at once. They looked at Horace, and back to the Swede.

"Don't talk about that here," Isobel said, and Lettie said, "How did you know?"

"I know many things," said the Swede. "I observe. I see. I think to myself: I will not interfere. But then I saw something that may be of worth."

Suddenly he turned to Horace. "Young man," he said to Horace, very politely. "Will you do me a great favour? Will you fetch from my cabin my small box of chocolates? My friend, Herr Doktor, will be there and he will give them to you."

"What'll you give me?" said Horace. "Will you give me chocolates?"

"It is chocolate for drinking," said the Swede apologetically.

"Well, what can I have for it?" said Horace.

"Horace!" hissed Lettie.

But the Swedish man only laughed. Horace held out his hand expectantly.

The Swedish man reached into his pocket and found two paisa. He put them into Horace's outstretched sticky palm.

"Never do something for nothing, hm?" said the Swedish man.

"'xactly," said Horace. "Which one's your cabin?"

"It is in the Row B," said the Swede. "You will see the door ajar, and my colleague Herr Doktor within."

Horace grinned. He did not have very many teeth at the moment, and it made his grin rather alarming: gummy and pink.

"Well," said the Swede very quietly to Lettie and Isobel, when Horace had gone. "I have seen, I think, that you are detecting something. No, no—" He held up a hand. "I do not know what. It is simply that you have the air of children who know things. No, you have the air of *people* who know things. Children are people, after all. I have known what it is to know things, and what it is to have a secret."

"We don't have secrets," said Lettie, and Isobel added, "It's everyone else that has secrets."

"Hm? Your notebook, no?"

"How do you know about the notebook?" demanded Isobel.

"I am very good at observing," said the Swedish man. "I have been a great policeman in my time."

"A real one?" said Lettie. She was impressed, Isobel could tell.

"This investigation isn't even to do with you," said Isobel. "Even if you were a detective."

The Swedish man laughed.

"I would not dream of interfering," he said, "in the detective adventures of small children."

"We aren't small children," said Isobel. It was at times like this that she remembered exactly why she disliked people so much.

"There is nothing in your detective adventures for a real, great detective such as myself. But nonetheless, I know a detective adventure when I see one. And I resolve not to interfere. But then, I see something. And I think: I will tell these children. I will give them a clue, when I see them alone."

"We don't want your pretend clue," said Isobel, hotly. "We don't want anything pretend. I don't play. I don't know why everyone wants children to play games all the time. It's such a waste."

"A waste?"

"A waste of all our time and energy," said Isobel.

"Nonetheless, young lady. The clue I offer you is not pretend. Indeed it is not so much a clue as a warning."

"A warning?"

The Swedish man nodded.

"I come to warn you that someone else is paying careful attention to your detective activities."

"What?" said Lettie.

"Who?" said Isobel.

"It is, I will tell you—" He lowered his voice. "Mrs Drake. Have you troubled her in some way?"

"Mrs *Drake*?!" said Lettie, astonished. "Diamonds Mrs Drake?"

"Diamonds Mrs Drake, as you call her. A very good name. Yes. I have seen her watching you, and I have seen her stand too near that lifeboat that you keep for your headquarters. Yes, you see, I also know about this.

117

And I tell you this for only this reason: detecting, even the mysteries of children, can be a dangerous business. People do not want even their smallest secrets unveiled. Do you understand? And here is your young brother."

Horace burst back into the room, clutching the box of chocolate powder. His mouth was gummed together with some kind of sweet.

"You got a secret," he said to Lettie, indistinctly. "But I got sweeties."

"Nougat, if I am correct," said the Swede, with a practised air. "Thank you, young man. You have been most helpful. As, I hope, I have also been."

"Well!" said Lettie, after. The dancing was finished; they were in their cabins, and getting into their nightgowns.

"Diamonds Mrs Drake!"

"He could be the murderer," Lettie said. "The Swede. Or she could be. It's all so jolly uncertain. Are you sure the captain wouldn't listen to us?"

"We tried," said Isobel. "They never do."

Lettie shrugged and undid her plait. She shook out all her hair, and Isobel gave her a mean look (which Lettie didn't see behind the hair).

"Diamonds Mrs Drake is suspicious, though," said Isobel.

"They are *all* suspicious," Lettie said, getting into bed. "Go on. Put out the light. We'll talk to Sam about it after breakfast."

She let out an enormous yawn. Isobel stifled her own. The case was very pressing, but the running and the jumping and the war and the sun had made them both sleepy.

"It would be better if we could talk now," said Isobel, but Lettie was already asleep. *Infuriating, infuriating girl*, thought Isobel. This was the bother with letting people into the investigation who weren't properly committed, but after a moment she, too, was fast asleep.

Chapter Nine: An Absolute Abundance Of Things

Week 2, Day 3

Very nearly at the Gulf of Aden

When Isobel woke, the decks were already almost dry, which made it well past eight. She lay in bed, looking at the deck drying (puddles dwindling as she watched, and dark patches fading to ordinary under the sun), and the pattern of the reflection that the water through the porthole made on the ceiling. It danced and swirled in coils of light, like snakes when a charmer plays, sometimes going this way, sometimes that. Lettie breathed softly in the next bed.

She didn't want to get up yet. Breakfast would already have started, but she was not hungry. Horace was always hungry; Lettie ate every scrap of her meals in an orderly fashion. Isobel had never been very interested in food. She thought she was just not a very hungry person.

Lettie yawned and stretched. "Mm," she said, contentedly. Lettie did so many things contentedly it made Isobel want to scream, even now. "Morning. Good morning. These beds are good for ship's beds, don't you think?"

"I don't know," said Isobel. "Some of us haven't been on a ship before."

Lettie didn't rise to it. "Well, I have. And these are jolly soft." She wriggled happily against the pillows. "Two pillows and a counterpane. And the counterpane is quilted. I thought a mail ship would have worse beds but I think actually they are better. What do you think?"

"We've got a murder to solve," said Isobel. She sat up in bed to make an example to Lettie.

"Oh, I know. I know that. Still, bed is lovely, isn't it?"

"No," said Isobel. She swung her legs out of bed. "I wonder why your mother hasn't come in yet."

"Headache, I expect," said Lettie. "She looked very pale last night. I do worry about her, you know."

Isobel did not know what to say. Mothers weren't for worrying about. Mothers were for – well. She did not pretend to know, really. Mothers were a mystery.

"It's partly because she misses Daddy – well, we all do – but partly she always gets headaches. She always has. We have to be very quiet a lot at home. Old home," she corrected herself. "Old home, old home, old home. We shan't be going back to India for a long time. Nor will you, I expect."

"Get up," said Isobel. She didn't like this kind of conversation.

"I'm starving," said Lettie. "Aren't you?" She stood up and shook out her hair. Even her nightgown was snowy white, and the blue ribbon threaded through the ruffly part at the top was real silk. Isobel was acutely conscious of her own nightie, which, while perfectly serviceable, had no ribbon – and it would not have been a silk one if it had.

"If we get dressed and go up to breakfast by ourselves," said Lettie, pragmatically, "we'll be able to signal to Sam and meet him afterwards. And we might get out without Horace following. Why he must be such a little pest I don't know. Can you do my buttons?"

"I can try," said Isobel. "But I can't even really do my own."

"We can try together," said Lettie.

Somehow, they managed it. It was not perfect – there were too many buttons and hooks for it to be perfect – but they both ended up in frocks and pinafores, with a stocking on each foot and a boot (mostly buttoned) over each stocking.

"What about hair? And faces?"

"We can wash our faces," said Isobel. She passed Lettie the jug and a sponge. "That will have to do."

They washed their faces with the cold water and the sponge; first Lettie, then Isobel.

"But my hair," said Lettie. Her hair was all around her face, like a picture in a book. She looked at her reflection critically in the glass of the porthole. "It's like a princess's hair, isn't it?" she said, in a self-satisfied way. Isobel threw the sponge at her and it made a wet mark on Lettie's pinafore. For a minute she wondered if Lettie was going to cry, but instead Lettie threw the sponge back at Isobel. She was a very good shot, and it hit Isobel on the forehead, splashing her with soapy and very cold water before falling to the floor. Isobel gasped.

"You'll be sorry," she threatened Lettie, and bent down to retrieve the sponge. Then she stopped.

There was a folded piece of paper on the floor by the door. It looked as if it had been pushed under the door in the night.

She said, rather uncertainly, "Lettie?"

"What?" said Lettie, suspiciously. "You got me once, I got you once. That's fair. Fair's fair, Isobel. Play fair."

"No," said Isobel. "Something else."

Lettie came over and looked at the paper too.

"Isn't it yours?"

"I would know if it was," Isobel said. "Not yours either?"

"You do all the writing," said Lettie. She added, slyly, "You made sure of that. You're the writing one. You won't let me even hold the pen."

"Don't start that," said Isobel. "Not without Sam here to make it all right." It was very important, she thought, to have all three of them together if there was going to be arguing. Arguing with just two of them felt much more dangerous, and she could not have said why. Safety in numbers, she thought of Sam saying. Safety in numbers.

Lettie, it seemed, felt the same. "All right," she said, peaceably. They looked together at the piece of paper.

"Well!" she said. "A clue?"

"Maybe," said Isobel.

Lettie bent down and picked it up. Then she said, "Bother! It would have had fingerprints on. Sam would have thought of that."

"What would we see them with, anyway?" said Isobel. "We haven't got anything useful."

"No magnifying glass," said Lettie. "No special powder. That's what they have in books."

"We've only got Sam's pipe," said Isobel. They exchanged looks. On this point they were in perfect accord.

"Awful," said Lettie, with a shudder.

"Disgusting," said Isobel. "I wish he wouldn't. Why couldn't he have a magnifying glass instead?"

"Too late now, anyway," said Lettie. She turned the paper over in her hands. It was ragged and small, as if it had been torn from something bigger, and folded very scrappily. "It's out of the handbook," she said. "There's a notes bit at the back. They've torn it out of the handbook."

"No clues there, then," said Isobel. "Anyone could get a handbook. We've all got one. According to you."

"We have," said Lettie. "In the drawer."

"Useless to us, then," said Isobel. She always felt very pinchy about the handbook. It still seemed most unfair that Lettie should have noticed it first.

"It *is* a clue, though," said Lettie. "Altogether, I mean. A mysterious note is always a clue."

"Open it, then," said Isobel. "This mysterious note."

Lettie unfolded the note and her eyes got very big and wide. She turned the paper round so that Isobel could see. And Isobel gasped.

There were only three words on the page, scrawled in

the middle of the paper.

They said, in shaky capitals:

I SAW YOU

"Whew!" said Sam. "What a lot of things. An absolute abundance of things. Overwhelming number of things to discuss."

"Absolutely overwhelming," said Lettie.

"Hand it over, then." Isobel was keeping the note in the back of her notebook, for safety. She took the notebook out and passed Sam the note. He unfolded it and looked at it. He swallowed hard.

"Gosh," he said. "A real mysterious note. A murder and a mysterious note and a mysterious warning. You wait all your life for just one and then all three come along at once." He was trying to sound brave, Isobel thought, but she could hear that he was just a little bit scared. He handed the note back to her.

It was, she thought, one of the most frightening things she had ever seen in all her life.

The letters were in black block capitals, and all over the place, as if they had been written by a child.

"Or written with someone's other hand," said Sam, grimly. "If I wrote with my left hand it would look just like that."

"To disguise the handwriting," said Lettie. "So we wouldn't be able to tell who wrote it."

"But saw us do what?" said Isobel. "And who?"

"Diamonds Mrs Drake, I suppose. If we can believe that Swede."

"We can't believe anybody," said Isobel.

They were sitting in the lifeboat after breakfast. They had lifted it, the three of them, just a little way up its ropes, so that they could see any feet approaching.

Lettie made the signal to Sam as they left breakfast: *HQ. Now.*

They had left breakfast before Horace could follow, and climbed quickly into the lifeboat.

"Right." Sam knocked his disgusting pipe lightly on the floor of the lifeboat, which was properly the floor of the deck. "Much to discuss. Put that back in your notebook, Petty. It might have fingerprints, or it might have done before you had your hands over it."

Lettie and Isobel exchanged looks. "We haven't got a magnifying glass," said Isobel, firmly. "So I said it was fine."

"I suppose so," said Sam. He didn't look convinced. "Still. We ought to be careful with evidence in any case. Back in the notebook."

"Don't tell me what to do," said Isobel, and Sam

looked suitably abashed. But she did it anyway.

Sam tapped his pipe again. "I call this meeting of the Petty, Lettie and Khan Detective Agency to order."

"Are we an agency?"

"Of course we're an agency. There's too many of us to be a consulting detective, like Holmes. Three detectives is an agency. Anyway, I call us to order."

"Order," said Lettie.

"Order," said Isobel. This seemed like the proper thing to say.

The morning sun was so strong that it shone through the upturned hull, greenish and pale, and it was quite light inside. There was just enough space for three, if they sat with their legs tucked up – although, Sam said, they ought to remember that it was still his office. Investigation headquarters, true, but Sam's office first and foremost. This seemed fair to Isobel.

"Our main order of business this morning is to find out who might be our victim."

Isobel opened her mouth to say something else about the Swede, and Diamonds Mrs Drake, and the note, but Sam held up a hand. She glared at him instead.

"Because until we find a victim, we can't hope to convince anyone that there's been a murder. And unless we can convince someone there's a murder, we can't convince someone there's a murderer. And unless we can convince someone there's a murderer, this ship is going to stop at the Port of Suez in three and a half days, and the murderer is going to escape. And where, I ask you, is the justice in that?" His voice had got louder and louder, as if he were making a speech to a great number of people instead of just to the two girls.

Isobel opened her mouth to reply again, but Sam kept speaking. He liked to speak, she had noticed, and he liked to make speeches.

"There is *no justice*," Sam declaimed, "unless we find this victim. And the only way to do that is to compare our list of people we have seen with the passenger list, to see who we are missing. We need to make a list of people we think might not be on the boat who ought to be on the boat. We have a clear objective, don't you agree?"

"Agreed," said Isobel. She felt better knowing there was a plan. "But—" And now it was her turn to hold up a hand. "What about Diamonds Mrs Drake? What about the Swede? What about the note? We have to be careful."

"The Swede didn't do it," said Sam. "I'm pretty certain."

"You weren't the one he warned," said Lettie,

fervently. "He frightens me. He knows things."

"He doesn't know what our case is, though," said Sam. "He'd have said if he did. He said it was kids' stuff. And murder isn't kids' stuff."

"Why are adults so pig-headed?" said Isobel crossly. "Why do they never think we might be doing something useful? They think they are completely different creatures instead of just bigger ones of us. I would rather die," she added passionately, "than ask them for help at all."

Sam nodded, but Lettie did not look sure. "Grown-ups are useful," she said, but the other two ignored her.

"And the note," Sam said. "That just means we have to work faster. Golly! We must get this murder solved absolutely as quickly as possible. It is… Well, it is exciting, isn't it?"

And Isobel had to admit that it was.

They pored over the lists together, the three of them, marking things here, checking things there. Once Lettie went to cross a name off the list in Isobel's notebook, but Sam whisked the pen out of her hand just in time. "We said Isobel would be the one to write in the notebook," he said, gently, and managed to make it sound as if it was neither Isobel's nor Lettie's fault.

When they had finished, they looked at the list they

had made. It was not a long list.

"Mrs Karamazova. Mrs Karamazova's maid. Two French sisters, but I don't know which ones, for they don't wear name badges. Four ladies. And everyone else is accounted for. Everyone else we have personally seen."

"Well, that's four leads," said Sam, trying to be cheerful. "That's four more than we had earlier."

"All ladies," said Lettie, thoughtfully. "Could it have been a lady? I suppose the one who fell might have been, but the one who came back didn't look like—"

She clapped a hand over her mouth. The other two stared at her.

"The one who came back didn't look like a lady," repeated Sam. "I know that, and Petty knows that, because we were both there. But you were asleep. Weren't you?"

"Well…"

"Didn't look like?" said Isobel. She could feel her temper rising. "Didn't look like what? You little *sneak*, Letitia Hartington-Davis. You little sneak, you—"

"Let her explain," said Sam. "Give her a minute, Petty." And Isobel would have been even crosser except that he put his hand in a reassuring way on her writing wrist.

"You *followed* me," Isobel said.

"You had better say it, Lettie," said Sam. "We've been jolly decent about letting you in on our secrets. It's not especially gentlemanly of you to keep one from us."

"It wasn't a secret," said Lettie, blushing. She really blushed: a pretty rose colour creeping up her cheeks, visible even in the green light of the lifeboat. Isobel wanted to kick her.

"When you came back the other night, I wasn't asleep. I got up and saw you weren't there. So I went to see where you were, to see what you were doing, in case it was interesting. But you weren't anywhere. So I deduced you must be on deck."

"You didn't *deduce*, because you aren't a detective," said Isobel, furiously. "You're just a follower. A creeping follower who could have ruined everything. Imagine if someone saw you. You might have ruined everything without even knowing. You probably did ruin everything."

"I didn't ruin anything," said Lettie, haughtily. "If you had been in bed I wouldn't have had to get out of bed to come and find you."

"You didn't even *find* me!"

"I heard you coming back across the deck so I ran and got into bed so you wouldn't *see*, that was what I was going to *tell* you—"

"What were you going to tell us, Lettie?" Sam's voice was quite reasonable; the girls had been almost shouting in furious whispers.

"I was going to *tell* you," said Lettie, looking only at Sam, "that it didn't look— They didn't look like a lady. The person who—" She looked a bit ashamed of herself. "Well. The person who came back."

Chapter Ten: The Curious Incident Of The Door In The Night-Time

Still Week 2, Day 3

The Gulf of Aden

"The person who came back?" said Sam.

"You *saw* the murderer," Isobel said, her mind working furiously. "You actually *saw* the murderer, and you weren't going to tell us because you didn't want me to think you were a sneaky little follower. Which you are. You followed me, and you listened to us talking, and that's how you knew to look at Sam the next morning. You – you—" She couldn't think of anything bad enough. "You friend-thief," she managed, after a moment. "You ... you ... adventure-thief. This was *my* adventure. You had no right."

"Petty," Sam said, gently. "She hasn't stolen any friends."

He looked at her, and she felt a small, quiet relief steal into her heart. "It's still our adventure," he said.

134

"It doesn't make it less of an adventure to have three of us."

"Exactly," said Lettie, smugly, and Sam shot her a look. "Sorry." She made an elaborate pantomime of zipping her lips shut.

"No!" said Sam. "That's the real problem here. You saw the murderer! And you were going to not tell us."

"I didn't think I saw anything you didn't see," said Lettie. "And besides, you said we had to find the victim first. You said this was a victim-first, first-of-its-kind murder case. So I didn't think it mattered."

"You didn't think the *murderer* mattered in a murder case?" What had Isobel been thinking? Letitia was the worst; she was the absolute worst and she should never have softened towards her in a thousand years. Poison ants. Poison ants for Letitia forever. And the worst part was that she was bedded in now; bedded in like a plant transferred to a new flower bed, all the roots woven into the soil, and you couldn't uproot her without uprooting the whole thing. Digging her out would be more trouble still. She had got in, Isobel thought, under *false pretences*. And she didn't even think it had mattered that she had seen the murderer.

"Well…" She really was pink now, a pink little flower with a golden halo.

135

"What exactly did you see?" Sam turned to face Lettie.

"Not very much," she said. "I came up after Isobel. I was just coming up to the deck, and the door was closed, but I saw a light through the little porthole, so I stopped. And then—"

"You following little *toad*," Isobel said, but Sam said "Shhh!" and told Lettie to go on.

"But I didn't see the murder. I was behind the door."

"You were behind the door?"

"Yes," she said.

"Interesting," said Sam, and Isobel had to agree that it was.

"And then the light went out."

"It did go out," Sam said. "I remember." They were silent for a few seconds, and they remembered, all three of them, the sound of the tussle, the sound of the waves, the way the gold light had played out over the water below. The shadows of the people, and the sea so far down that any splash was lost in the churn of the waves in the storm. It had been so horrible that they had all three tried not to think about it: to think only of the puzzle, and the mystery, and the glory of the investigation. It was much worse when one thought about it as a real actual person. Isobel shook her head to

136

try and put it out of her mind.

"And then what, Lettie?" In thinking about that night Isobel had almost forgotten to be cross.

"Then I was standing behind the door, and someone banged it open and rushed past me in the dark."

"Right next to a murderer," Sam said, marvelling. "And did you see anything?"

"Nothing," said Lettie, hopelessly. "I am sorry, honestly I am. They banged the door right into me. It bruised my leg."

Isobel thought of Lettie putting on her stocking very, very slowly the next morning.

"Look." Lettie rolled down her stocking. Her leg had a deep blue bruise along her calf. "I didn't know it was murder. I didn't know that until it was the morning."

"You heard me come back with Sam, didn't you?" said Isobel. She just had a hunch, and Lettie nodded.

"That's why you asked the next morning if I knew him. Because you heard him say goodnight in the corridor." Lettie nodded again.

"You do notice things, don't you?" said Sam, more admiringly than Isobel would have liked.

"Not when it's murderers, apparently," said Isobel.

"Shut up a minute, Petty, will you? Lettie's on to something."

"Oh, I didn't have anything else to say," said Lettie. "Sorry. That was all."

"Wait a minute, though. Hold on. I'm getting a sort of magnificent idea."

"Are you?"

"The Curious Incident of the Door in the Night-Time," said Sam thoughtfully. "Holmes! Petty! Tell me I'm a genius! Lettie! Did you hear the door?"

"The door?"

"The heavy door between the corridors. Between A and B. It can't be opened silently, can it?"

They looked at him.

"That big door. They keep it open with a cannonball in the day, so the people in Row B can get out on deck whenever they want. But they close it at night in case of fire. If it was closed, like it is every night, and Lettie didn't hear it open … the murderer must be from Row A. Or at least have been able to hide somewhere on Row A after he'd done the murder."

"Or she," said Isobel.

"Or she," said Sam. "Or she."

"So if the door can't be opened silently," said Isobel, slowly, "we've narrowed down our pool of suspects by half. If the door can't be opened silently, one of us would have heard it open to let them come through.

Because I wasn't asleep, and nor were you, Sam. And if the door can't be closed silently, Lettie would have heard it shut behind the murderer, leaving. If the door makes a noise when you move it…"

They looked at each other. "Let's go and see," said Isobel, and as one they scrambled out from beneath the lifeboat and ran down into the ship as discreetly as they could manage.

The French sisters were with their parents in the dining room, arguing again. "Céline," she heard one say, loudly, and immediately be cut off by a wail of "*Mais, Cendrine!*" But they shut up quickly when they saw the children come past the open door, and they all glared, as if they didn't want anyone to know what they were fighting about.

"Or they don't want to argue in front of people," said Lettie. "It's not very polite or well brought up to argue with your family in front of people. I never argue with Horace in front of people. Or I didn't, anyway, before Isobel came."

"Perhaps you'd always argue if you had so many sisters," Sam said, but since neither Lettie nor Isobel had any sisters they didn't know.

"I do wonder what it's about," said Lettie, but there was no time to stop and eavesdrop.

"Besides," Isobel pointed out. "We shouldn't understand because it's in French."

But they saw nobody else in the corridor. The door was held open by a brass cannonball, pitted and worn, and so heavy that it took Lettie and Isobel together to push it out of the way so that the door could slam shut with the pitching of the ship. It made an enormous crash as it did so, louder because the corridor was so little and narrow, and both girls jumped.

"Interesting," Isobel said.

"Very," said Lettie.

Sam was on the other side, and they saw the handle turn. But the door did not move.

"Interesting again," said Isobel.

"Very," said Lettie.

They took hold of the handle on their side, and Sam on his, and together they pulled it open. It creaked.

"That!" said Sam, looking triumphant, once they'd rolled the cannonball back before the door to keep it open. They were all panting a little bit. "That noise! Did you hear it?"

"Of course we heard it," Isobel said, but Sam shook his head.

"Lettie, I mean. Did you hear it the other night?"

Lettie screwed up her face and thought. "No."

"Are you *sure*?"

"Positive. I didn't hear it. I heard footsteps and then a door open, but it wasn't that creak at all. It was a handle turning, and a click. But the corridor was so dark I couldn't see anyone."

"Don't you see what this means?!" Sam was practically dancing from foot to foot.

"What?"

"No, wait a minute." Isobel was thinking. "You think this rules someone out."

"It does rule someone out. It rules out two someones."

"What?"

"If the door was opened, we would have heard it. We didn't, so it wasn't. It wasn't opened to let the murderer in to the corridor and out on to the deck; it wasn't opened to let the victim into the corridor and out on to the deck; and it wasn't opened to let the murderer out and into Row B. The murderer could have hidden in someone else's cabin, I suppose, but why would you? Why would you complicate it by getting someone else involved? And the murderer couldn't have known that your cabin would be empty. Even Isobel didn't know that. Occam's razor."

"Razor?" said Lettie. She looked rather lost.

"It means the simplest option is likely to be the right

141

one. The door didn't open. Nobody went through the door. The victim and the murderer – and the detectives! – came from Row A."

"Which means," said Isobel, "that the missing person isn't one of the French sisters. It means…"

Sam did a little pretend drum roll on his knees.

"It's the Karamazovas!" Lettie said, and Sam and Isobel both reached out to shove their hands over her mouth.

"Not here!" muttered Isobel.

"To the lifeboats!" called Sam, and they ran back up the stairs, the way they had come.

Far away in the distance was a coastline. "Is that Africa?" said Isobel.

"Arabia," said Sam. "Where all the perfumes come from. *All the perfumes of Arabia shall not sweeten this little hand*. That's from a play about a murderer," he added to Isobel. "It's by Shakespeare. It's supposed to be rather good."

"A lady murderer," said Lettie.

"Exactly. That's a lady murderer, and that's Arabia." It was greyer than the coastline of India, Isobel thought. Everywhere seemed to be greyer than India, the further they got from her home, and she thought with a start of how grey England must be.

Major Bourne and Diamonds Mrs Drake were talking together in low voices by the railing. Her turban was the colour of the sunset, deep, rusty orange, and her diamonds were pinky-peach in the reflected silk. She did not look suspicious. She didn't even seem to look round when they ran past; she was looking at Major Bourne.

"He does love her," Lettie said. "You can tell. He has fallen in love with her on this voyage."

"How can you tell?" Isobel frowned.

"He watches her all the time now. He didn't to start with. He adjusts her parasol for her when she's in a deckchair. He brings her things. And it would be nice for him to have a wife."

"Hmm," said Isobel.

"Maybe that's what she was looking at," said Lettie, suddenly. "Maybe that's what she was looking at when the Swede thought she was looking at us. Major Bourne. To see if he was in love with anyone else."

"Maybe," said Isobel.

"He does talk to those Frenchies too. And they've got money. Their grandfather invented the suitcase."

"The suitcase?" said Isobel, momentarily interested.

"The suitcase," said Lettie. "Imagine."

The Karamazova sisters were on deck too. Thin Miss

Olga was asleep in a deckchair with a bonnet tied over her face to protect her from the sun. Huge Miss Natasha was staring out to sea, to the horizon where Suez waited.

"Planning her getaway," said Sam, from the side of his mouth.

"You think it was her?"

"She's as big as a man, isn't she?"

Isobel turned to look at Natasha Karamazova. She thought about her biting the beetroot from her knife, and the red juice dripping down her chin. She thought about her clutching her sister's hand by the railing, and thought about her doing press-ups in her striped bathing suit, and the Madame Hercules Cup, and thought about her mother, perhaps downstairs in her cabin, and perhaps … somewhere else. Isobel shivered and ducked under the lifeboat to join the others.

"Well," said Sam.

"Well," said Isobel.

"Well," said Lettie.

They sat. The light was different now, and the deck was quieter. People were in their cabins changing for dinner, and the lap of the waves against the hull of the boat was more clearly audible. The engines made a steady beat underneath it all, and the deck seemed to hum a little more than usual as if it too knew that they had nearly caught a murderer.

"What happens now?" asked Lettie, humbly. "I've never caught a murderer before."

"Nor have I," said Sam. "It's not the sort of thing that happens to children particularly often. Even if you read all the right papers and spend all your time looking for one. I've waited years to catch this murderer. Since I was younger than Horace."

Isobel made a face at the mention of Horace. So, surprisingly, did Lettie.

"He is a very sticky child," said Sam. "When I was his age I already knew I was waiting for this moment to come. I was prepared. I have always been prepared, like an English Boy Scout. We don't have them in India. At least, I didn't. Did you?"

The girls shook their heads.

"His middle name is Dignity," said Lettie. "After a ship. And you'd think he'd live up to it once in a while, but he never does. He eats things he finds on the floor."

"Dignity!"

"Isn't it awful? Mine is Lucrezia."

"*What* a name," said Sam, admiringly.

"I think we should talk about the murderer," said Isobel quickly. She did not like it at all when Sam was nice to Lettie. The truce between them was a truce for catching murderers, but they were not friends. She had not and would not forgive Lettie for not telling about seeing the murderer. Who knew what other secrets she might be keeping?

"Miss Karamazova," said Sam. "Miss Natasha Karamazova is the murderer. And she murdered … her mother?"

"The bigger one pushed the smaller one overboard," said Isobel.

"Mothers can be small," said Lettie. Sam and Isobel did not look at each other. They had never agreed not to look at each other when the subject of mothers came up, and they had never spoken about it. Still, when Lettie said the word "mother", it seemed simpler to them both to look away.

"They can be small," said Sam, still looking away. "Especially when they are old."

"The little one didn't seem like an old lady," said Isobel. "And surely if they were both Russian they would speak in Russian."

"We have ruled out everyone else," said Sam. "And when you've eliminated the impossible, whatever remains is the truth. Of course."

"What?"

"When you've eliminated the impossible, whatever remains must be the truth. I thought you knew about Sherlock Holmes." He drew a satisfied drag on his empty pipe.

"That is absolutely horrible," said Lettie, looking at it.

"I do know about Sherlock Holmes," said Isobel, crossly. "I do. I just don't know everything he ever said."

"That's a very famous bit," said Sam. "And, as it happens, pertinent to our situation. Pertinent means relevant, which means it matters. Do tell me to chuck explaining things if it gets too much, by the by. Father won't let me do it at all. He refuses to take me seriously as a manipulator of language."

"It is such a horrible pipe," said Lettie. "And the sound is awful."

"Don't be a priss," said Isobel, and Sam looked at her in amazement.

"You hate this pipe," he said. "Don't side with me just because Lettie isn't. Have some courage of your convictions, Petty."

Isobel made a face at him, but he only laughed. "Anyway. The point is: we've got four people we haven't seen. Two of them are the French sisters, who couldn't have opened the door without Lettie hearing it open. Two of them are the Karamazova mother and the Karamazova maid. Miss Natasha Karamazova is famously enormous and famously strong."

"Why would she kill her mother?" said Lettie. "People love their mothers."

Sam and Isobel looked extremely solidly at the walls of the lifeboat. The light was even paler now, and moving with the reflections of the water far below, bouncing up from the sea to the white-painted metal of the ship walls and reflecting back on to the lifeboat ceiling, casting patterns on their faces.

"Some people love their mothers," said Isobel, sternly. "Some people do."

"Everyone loves their mothers!" said Lettie, and Isobel felt something hot and desperate rise up behind her eyes and a queer sickish feeling in her throat, and all around she thought for a moment she could hear the dead silence of the long low white house in the green hills, and feel the small brown snake moving through her hands as she sat under the table there, and knew nobody would come.

"Not everyone," said Sam, firmly. He put his hand on Isobel's shoulder, and his hand was warm and dry and solid, and the sickish feeling receded a little, and she was on the ship and they were solving a murder, and that was what was true, after all.

"We don't need to know all this stuff about mothers," Isobel said quickly. "She might have pushed the maid overboard. She might even," she said, with a sudden brainwave, "have pushed her sister. Miss Olga. Remember? She had a bonnet over her face when we came past. That might have been the maid in disguise. And she might easily have had a quarrel with her sister. People do, you know. I stayed with a family that were always quarrelling."

Sam sucked noisily on his pipe. "She could have murdered her sister," he said, mildly. "That's a point. A veritable point."

"So what next?"

"We need proof, I think. Or at least, we need to see if the mother and the maid are really missing."

"We need to check their stateroom. After dinner, while there's music on the gramophone in the dining room. They usually sit there for ages listening."

"Yes!"

"And," said Lettie suddenly, "their handbook will have a page torn out. To match with the note. An empty stateroom and a torn-up handbook. Or a missing handbook, I suppose, if that's overboard too."

"Yes!"

They grinned at each other.

Then Lettie said, suddenly, "Oh, help. What's the time? We're dining with the captain tonight and it means clean frocks all round."

Sam checked his fob watch, and they shimmied out from under the lifeboat, beaming, and ran lightly across the deck and round the corner and straight into Miss Natasha Karamazova.

Lettie yelped and grabbed Isobel's wrist, pulling her to the side and back round the corner. Isobel went to pull Sam with them, but it was too late. Miss Natasha had caught him by the shoulders. The deck was deserted and the sun was setting over the sea, tinting it pink and scarlet.

She put her enormous hands on either side of Sam's face. They were very pale and huge, like dinner plates, and you could barely see Sam's head between them.

What if she pulls his head off? Isobel thought, and she could feel Lettie thought the same by how tightly she was holding her hand.

"So," said Miss Natasha Karamazova in her thick Russian accent. "You children are … having fun? You are … safe?"

"Very safe, Miss Karamazova," Sam said, and Isobel admired how steady his voice was. Lettie's hand was hot in hers and she clutched it tighter. Not because she was scared, of course, but because Lettie might have been.

"If some children being so naughty on this ship, it might … cause an accident," boomed Miss Natasha. "Are you understanding me?" She said "understanding" as if it had a k on the end: *understandink*. And all her "s"s came out like "z"s. *Zome children. Zo naughty.*

"There will be an accident if you run so fast," she told Sam. Her face was very big and white, like a pancake made with wheat flour instead of gram, and her teeth were very yellow, like little chickpeas. "An accident like you might … fall into the sea. Are you understanding me?"

"I understand you very well, Miss Karamazova," Sam said. Isobel's heart was beating very fast. She could feel Lettie's heart beating in her hand, in the soft bit below the thumb, and she was glad to have Lettie there: glad to have two hearts beating, watching this, instead of just one alone.

"Be careful in future, boy," said Miss Natasha, and released Sam so hard that he staggered backwards. "Go to your father, or I will, to tell him you have been running."

Miss Natasha did not look at the girls, and nor did

Sam: he merely walked briskly ahead of them to the cabin doors.

"Why isn't he speaking to us?" Lettie hissed, and Isobel nodded at his hands. He was signalling with his thumb and forefinger, bent round to make a C. *C for cabin*, Isobel thought. But whose? Theirs? His? She watched his hands: forefinger pointing straight, then the thumb jerked out at a right angle. *I, L, C. Isobel, Lettie, Cabin.*

They waited until Sam had gone inside, and watched Miss Karamazova look out over the ocean. Then she sighed, heavily. She leaned on the barrier between the deck and the drop to the sea, and covered her own face with those dinner-plate hands, and said something almost inaudible to someone who wasn't there.

"That's Russian," whispered Isobel. "She's speaking Russian to herself."

"She looks so sad," whispered Lettie.

They were frozen in place until Miss Natasha moved, unless they wanted to tiptoe behind her. They were both too afraid to move at all. And then something strange and odd happened: Miss Natasha began to cry. Isobel had never seen an adult cry, and certainly never someone as huge and strange as Miss Natasha. Her shoulders, broad as a barrel, strong as an ox pulling a cart, shook slightly in her striped bathing dress, and her bare elbows quivered on the mahogany bar, and they could hear her – a dreadful, queer little sound that seemed too small to come from someone so enormous. Then she stood and mopped her face with the sleeve of her garment, and shook herself off like a wet dog hoping to come inside.

"Enough," said Miss Natasha Karamazova in English, and went down into the corridor where the cabins were. Lettie and Isobel stared at each other in horror and amazement and utter, utter confusion.

Chapter Eleven: A Regular Lady Macbeth

Still Week 2, Day 3

The Bab-el-Mandeb Strait

There was no time, when they got back to the cabin, for Sam to come. There was no time for a proper plan, which they needed now more than ever. No time, no time, no time to think. No time before Suez, no time before dinner, no time to plan.

They ate dinner that night at the captain's table. You took it in turns, on board ship, to eat with the captain like a sort of treat. Isobel lived in horror during that meal that he would say something about the way she and Sam had come to his cabin; that he would turn to Mrs Colonel Hartington-Davis and ask her what her little orphan ward was doing running amok on his mail ship, and whether Mrs Colonel Hartington-Davis ought not to take better care of her. But he did not: he patted Mrs Colonel Hartington-Davis on the shoulder, often, and told her how lonely it was to be a sea captain on a mail ship. He asked her how lonely it was to leave your husband in India, and he asked Horace about whether he wanted to be a sailor when he grew up (no, the army), and he asked Lettie and Isobel whether they wanted to be sailors' wives (and they looked at each other with a kind of horror). The captain laughed and said that Lettie was a very pretty little girl, and he looked at Isobel and told her that she seemed a smart young thing, and although Isobel didn't care at all whether the captain thought she was pretty she still wanted to kick both him and Letitia in the shins, under the table. She was trying not to listen to any of it.

"All well otherwise, I trust, Mr Purser?" said Mrs Colonel Hartington-Davis.

"Can't complain, can't complain. Everyone on board, that's what I like to have, and all in budget and on time. We've run out of kippers, and one of the passenger chaps using more of the hot water than he ought," said the purser. "But when that's the most of your worries, it's a blessed voyage, isn't it?"

Lettie looked at Isobel when he said "everyone on board", but Isobel didn't want to look back.

And all the time that she was thinking about

whether the captain would say something to Mrs Colonel Hartington-Davis about her visit to his cabin, and all the time that she was trying not to mind about being called "smart" instead of "pretty" there was a little ticking metronome in her head, like the thing that sits on top of a piano so you can play at the right speed, or the pendulum inside a grandfather clock, saying: *no time, no time, no time…*

For it was true there was no time. For it was true that if Miss Natasha Karamazova was a murderer, (and really, who else could it be? Why else would she have said what she had said to Sam? And why else would she have wept?) For if it was true that Miss Natasha Karamazova was a murderer, and if it was true that Miss Natasha Karamazova knew that they knew, (and really what else could she have meant by what she said to Sam?) For if all those things were true, it was true too that they were in danger.

The sisters Karamazova dined alone, as usual; Miss Olga (thin) facing out through the porthole into the ocean; Miss Natasha (murderess?) facing into the room, spearing individual fine white flakes of smoked fish with the point of her knife and lowering them one by one into her wide red mouth.

If Miss Natasha Karamazova had murdered her

mother (or the maid, or her sister, who had had the bonnet tied across her face, who still faced the ocean, whose face Isobel could not see), she had got away with it, and would continue to do so if it weren't for three meddling children…

If she, Isobel Petty, were Natasha Karamazova, and the only thing that might spoil her successful murder were three children, she would not hesitate to push them into the ocean too. She was trying to communicate this to Sam by thinking, but she wasn't sure it was working. She wished that she knew the signing language from the back of the boat book, but perhaps there wasn't a signal for "we need to find proof that the big Russian lady is a killer before she kills us too". She doubted it, anyway.

No, there was only one thing to do. Boldly, she reached for Mrs Colonel Hartington-Davis's hand. Mrs Colonel Hartington-Davis looked at her in shock.

"I am afraid I must – I must— May I go to the—"

Mrs Colonel Hartington-Davis blushed a furious shade of crimson. "Dear! We never mention such things at dinner!" she hissed through gritted teeth, and hoped the captain hadn't heard Isobel's awful manners. "Go then, dear. If you must."

Behind the captain's back Isobel made a small hand

signal to Lettie: thumbs-up. Lettie nodded, a tiny little nod that neither the captain nor Mrs Colonel Hartington-Davis would notice.

Isobel stood. As she did so, she caught the carafe of red wine with her elbow; it tipped and smashed noisily on the table, spilling wine all over Lettie's beautiful white pinafore. The crimson stain bloomed like a poppy and Lettie burst immediately into noisy sobs.

"That horrid little girl," Lettie wailed. "That horrid clumsy brat has spoiled my-y-y pretty dre-e-ess!"

She put her hands over her face, then dropped them slightly and very briefly to delicately wink at Isobel. "I ha-a-ate her, Mummy! I ha-a-te her! She spoiled my dress!"

"She did it on *purpose*," said Horace. "She's made of snakes. That's what I think. She's a horrid snake with legs."

"Children," said Mrs Colonel Hartington-Davis. "Please, children." She put a hand to her temple. "Captain, I am so dreadfully sorry."

"An accident, I'm sure!" The captain raised his hand to call for a fresh tablecloth and a new jug of wine. "I'm sure such a nice little girl can go and pop on a clean frock and be back for pudding as pretty as a daisy, what? Perhaps you could help her, miss?" He nodded at

Isobel. "Put right your wrong, what?"

"Shouldn't I—" Mrs Colonel Hartington-Davis made a move to stand up, but the captain put his hand on her shoulder to stay her. "Nonsense! These little girls can help each other!" And Isobel had to stifle a smile.

Isobel and Lettie went across the dining room together, Isobel with her hands folded crossly before her, and Lettie crying the whole way. Sam, Isobel was pleased to see, had already got up from the table and gone too. He probably hadn't even had to ask to go; Dr Khan sat, reading, as usual. He was making notes in the margins of his papers in spiky black handwriting, and did not look up as Isobel and Lettie went past on their way out.

Sam was waiting for them on the stairs.

"Wisest, wisest of women! What judicious casting of wine upon the waters, and by wine I mean wine and by waters I mean tablecloth and also Lettie's pinafore. You look like you've been stabbed," he said, admiringly. "Bloody all over. It's a shame you didn't get any on your hands. Then you'd have been a regular Lady Macbeth."

"That play again," said Isobel.

"Precisely," said Sam. "Anyway, an excellent distraction. Buys us some time to search the room, don't you think? To find that there is no Madam

Karamazova? Or no maid?" He produced his pipe from the sleeve of his jacket. "Watson –" (he nodded at Isobel), "Watson –" (he nodded at Letitia), "It is time to find some clues. As I am sure you have already deduced from my small contretemps (that's a run-in, by the way, in this instance, or an unexpected and unfortunate occurrence) with Miss Natasha before dinner, I suspect we may well be in danger."

"Obviously," said Isobel, crisply.

"What?" said Lettie.

"What Sam means," Isobel explained, "is that Miss Natasha knows we know. What else did that speech mean about pushing us into the ocean?"

"What else could she possibly have meant?" said Sam.

"She knows we know," Lettie said, slowly.

"She knows we know," Isobel agreed. "We can't wait; we need proof. We're in danger."

"We need proof now."

"Now. If she's not in the dining room, she must be in the stateroom. The maid and the mother. And if they aren't in there, or if only one of them is…"

"Lettie! You had better go and change out of your Lady Macbeth get-up. Or they will know."

Lettie nodded ruefully. "I thought of that. But you

two search the rooms."

"You'll have to come and do my buttons, Isobel, after you've finished." Isobel nodded. She was getting better at buttons, she thought.

They had been talking in frantic whispers and walking as quietly as they could manage, by common consent, and they had come now to the large door that separated Row A from Row B. In one of the rooms – Major Bourne's – one of the babies was crying, and then it stopped.

"That means the maid is in there, probably," Sam said. "Babies don't just stop crying on their own. So we must be quiet."

"You go now, Lettie, and I'll come in a minute. Once we've made sure there's nobody in the room," said Isobel.

But both doors were locked shut, and the handles would not turn at all. It seemed impossible to Isobel that they had not thought even a little bit of this eventuality, and she thought of the keys on the chain round Miss Natasha Karamazova's neck, shining in the sun, and wanted to scream.

The babies in Major Bourne's room were crying again. Isobel knew exactly how they felt.

Chapter Twelve: The Depths Of Despair
Week 2, Day 4
The Red Sea

"No proof; no victim; a murderer who knows we're on to her."

Lettie gave a huge sigh and rolled over so that her face was pressed up against the canvas side of the lifeboat. "This is *ghastly*."

Sam was eating condensed milk out of the tin with a spoon. He offered some to Isobel, who shook her head. "Suit yourself," he said, and went on.

"What did you *think* detecting was going to be?" Isobel was sitting with her knees drawn up to her chin. There was a run in her stocking and she couldn't leave it alone. The hole was exactly the size of her little finger, and every time she poked it the ladder ran on and on, down her leg, exactly like tracks being laid for a train. There were no holes in Lettie's stockings. She thought fondly of the red wine ruining the white frock the night before. She said, sternly, "This isn't a game, Letitia. I don't play."

"You played hopscotch," said Lettie, slyly. "You *liked* hopscotch."

Isobel glared at her, but as Lettie's face was turned to the wall she didn't even see. *What a waste of a glare*, Isobel thought. A good glare, at that.

"I don't play," said Isobel. "That was necessary for the investigation. We were distracting Horace."

"He's being very unlikely, lately," said Lettie. "He never wanted to play with me in Calcutta, anyway. Perhaps he wants to play with me in England. Who knows?"

"I thought you knew all about England," said Isobel. "I thought you'd been to England so many times it made you English."

"We are English," Lettie said quickly.

"I'm not," said Isobel.

"You can be if you want," said Sam, and Lettie opened her mouth to say something and shut it again. "I'm Indian because my father is, and English because my mother was, and so I'm completely both."

Sam did not say things about his mother very often; it felt to Isobel like a sigh when he said it, like something

163

precious breathed out into the stale air of the lifeboat and the salt air of the sea. "She was English and very clever and she died when I was just a baby."

"Isobel's mother passed on as well," said Lettie, and Isobel said, quickly and without meaning to, "My mother *died*." She dug her nails into the palm of her hand so hard and swiftly that the run in the stocking tripled in size. She did not want to look at Sam.

"I was just being polite," Lettie said, and her voice was apologetic. Isobel felt suddenly too tired to have a quarrel about it.

"I knew you were an orphan," Sam said. "I knew you were before I even talked to you. You look like an orphan."

"What do orphans look like?" Isobel said, but she knew really what he meant. It was the scrawniness, and what they called the sallowness of her – although she had been the same yellowish-cream colour all her life, and she had never been a plump child. It was the way nobody had taken care over her frocks. It was not having anybody to brush her hair. She didn't mind any of these things, but it was clear to her that other people did.

"Who tidies *your* clothes, then?" she demanded of Sam. He looked a little bemused. "Who brushes your hair and tidies your clothes? Who makes you look so neat? Your hair stands on end but it still looks neat! It still looks brushed! I can't help it if I haven't any mother or any father or any ayah to do these things for me!"

"I do it myself," said Sam, and Isobel was entirely disarmed.

"Yourself?"

"I do everything myself," said Sam. "I am remarkably independent. I have had to be. My father isn't the domestic sort, if any father is. I expect I'd be much lazier if my mother hadn't died. You might be much more independent now, you know. Which would be a good thing."

"That is a dreadful thing to say," Lettie said, sternly. "You mustn't be glad that people have passed on."

"Glad!" Sam stared at her and put his condensed milk can down on the ground. "Glad!"

"Well – you said it might be a good thing…"

"Glad! There can be good things that happen because terrible things happened, you know! I can be pleased I learned to do all my own buttons and to run a newspaper because I never had a mother to stop me, and still never be glad that I haven't had a mother since I was so small I can't remember! Glad! I wouldn't ever be glad!" It was the closest Sam had ever come to shouting, and Lettie looked as if she might cry.

"Things," Isobel said, very carefully, trying her best to explain to Lettie (who would never understand, who had a mother who loved her, who had a father who missed her, who knew all about people). "Things are just a bit complicated."

"Complicated," said Sam. "Complicated is *exactly* the word for it." He sighed one big long breath out. "I didn't mean to snap, Lettie. But I'm not glad. And it is complicated. And I don't really know the words to explain it. And if I don't know a word, it doesn't count. I am," he said, with a touch of his usual dazzle, "extremely magniloquent."

"Magniloquent?"

"It means that I like big words," Sam said. "Which I do. Magni is Latin for big. Loquent is Latin for … well, something like speaking But you don't do Latin at girls' schools, probably. And Isobel is never going to school at all."

"Never," said Isobel. She shuddered. "Don't talk about it. I don't want you to. That's a different life."

"It's all one life," said Lettie, as if it was simple. "You can't just divide it up into bits and say that's one bit, that's another bit."

"I can do exactly as I please," said Isobel, crossly.

"We can all do as we please," said Sam. "Except that we're trying to catch a murderer. This meeting of the Petty, Lettie and Khan Detective Agency really is a dismal one. And we'll be in Suez tomorrow evening, if the sea stays calm."

"Tomorrow!"

"She'll get away!"

"Why should she even try? She can just say that her victim got off the boat, if anyone asks where they are. Nobody would even know."

"This is bad," said Lettie.

"We know," said Isobel.

"It must be her. But how can we prove it? It has to be her! She threatened Sam."

"She's the only one with a victim in Row A," said Isobel.

Sam sat up and banged his head.

"I have just had," he said, "a truly horrendous thought."

"What is it?"

"Just because the murderer is in our part of the corridor, it doesn't mean the victim is."

"What?"

"Oh, no," breathed Isobel. "Oh, no. You're right."

"Of course I'm right. The victim could have been

lured outside earlier by anyone in Row A. The German doctor seems suspicious to me. He drinks salt water. And he had a disturbed night, remember? He told the steward the morning after. Hugo Trimlingham. His manservant, even. My father. Your mother. Major Bourne, a big man who speaks very good English. Even if the victim is one of the missing Karamazovas – maid or mother – it doesn't prove that Natasha Karamazova did it."

"They could have met on board ship."

"They could have known each other from somewhere else. Your mother knows my father, doesn't she? Or she knows who he is. That Swedish man seems to know who everyone is."

"Knowing who the victim is—" started Isobel.

"Doesn't tell us who the murderer is," finished Sam. "It doesn't even narrow it down by very much. Because they might have met anywhere. This isn't a special murder mystery at all. It's just an ordinary one, only much harder. This is the depths of despair, and I am in it."

Sam flung himself backwards on to the heap of lifejackets. They made a sort of unpleasant rubbery squishing sound.

"But Natasha Karamazova was crying," Lettie said, after a bit. "She was crying. And she was angry with you. Surely that's – that's something?"

Then, like a kraken emerging from the waves, Sam sat up from the jackets so suddenly he bumped his head again on the rib of the lifeboat.

"Letitia," he announced. "You may be a genius."

Isobel bristled. Lettie had said nothing new. They knew that already.

"We are," Sam said in his declaiming voice, "going about this all backwards."

"Backwards?"

"We need to think of other people who were acting strangely. People who were upset in some way. Like crying, or being angry. Those are both signs of being a murderer – and reasons you might do a murder in the first place. Motives."

"Motives?"

"Like headlines," said Sam. "Why do people do murders in books?"

Isobel shrugged. "I don't read books."

"You really should," Sam said, mildly. "Some of them are good. Sherlock Holmes is a book."

"I don't like books," said Isobel.

"You said you didn't like lots of things," said Lettie. Isobel shot her a glare, but Lettie didn't even seem to notice.

"You don't read books *either*," said Isobel to Lettie.

"I do. But not," she admitted, "ones that will be very useful to us now. Nobody gets murdered in books for little girls."

"Nobody?" Sam was horrified.

"No. They don't think little girls are interested in murder."

"But you are!"

"They don't know that," said Lettie. She smiled a sickly-sweet kind of smile; the kind of smile that made her dimples jump in her cheeks and her eyes seem a brighter blue than ever. She looked like a painting of a little girl: a painting of a girl in a story about being well behaved.

"They think I'm interested in dollies and skipping and sewing, which," she added, thoughtfully, "I am. I'm very interested in skipping, quite interested in sewing and I like dolls an ordinary amount. There's nothing wrong with being interested in those things. It's just that I am also interested in murder."

Her face went back to normal again. Isobel was deeply relieved. It was unsettling, honestly, how quickly Lettie could put on a grown-up-pleasing face.

"Motives," said Isobel quickly, because she didn't want to talk about books any more. "What are motives?"

"Well…" Sam stopped and thought about it. "There's money, of course. People do murders to get money. Sometimes just to steal it, and sometimes to steal it in complicated ways. Like they would get it in a will or something, if the person died."

"The Discount Viscount!" said Lettie suddenly. "Trimlingham! He got money! From a will! The will was in the papers and everything, so you know it's true. *And* he needed it, too. For space."

"For space?" said Sam, interested.

"He's an astronomer. He wants to explore space."

"How could anyone explore space?"

"Like with a ship," said Lettie. "He wants to sail through space like we sail through the sea."

"That," said Isobel, scornfully, "is absolutely impossible."

"I know *that*," said Lettie. "I'm not stupid."

"She knows you're not stupid," said Sam. He reached out and patted Lettie's shoulder. "Go on about the Discount Viscount."

"They call him that because he didn't have any money," said Lettie. "He needed money, and then his father died and he got some."

"He might have murdered his father!" said Sam excitedly.

"For the money!" said Lettie.

Isobel said, "But his father wasn't on the ship, and you wouldn't get money in a will if you didn't know the person was dead."

"What?" Lettie looked at her.

"You get money in a will after a person's dead. But our whole problem is that nobody *knows* this person is dead. They don't even believe us that somebody died. So it can't be Lord Trimlingham. Besides, we saw him. We saw him and his valet yesterday morning on deck. So they can't be dead."

"True," said Sam. He sighed. "He's out, then. Shame. I thought Lettie was on to something there for a minute."

"So did I," said Lettie. "Why else do people do murders? Who else was sad? Who else was angry?"

They thought. Then she said excitedly, "Diamonds Mrs Drake. Diamonds Mrs Drake was crying. And that Swedish man said she was watching us. She's got something to do with it."

"She might have," said Isobel, "but those French sisters were arguing. Which is a second mark against them. If they knew one of them had been murdered."

"Accomplices!" said Sam gleefully. "Maybe they were in cahoots with someone in Row A to murder their sister. Major Bourne, for instance. He's a jolly good suspect."

"He might have been in league with Mrs Drake!" said Lettie.

"You said they ought to get married," said Isobel, slowly. "They could be in cahoots, if it were true."

"Perhaps he was already secretly married to the Karamazova mother."

"Or the French sisters," said Lettie.

"They'd recognise him," said Sam.

"Perhaps they thought he was already dead."

"Perhaps his beard is false."

"Perhaps they aren't his babies at all."

"Perhaps he stole them."

"Perhaps they are mysterious twins!"

"Kidnapped at birth!"

"A long-lost sister!"

Isobel watched this conversation with something like horror. "You're just making all this up," she said severely. "None of that can possibly be true. You couldn't know it even if it was."

"That's newspapers!" said Sam, grinning.

"Nobody is mysterious twins," said Isobel. "I have never met a mysterious twin."

"There could be mysterious twins," said Sam. "There

could be a long-lost sister or a long-lost brother. There could be kidnapping. There's been a murder, Petty. It doesn't get more exciting than that. Anything is possible now."

It all felt, to Isobel, as if things were spiralling too far and too fast out of control. She felt a little as if she might cry again. What was happening to her? She did not think she had ever cried before. She had not cried at all when they told her everyone was dead. She did not even think about crying then.

"But you didn't mind making stuff up about Karamazova," said Lettie. "Detecting is all making things up and seeing if it's true or not."

"Detecting is noticing things," said Isobel. There seemed, once again, to be a wide gap between them, which she could not jump across. They were playing a game that meant nothing to her. "I didn't make anything up about Karamazova. I simply detected what was true."

"Do admit that Major Bourne is a suspect," said Sam. "Do admit, Petty."

"I agree that Major Bourne is a suspect," said Isobel. "He is a very angry man."

"Yes, all right," said Lettie. She seemed a little put out; her cheeks were pink from the thrill of the conversation. Isobel wanted to stick a pin in her, to burst her like a bubble on a thorn. Lettie was too happy, Isobel thought, that was the problem. She was too happy and too pretty and too pink and too pleased. She ought not to be allowed to have the excitement of a murder too. She ought not to be allowed Sam. It wasn't fair.

"Go back to your list, Petty. I knew we ought to have one. Give us a new column. Give us a column that says *Motive*. Oh, I know we haven't got anything to put in it yet. But give us time. God, give us time."

"That's exactly what we haven't got," said Isobel. "Time. We'll be in Suez in two days – and that's the lunch bell, isn't it?" It was, and it rang out clear and loud across the deck, and they looked at each other and felt the time slipping away from them all. It had never felt so precarious to any of them – and never would again, thought Isobel. If she had seen any art, or read any books, she might have thought of sand falling through an hourglass; but she had not, so she did not, and thought instead of earth falling through her fingers, and of water caught in cupped hands, evaporating away in the heat of the sun before you could pour it on the thirsty ground.

175

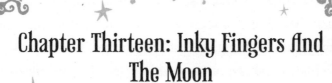

Chapter Thirteen: Inky Fingers And The Moon

Still Week 2, Day 4

Still the Red Sea

"After lunch," Sam said, "let's meet back here. We'll pick a suspect each. And we'll trail them."

"Trail them?"

"It means to sort of follow them about. See if they do anything."

Somewhere across the deck, Mrs Colonel Hartington-Davis was calling for the girls.

"No grown-up detective would ever realise how difficult it is to run an investigation when people keep bothering you," said Sam. "We could just live up here on condensed milk."

"Ugh," said Lettie. "You and your condensed milk."

"Eating just takes up so much *time*," said Isobel.

"Always having to stop and eat a bowl of kedgeree just as things are starting to get interesting. But then, that's mothers!" said Lettie cheerfully. "Always wanting you to do things."

Sam and Isobel exchanged motherless glances.

"That's mothers," said Sam, grimly. "I suppose we'd better go."

So they went.

At the dining-room door they split: Sam to his father, who was working as usual. He nodded to Sam when he sat down, and put his hand quickly and tenderly on his son's head. Sam ducked, but even across the room, Isobel could see he was pleased. People were so funny, she thought. Parents were so funny, and all of them different.

When Isobel and Lettie got to their table, Mrs Colonel Hartington-Davis made the usual fuss about them washing. "Go back downstairs at once," she said. She looked brighter than she had that morning. "Lord Trimlingham is going to eat lunch with us and I won't have you little girls showing me up. Especially not you, Lettie, precious. You have always been such a pretty little girl." She looked Lettie up and down in a troubled sort of way. "Get a pressed ribbon from the drawer."

Then she looked Isobel over and sighed. "Well, there isn't much to be done with you, Isobel, dear. Just wash your hands and face and do your best."

Sam was watching from his table with amusement.

"For someone who's supposed to care about hygiene," Isobel said crossly to Lettie on the way down, "Dr Khan doesn't seem to care much about whether Sam washes his hands and face before lunch."

"It's nice to wash," said Lettie. "I like being clean."

"Of course you do," said Isobel. "Grown-ups like it. That's why you like it."

"I just like to be tidy," Lettie said, primly.

"*I just like to be tidy,*" Isobel said, in a feeble imitation. She bit her lip, looked down at her own stockings with the hole in them, and sighed.

"Isobel!" There was a note of alarm in Lettie's voice. She looked up.

There was something white tucked into the thin space between the doorknob and the door.

A scrap of paper with a torn edge, folded in two.

"Is it … another one?"

"Another one," said Isobel. She moved forward and stopped herself.

"Sam will want to know if there are fingerprints," she said. "Not that we can see them. But we should be careful. Give me your hair ribbon."

"What?" said Lettie, and then she understood. She pulled out the crumpled ribbon from her hair and handed it to Isobel, who folded it between her finger and thumb. Then she pulled the sheet of paper free.

She looked at it closely, and as she did so she noticed a faint and peculiar smell. Waxy, almost. Like candles, maybe, or oil. But someone upstairs opened the dining-room door, and the strong smell of boiled cabbage wafted down, and it was gone. Perhaps she had imagined it.

It was obviously the same kind of paper as before: ripped and heavy, from the handbook. She turned it over.

"Look!" There was a black smudge across one corner.

"Ink," said Lettie. "Off their hands."

"Lettie! It might still be on her hands! Or his hands!" They looked at each other in amazement.

"If it's on Karamazova's hands," said Lettie, "that's it. We have to have proof. Go on then. Open it."

Isobel unfolded the note.

Only two words this time, in the same shaky black capitals. Same wrong-handed scrawl.

WATCH OUT

Upstairs everyone was still waiting for them to come back up to lunch, clean and tidy. First:

I SAW YOU

she thought. And now:

WATCH OUT

She tucked the second note into her notebook with the first, and stashed the notebook into the top of her knickerbockers. She washed her face as best she could, and helped Lettie tie her ribbon.

"D'you want a ribbon?" Lettie offered, and Isobel thought about it, and then she shook her head. Some girls, she decided, were meant for ribbons. And some were not.

"You would look pretty with a ribbon," said Lettie.

"I'm only supposed to wear black," said Isobel, because nobody had ever said she might look pretty before in anything. She was not a pretty girl, and she knew it.

"I think you'd look prettier in a colour," said Lettie. "You might look lovely in red. No, not really red…" She thought, considering. "A sort of wine colour. Like the one you spilled. Black makes you look much worse."

"Thank you," said Isobel. She meant it to sound sarcastic but it came out sincere.

"We'd better go back up," said Lettie. "We need to see if Miss Natasha has inky fingers."

"If *anyone* has inky fingers," corrected Isobel. "It isn't just her now, remember? We went back to the beginning."

"So we did," said Lettie. "But I still think it's her. We haven't really got time to suspect anyone else. Lunch first, anyway. Gosh I'm hungry. I wonder what it is."

Suddenly Isobel felt very tired. There was so much still to do, and they had to waste so much time sitting at meals, and being polite, and saying things that didn't need to be said, and she felt very faraway and like she didn't understand any of them at all. Once, she thought, she had had a different kind of life. Once she had known nobody, and it was not that that had been better (*no Sam!* she thought with horror, and then, to her surprise, *no Lettie!*). It had just been easier to understand.

"Come on," said Lettie, and they went upstairs together, Lettie half running because she was so hungry, and Isobel dawdling because she was suddenly so tired and sad.

The Karamazova sisters were sitting at their usual table and it was impossible to see whether their hands were inky at all. They couldn't even tell Sam about the note so that he could look, because of course he was eating with his father, and they had to sit with Mrs Colonel Hartington-Davis and Lord Trimlingham. There was wine in Trimlingham's moustache.

Horace was eating with his mouth open again.

"That's not even *lunch* that you're eating," said Lettie in disgust.

"Sweeties," said Horace, indistinctly. "Everyone gives me sweeties. And I've eaten all my lunch."

"Nobody gives you sweeties," said Lettie, in a superior voice, and Horace stuck his tongue out.

"They do too. Nearly everyone. Doktor Weiss had some chewy nut ones, but I've et them all. That funny Swedish man give me some chocolates. That lady –" he pointed at Miss Natasha – "gives me waxy black ones like the bottom of a lamp."

"*She* gives you sweeties?" said Isobel, in alarm.

"She does good exercises and gives me sweeties that taste like lamps," said Horace. "And lots of Turkish delight from Lord Trimlingham. Major Bourne said he would give me sweets when we were next in port because he said he didn't have any and I said he had to or else, and grown-ups don't like to talk to me too much because I'm sticky all over."

"You greedy little pig," said Lettie, disgustedly.

The French sisters – still only four – were arguing again. One was crying. Isobel tried to linger by their table on the way to her own, to listen to their argument even though she spoke no French, but one of them snapped, "May I 'elp you?" and they all looked at her

182

under their matching purple bonnets with cross, narrow eyes, and she had to pretend she was just looking for some extra napkins. The German doctor had barely touched his lunch; he never seemed to eat much, thought Isobel, and nor (now she thought of it) did Lord Trimlingham. He was drinking quite a lot of wine instead. Two – three? – things to note down. She wasn't sure what they meant, exactly. But it seemed worth noting them down.

"You'll do anything for sweeties," said Lettie to Horace.

"Not just sweeties," said Horace. "I like money, too."

"Why are you so greedy?"

"'Tisn't greedy," said Horace. "It's *sensible*."

Major Bourne's babies were still crying in the corridor, making an awful racket, and it fitted exactly with Isobel's mood. There was so much noise; so many people talking. It made it hard to feel anything about anything else. Over the crying was the noise of the knives and forks on plates, and the people chewing, and Horace and Lettie still bickering about whether Horace could go and ask Major Bourne for sweeties, and whether Horace was ghastly or not; and Trimlingham and Mrs Colonel Hartington-Davis having a conversation about why Mrs Colonel Hartington-Davis had had to come *back* from India, and why Trimlingham had had to go in the first place, and what somebody they both knew had said about somebody else, and whether Trimlingham's father had known the wife of the archbishop when he was in India, and whether Mrs Colonel Hartington-Davis's mother had known Trimlingham's father's uncle who was the ambassador at Calcutta, and why the cousin of the viceroy had made such a fuss at supper because he was seated a little lower than his older sister, and why older sisters had to sit below younger brothers, and whether it was a good thing older brothers always inherited, and whether it was a good thing that estates stayed in the family, and whether it was a good thing that the world was generally the way it was, everyone in their place, *high and lowly and each to their estate*, noise and noise and noise and on and on and on it went, with Mrs Colonel Hartington-Davis's voice rather higher and flutier than it usually was, and it ran along Isobel's nerves like a knife scooping seeds from a vanilla pod.

"What a trouble for you, to have to go all that way just to sort out such a silly thing!" Mrs Colonel Hartington-Davis was saying, with her hand on Trimlingham's linen sleeve. The air was thick with imaginary vanilla, sweet and overwhelming, and Isobel felt dizzy with all of it.

"Dreadful," said Trimlingham. "Really dreadful. I mean to do such good with this money, you see. I'm a scholar of the stars. To study the stars properly – scientifically, I mean – one needs money."

"You see?" Lettie mouthed to Isobel, but Isobel shrugged. She was trying to think about something outside of the dining room: something clean and solitary and quiet. It was irrelevant. Trimlingham's father had not been on the ship, and could not have been on the ship, since he was dead before the ship even left. You couldn't murder people who were already dead.

"Are you interested in the stars?" It was a moment before Isobel realised Trimlingham was talking to her.

"Don't know," she said. She didn't want to like Trimlingham: he was too nice. It made her not want to trust him. He looked disappointed.

"There's women astronomers now, you know," he said. "It's a new century coming, and you'll find your place in it."

Isobel shrugged, but she was interested all the same.

"No reason women shouldn't be interested in the stars. Or the cosmos. Or the world." He sighed. "Well, there's no reason a girl should be. It might be the modern world, but I can't force it. Miss Letitia?"

"*I* don't know," said Lettie. She dimpled up at him, the way she did to all grown-ups.

"I'll show you this evening, if you like. Both of you! And that little pal of yours. Nice boy. And this fine young man here, what?"

Horace had never looked less like a fine young man. He was licking his knife, like Natasha Karamazova, and looking at them with those blue-button eyes. "I've got a *secret*," he told them.

"Shut up, Horace," Lettie said, and Mrs Colonel Hartington-Davis said, "Letitia!" and glared at Isobel as though it were Isobel who had said it.

"You don't have a secret," Lettie said.

"I know *Isobel's* secret," said Horace.

"Go on, then," Lettie said boldly, and Isobel held her breath.

"Isobel…" Horace said, slowly, tauntingly. "Isobel … Isobel is a *snakey* girl. Her secret is: no legs!" He laughed and laughed until Isobel thought he might be sick. "No legs under her dress!" he said, choking on a bit of kedgeree. "No legs!"

"Honestly, Horace, can't you grow up?" Lettie put her nose in the air. "Really, Mummy, can't you do anything with him? I'm trying *so* hard with Miss Petty, honestly I am, Mummy, and he's making it much harder."

"Horace, darling," said Mrs Colonel Hartington-Davis, ineffectually. "Lettie, precious, if you'd only play with him he wouldn't taunt you so."

"Don't want to play with the girls," Horace said. "Snakey snakey girls. I've got my own game. They can't play with me."

"I didn't want to play with you anyway," said Isobel, with dignity. "You're much too young."

"You played the other day," said Horace. "You *liked* playing. You think you're special but you're a snakey girl really. No legs!"

"Can't you stop him saying that?" Lettie appealed to her mother, and Horace was still laughing so much he seemed as though he might be sick.

"I have just the thing," said Trimlingham. He winked at Lettie and held out a rose-scented paper bag to Horace. "Have a sweet."

Horace took two, and – for a perfect moment – there was perfect silence.

Chapter Fourteen: Everything Gets Eaten By Something In The End
Week 2, Day 5
Still the Red Sea

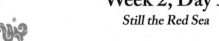

The deck was very full of people after breakfast. The sun was hot, and the deckchairs were full, and it seemed that half the ship was crowded at the balustrade trying to see the coasts of Africa to one side and Arabia to the other.

"Everyone's on deck," said Sam, but Isobel shook her head.

"Not everyone. No Mrs Karamazova. No Karamazova maid, obviously. That Swede is talking to the German doctor. Four – no, five! Five French sisters! That's one missing person found! She's the one in purple so pale it's almost beige! I haven't seen her before!"

"Very *good*, Isobel," said Lettie. Isobel glared at her.

"Oh, splendid work, Petty. One down. Father's not

here – too busy drawing up plans for sewers. He's got an audience with the prime minister when we get to London. He's going to show him all his sewers. But is everyone else on deck?"

"Major Bourne's here, without his maid – she's probably with the other servants, because Trimlingham's valet isn't here either. Trimlingham is, though, over there with Horace. Look, Lettie! Major Bourne is talking to Mrs Drake."

Mrs Drake's diamonds glittered in the sun. Her turban was emerald green today, to match her gown. She looked like a very expensive mermaid.

"Perhaps they *will* get married," Lettie said, dreamily. "Imagine! A wedding on board ship!"

"Captains can marry people," said Sam. "They can do weddings, I mean. They can do funerals too." He stopped. "Rather grim when you think of it. There's us watching a murder, but if someone died, they'd throw them overboard just the same."

"Eaten by sharks!" said Lettie.

Isobel pressed her lips together. She thought about the long low white house, the little brown snake. The way the wine had dried in the cups to a kind of reddish dust. Then she said: "Everyone gets eaten by something in the end. Sharks. Worms. It's all the same."

Lettie squealed. "Don't say that! Sam, make her not say that!"

"I don't make Petty do anything," Sam said. "Petty is her own man. Nobody makes Petty do anything. Besides," he added, "she's right. Unless you get burned on the river, like Hindus. The Parsees get eaten by vultures. They have special towers."

"Special towers?"

"Special towers," said Sam. "They get taken up there specially. The towers have no roof on, so the vultures can get in. And the sun, to make it all bleached clean." They thought about this for a minute.

"How disgusting," said Lettie.

"How interesting," said Isobel.

"How irrelevant," said Sam. "The question is, how can we get past this hideous throng of people to our HQ without them all noticing? I know they are all looking at Africa, but it only takes one."

"It only takes Horace," said Isobel, grimly. "He's determined to tell about HQ. He keeps pretending he has a secret and I know it's about the lifeboat."

"He really is being rather awful," said Lettie. They all looked at Horace, who was standing with Lord Trimlingham. Lord Trimlingham was showing him something through the telescope. Horace put his hand up and pointed, and yelled something that was snatched away by the sea breeze.

Sam said, suddenly, "Wait a moment!"

"What?"

He screwed up his face against the sun. Then he said, "Oh, nothing. I just thought – I thought something reminded me of something, but I can't think what."

"Horace shouting?"

"No. Yes. Maybe. I don't know. Perhaps it was just thinking about the telescope."

"Oh. I thought you'd seen something."

"I did," he said, but he didn't sound sure. "I'm sure I saw something. It reminded me of something, but I— It's gone now. Blast and bother. I thought I had it, but it's gone."

Isobel shrugged. "It probably wasn't important. Or I would have noticed."

"So would I," said Lettie quickly.

Sam put his hand over his eyes theatrically. "You two! It never ends!"

Lettie laughed, and Isobel did too. She didn't want Sam to think she was a bad sport.

Just then the ship's horn gave a long, low hoot and a moment later the captain appeared at the doorway to the cockpit. "Clear the decks, please! We are entering a particularly busy course and I expect there to be some swell! Clear the decks!"

The last person to leave the deck was Diamonds Mrs Drake, followed closely by Major Bourne. Lettie nodded at them meaningfully, but Isobel ignored her.

Then Lettie gasped. "Isobel!" she said, grabbing her hand. "Another one!"

"Another what?" said Sam, but Isobel and Lettie were already rushing forward.

There was a piece of paper lying on the deck where Major Bourne had been standing. Lettie yanked the ribbon from her hair and passed it to Isobel, who stooped down and picked it up. It was damp, and folded very small, and it was clear at once that it was nothing like the previous two notes. It was written on expensive letter paper, and was not torn at all, and instead of the blocky, scrawly capitals it was written in an elegant deep blue curly script.

"*C – Meet me at midnight*," Isobel read, slowly. "*By the telescope. Bring this note with you. We must talk about what happened. E.B.*"

"What?" Lettie opened her eyes very wide. "That's not what I expected."

"Nor me," said Isobel. "There was another note," she explained to Sam. "On our door."

"On your door? Not under it?"

"Wedged in the doorknob."

"What did it say?"

"It was like the first one," said Lettie. "All scrawly like someone who couldn't really write. This one said *WATCH OUT*."

"Watch out?"

Lettie nodded. "Quite horrible, really. But we forgot, because of the captain's announcement."

"And not like this one?"

"This one is quite different," said Lettie, leaning over Isobel to see it. "Read it again, Isobel?"

"*C – Meet me at midnight*," Isobel repeated. "*By the telescope. Bring this note with you. We must talk about what happened. E.B.*"

"What does it mean?"

"What does it *mean*?" said Isobel, sneeringly. "You can see what it means. It means what it says."

"Oh, for goodness' sake!" Sam snatched it from her hand. "Do neither of you know a good clue when you see one?

"I knew it was a clue," said Lettie, smugly. "That's why I pointed it out."

"I noticed it too," said Isobel.

"Well, I noticed it first—"

And they would have gone on like this if Sam had not dropped his pipe into his pocket and grabbed both of them by a shoulder apiece.

"Do neither of you care about this investigation?" he hissed furiously. "This bickering! I hate it! Neither of you are taking this seriously! A real clue!"

"But it's not a clue," said Lettie quickly. "It's not like our notes at all. It's quite different. It's a love letter."

"A love letter?"

"From Major Bourne to Mrs Drake. Ellams Bourne is his name. E.B. And Mrs Drake's name is Caroline."

"And why," said Sam "should a love letter not be a clue? Love is a motive. We didn't think of it as one in our list, but it is. If you wanted to marry someone else, for instance."

"But they could marry each other without a problem," said Isobel. "Her husband is already dead. His wife is already dead. She's absolutely dripping in diamonds. They could be married very easily. Why should they do a murder?"

"Who would they murder?" said Lettie. "Who is there to murder? She's got all her diamonds. She could marry him tomorrow, remember. The captain can marry people if he wants to and if they ask him. They would be a perfect match. I've said it all along."

"You have," said Sam, thoughtfully. "Still. It's a clue."

"A clue to their romance," said Lettie. "I do rather think this is private, actually. It isn't nice to pry into other people's business."

"What do you think detectives do?" said Sam. "What do you think newspaper proprietors do? If we didn't pry, we'd be out of a job."

"It's not very nice," said Lettie.

"Don't get cold feet now," Sam said. "We're in too deep. Natasha Karamazova threatened me with going overboard if we didn't stop."

"We haven't stopped," said Isobel. "We haven't even talked about stopping."

"Of course not," said Sam. "We're detectives. We detect at great personal risk." They grinned at each other.

"See?" Sam said to Lettie. "Petty is always smiling. It changes her whole face."

"It does, rather," said Lettie. She looked at Isobel's face thoughtfully. "You're much prettier when you smile. If you smiled and wore a dress the colour of that wine, I think you'd be completely normal medium-pretty. You're not really ugly at all, are you?"

"I don't care for being pretty," said Isobel.

"It gets you what you want," said Lettie. "Grown-ups

like prettiness. That's why they like me so much."

"You're a monster," said Sam, affectionately and rather admiringly. "Pretty, but a monster. It's a wonder no grown-ups have noticed. They think Petty's the monster – sorry, Petty, but they do – but really it's you, just going around using being pretty to make people do things for you."

"You have to have something," Lettie said, complacently. "You have to have something. Mine is being pretty. Yours is being a newspaper proprietor and a detective."

"What's mine?" said Isobel. She felt rather pathetic, asking.

"Noticing things," said Lettie instantly.

"Writing things," said Sam only a second later. "Telling the truth. You're very clever. And you're funny."

"Funny!"

Funny little thing, she thought. *Funny little thing.*

"Yes. You make me laugh a lot. With you," he added, generously. "Not at you. Never at you." And Isobel felt better.

Just then the door to the deck opened and Major Bourne came out. He looked very worried. He was looking around for something on the floor and didn't notice them immediately. When he did, he looked extremely surprised, and even more surprised to see the note, unfolded in Sam's hands.

"But that's mine," he spluttered angrily. "I was just – I was looking for it! Where did you get it?" He took it briskly from Sam. His face was very red and cross. "Reading other people's personal letters," he said stiffly, "is a criminal offence in England. Perhaps it isn't where you children come from."

"I'm from England," Lettie said, but he didn't listen. He was looking at Sam and Isobel as if they were a different species.

"You two," he said. Spat, really. "I can tell just by looking at you the sort of children you are. Sneaking around. Looking at things."

That, Isobel had to concede, was true.

"That is *private*," he said. Little flecks of spittle came from his mouth and quivered on his moustache. "That letter was my business. Do you little brats understand that?"

Sam nodded; Isobel nodded too. Lettie nodded, but he still wasn't looking at her. Curiouser and curiouser, Sam had said. And it was.

"Don't you think of poking your noses in anywhere else," Major Bourne said. "Don't you think of mentioning this note to anyone. Do you understand me? I forbid you to." He drew himself up to his full height and tucked the letter into his pocket. It was easy to see that he had been in the army.

"And you, boy." Sam flinched as if Major Bourne might hit him. "You, boy, you should know it isn't the actions of a gentleman to read another gentleman's letters!"

"I'm sorry, sir—" Sam began.

But Major Bourne carried on. "You little brats," he said, "had better learn to behave yourselves. Whatever would your fathers say?"

"Mine is dead," said Isobel.

Major Bourne looked surprised, as if he hadn't expected her to speak. "Your mother, then."

"She's dead too. That's why I'm here with Mrs Colonel Hartington-Davis."

"Colonel Hartington-Davis?"

"My daddy," said Lettie.

"Hartington-Davis's girl? I expected better from you. Your father's a fine man," he said to Lettie, softening a little. "A fine man. Don't you run around with this nasty pair. Your father's no better than he should be, I suppose," he said to Sam, and Sam's face went pink with anger.

"My father is a scientist," he said. "A very good

scientist. He saves lives."

"Your father lets his brat run around this ship looking at people's letters," said Major Bourne. "Your father should spend a little less time saving people and a little more time disciplining his son. I've a mind to tell him."

"We just picked it up," Sam said. "You left it on the deck."

"You nasty little sneak," said Major Bourne. This time some of the spittle flew on to Sam's cheek. "You'll tell nobody about this! Do you hear me? Do you hear me?"

Sam nodded again. Isobel followed.

"You," he said to Lettie. "Go and find your mother. You shouldn't be hanging around with kids like this. They'll influence you in bad directions, you mark my words. Pair of grubby little brats."

He gestured with his hand to the captain's deck and Lettie, looking helpless, obeyed.

Then he turned on his heel. "Sneaking kids," he said, as a parting shot, and went back the way he had come.

"Whew!" said Sam, as soon as the door was closed. "What was *that*?" He wiped Major Bourne's spittle off his cheek. "Surely nobody would be that cross out of just *embarrassment*," he said. "Surely nobody would worry *that* much. She's a widow. He's a widower. Surely if Lettie's right, and they could be in love, they would just be in love. Why would they want it to be a secret?"

It was intriguing, Isobel thought, how quickly they had begun to make enemies on this ship as soon as they started looking into things. And intriguing how many people appeared to have secrets they didn't want known. The French sisters and their argument, glaring at her. Crying Natasha Karamazova, holding Sam's face in her big white hands. And now Major Bourne. Did all adults have so many secrets? Did all adults have so many things they were afraid to have people know? And one of them, of course, had a murder to keep secret – which must be harder to keep than the ordinary kind. Or perhaps it was easier, since one of the people in the secret couldn't tell anybody. They had stumbled, Isobel thought, into such a strange world. There had been so few adults in her life; there had been so few children. There had been so few people, and now there were so many, and the sea was so endless behind them, and in front of them was Africa. And on the other side of Africa was Europe, and at the end of Europe was England, and at the top of England was Yorkshire, and in Yorkshire was her strange uncle and a strange dark house, and that, too, was full of secrets. Or things she did not know yet, and that – Isobel thought – amounted to the same thing.

Chapter Fifteen: Tomorrow On Shaker Island

Week 2, Day 6

Still the Red Sea

Miss Natasha was not doing her exercises this morning, she was knitting. She had not seemed like a knitter to Isobel, but there she was, on deck, with Miss Olga watching her anxiously.

She was knitting with thick, dirty white wool and very long, very sharp needles. They shone silver in the light, and so did the keys dangling round her neck. There was a shine in Miss Natasha's eyes too; they seemed very bright and very cold and very blue. Had she always had such blue eyes? Her eyes were bluer than the sea. "The Red Sea," Sam said, but it wasn't: it was blue, and there was no coast to be seen now. This was a wide part of the sea, and they were far away from everything, and Miss Natasha was knitting, and her eyes were shining, and it was not a kind shine. Each time she dipped the knitting needles (which she did, like her press-ups, very fast) her eyes flashed as the needles did.

"What's she making?" said Isobel.

Sam was eating condensed milk again, and not looking properly. He had a face like he was thinking, but Isobel knew he was mostly thinking about condensed milk. His pipe was hanging from his mouth, and getting stickier by the minute, as if he were Horace.

"It looks like a kind of net," said Lettie, and it did: a sprawling shawl of a net that lay across the wicker of the deckchair and shrouded it in a kind of unhappy grey mould.

"We need to get into their rooms," said Sam decisively. "We know that. We need to make absolutely sure that the mother or the maid is missing. Then we go straight to the captain. Tell him. Make him look. They couldn't ignore us if we showed them someone was missing."

"We could just ask them to look," said Lettie, and Sam and Isobel looked at her in disbelief.

"They won't start disturbing an old lady – what they think is an old lady – because we say so," said Sam.

"Of course not," said Isobel, scornfully. "We'll need to go ourselves."

"But the rooms are locked," said Lettie. "And she wears the keys round her neck."

There was something in her voice that made them both look at her.

"Lettie," said Isobel. "Have you had an idea?"

"I read in the handbook—"

"You really should read the handbook," said Sam, catching Isobel's disgruntled look. "It's very useful."

"I—"

"Don't *read*," said Sam and Lettie, together. "We know."

"It says in the handbook," said Lettie, taking pity on her, "that the purser has a spare copy of all the keys in case of emergency. Like if you drop yours in the sea. You can just go to his office and ask him and he keeps them all there."

"We can't make the Karamazovas go and ask for their keys, though," objected Sam. "Then they'd know. And why would they, when they haven't lost theirs?"

"We will have to take them from the office, then," said Isobel. It was the only solution that made sense. It was obvious.

"When you say we," said Lettie, heavily. "Do you mean ... me?"

"Of course we do," said Sam. "You did a heist once, you can do it again."

203

"*Could* I do it again?" Lettie didn't sound sure.

"You could do it," said Isobel. "You could do it again." She patted Lettie reassuringly on the shoulder – not because she wanted to, but because she knew it would make Lettie feel better.

"It's just that last time it was sort of like a game. And stealing papers isn't like stealing keys. Papers get lost all the time."

"So do keys," said Sam. "Have you never met a grown-up? It's all losing keys, as far as I can tell. All losing keys and saying someone else must have moved them. My father thinks I move his things all the time, but I don't. Wouldn't dare. He puts them down and puts papers on top of them."

"He'll think he lost them with the papers," said Isobel.

"We never heard anything about the passenger list," said Sam, thoughtfully. "But you're right, Letts."

"Letts?" said Lettie. "Letts?"

"Quicker," said Sam. He grinned at her. "Speed is of the essence in a heist. As you well know, heist queen."

"I'm *not* a heist queen," said Lettie.

"No?" said Sam.

"You could be," said Isobel. "If you did this."

"I don't know," said Lettie. "I don't know. Keys aren't

204

papers. Keys is proper stealing." She had gone a little bit white. "I just don't really think I can do this," she said. "I think … I don't think I like it any more. I mean, look at her. She scares me. I mean, really scares me."

"She scares me, too," said Sam.

"And me," said Isobel.

"That's sort of why we have to do it."

"Is it?"

"Do you want her to scare anyone else?"

Lettie shook her head doubtfully. "No. But…"

"What if she scared Horace?" said Isobel suddenly. "I know he's sticky and horrible. But he's only six. And what if he got scared? What if she threatened him?"

"Why would she do that?" said Sam, but Lettie was looking thoughtful.

"I would hate that," she said, slowly. "I would really hate that. He is only six. And he would do anything for sweeties. She's been giving him sweeties, you know," she told Sam.

"Suspicious," said Sam. "Why would she give him sweeties?"

"Everyone gives him sweets," said Isobel. "He just asks for them and he gets them."

"Anyway, Letts, how about it?"

Lettie pressed her lips together.

205

"Oh, go on," said Sam. "You love it really. Just a little heist."

"Well," said Lettie. She sucked in her breath. "Just a very small one. Maybe. Possibly. Perhaps." She stopped and thought.

Then she said, "But what about Bourne?"

"What about him?"

"He was so cross."

"So?"

"He was too cross. For just a love letter. And if it were one of those Frenchies who were missing, it might be him, too."

"Why, though?"

"Jealous of Diamonds Mrs D," said Lettie, wisely. "They always are. And Diamonds Mrs D is very beautiful. And rich."

"He could just marry her any time he wanted," said Isobel. "He wouldn't need to push the Frenchie overboard. We all know that they might get married at any time."

"Love affairs are very complicated," said Lettie. "If she had betrayed him, or he betrayed her, and they didn't want anyone finding out. But he was suspicious, too. Even if we leave off everyone else, they are both suspicious figures."

"Search his room too," said Sam, airily.

Lettie looked at him. "You mean a second heist."

"Just one," he said. He was grinning. He took a big, bubbly drag of air through his empty pipe.

"Two sets of keys," said Lettie.

"Three, actually. At least. Four, because we need to know why that Swede said that Diamonds Mrs D was watching us."

"What?"

"You steal one set. Petty and I do the rest."

"Heists are *my* job," said Lettie. It sounded as if she hadn't exactly meant to say it.

"The heist part is all on you," said Sam. "You need to get the purser's keys. From him. So that Petty and I—"

"Can go into his room, into the key cabinet, and take all the spares to the suspicious cabins!" said Isobel, excited.

"Exactly," said Sam.

"That *is* good," said Lettie, admiringly. "But keys are harder to steal than papers. He keeps them in his pocket. I'll have to think about it. And it's almost lunch."

"It is *always* almost lunch," said Isobel. It seemed to Isobel that the worst part of being a child was always being interrupted. You were never allowed to explain that you had other business: grown-up business always came first, and it was never important at all. It never *mattered*.

At lunch the dining room was very full. Dr Khan nodded briskly at Sam, who went to him at once.

The German doctor and the Swede were sitting together again, one sipping salt water, the other hot chocolate. It really was much too hot, Isobel thought. The Swede winked at them, but Isobel was not in the mood.

Diamonds Mrs Drake was there, and she was holding one of Major Bourne's crying twins. The twin was not, in fact, crying. Diamonds Mrs Drake looked at Isobel and did not smile. Then again, nor did Isobel. Major Bourne was holding the other baby, and that twin was crying.

"Well, I suppose one is better than two," Lettie said. "Is this everyone?"

"Everyone except the Karamazovas," said Isobel, significantly. She didn't even need the passenger lists now: it was like learning a language and realising you didn't need to look anything up in the phrase book.

Isobel gasped suddenly and put her hand over her mouth. "Look!" she whispered to Lettie, as soon as Mrs Colonel Hartington-Davis wasn't looking.

There at the table in the corner were the French sisters: one in lilac, one in violet, one in hyacinth, one in heliotrope, one in a puce so pale it was almost beige, and one – the sixth and the last – in deep, noticeable, stand-out royal purple like an emperor. There, in every shade of purple, sat the six French sisters, still bickering, still glaring, but all present and correct and alive. They all looked most unhappy.

"Six!" whispered Lettie, and Mrs Colonel Hartington-Davis looked over in alarm. Isobel squeezed Lettie's hand in warning under the table. Lord Trimlingham was sitting with them again. He was telling Horace about something. "Two years ago," he was saying, "a magnificent German man called Hermann Ganswindt came up with a marvellous idea."

Horace was spellbound. "What was it?" he said.

"He wants to make a galactic vehicle," Trimlingham told him, his eyes shining behind his glasses. "He wants to let man walk on the moon!"

"On the moon!" said Horace.

"On the moon!" said Isobel, somewhat against her will. "But that's impossible!"

"Not impossible," said Lord Trimlingham. "Expensive, but Ganswindt has the right idea. Man will walk on the moon, you mark my words. And I'll be the man to put him there. That's the focus of my work: my life's work, my great work. I saw Ganswindt give his speech, and I told him: when I get my inheritance, I'll help you out. I promised him. And now I'm on my way back to do just that. When I get to Europe, I'll be keeping my promise. I'll be selling my home, as I told your mother, and I have tidied up the last of my father's affairs in India, and now – well. Man will see the stars, young Horace. And woman too, Miss Letitia! And you, Miss Petty. You too. Space is for all!" His eyes were very bright behind his little gold glasses, and his face was very eager, and there was something in his voice that made Isobel a little bit afraid. It was strange to see someone talk about something they truly loved, she thought. Mostly people didn't. She had never heard anyone talk like this about anything – not a grown-up. Grown-ups never loved things. Trimlingham, she thought, really loved the stars, and she looked at him as if seeing him for the first time.

Lunch was rice pudding, and it was not very nice at all. There was a thick skin on the pudding, and Isobel felt sick just to look at it. Horace ate hers.

The door opened, and the captain came into the room, followed by the Karamazova sisters.

"She can't get out of bed," Miss Olga was saying in her thick accent. "Our mother, she cannot get out of bed. She must not be disturb by doctors, she must not be disturb by paperwork. She is going to England for see a doctor who can help. Tomorrow, when the health checks are made…"

"Here is her certificate, and she must not to be disturb," said Miss Natasha.

Isobel shot a triumphant look at Sam. *Everyone is here but the old lady*, she tried to telegraph, but she knew that Sam was watching too. *It must be her*, she thought. *We were right all along.*

The captain nodded and put his hand soothingly on Miss Natasha's shoulder, thought better of it, and took his hand away again. "Quite so, quite so," he said. "Quite so, Miss Karamazova." He patted Miss Olga this time, but Miss Natasha looked at him hard and he stopped that too.

He said, "Quite so" again, as if that meant anything. The Karamazova sisters were still looking at him. "Quite so, quite so." He held out his hand, as if he was showing them the way to their table, and they went, Miss Natasha still looking at him hard.

The captain cleared his throat, and then again, louder. Everyone looked at him, and he cleared his throat a third time.

"Ladies and gentlemen," he said. "There has been a small change to our schedule. Nothing to worry

211

about, nothing to worry about! As you are aware, I hope, tomorrow we will enter the Suez Canal – the so-called gateway to Europe and the Mediterranean. You all know, of course, that the outbreaks of cholera in Calcutta have been very hard, very hard indeed, and you know too that we must keep a healthy ship, for a healthy Europe and a healthy England!" He paused, almost as if he was waiting for applause. Nobody applauded. "Tomorrow on Shaker Island, in the mouth of the canal, a British doctor will be coming aboard to check the health certificates given by the doctor as we left Calcutta. We will put in at the island for perhaps half an hour, no more. This stop will mean a small delay to our schedule. Since we have made good time thus far, I anticipate no significant changes to our London arrival or, indeed, that of our mail stop in Gibraltar. With regards to the mail…"

He was still talking, but Isobel wasn't listening. *Tomorrow on Shaker Island*, she thought. *Tomorrow. Tomorrow on Shaker Island, and so it has to be today*, she thought. *It has to be now. We have to get the keys today. Or she might escape at Shaker Island. She might go free.* Isobel thought, and she looked at Lettie, and she thought, and she simply could not see what they were going to do next.

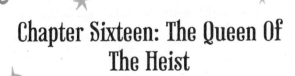

Chapter Sixteen: The Queen Of The Heist

Still Week 2, Day 6

Still the Red Sea

It was after lunch. They were lying under the lifeboat, as usual. Sam was chewing on his pipe. Lettie was eating a bit of ship's biscuit, which was really just a rusk. She was dipping it meditatively into Sam's discarded condensed milk can, swiping it round the sharp edges to get the most condensed milk, and then sucking it off. Isobel was writing in her notebook: nothing particular, but it did help her think. They had got very good at fitting the three of them into the lifeboat, like jigsaw puzzle pieces tessellated around each other. This time Isobel was sitting up and using her knees to balance her notebook on, Sam was lying at her feet, and Lettie was curled up at the other end.

"The first problem is where the keys are in the purser's room," said Sam, after a bit.

"And the second problem is how to get into the purser's room without the purser," said Isobel. She was drawing a rather good picture of a bunch of keys.

"We need the purser's keys," said Sam. "We need the purser's keys to get the Karamazovases' keys. It's a double heist sort of day."

"One was bad enough," said Lettie, but she didn't seem nearly as unhappy as before. Like all frightening things, it was better looked at. And there simply was no other option.

"It has to be you," said Isobel. "He doesn't like me at all. Or Sam."

Sam nodded glumly. "It all falls to you," he said. "You're the only one that looks good enough. Which is awful, really, because you're in it just as much as me and Petty. Still. Looks always matter, even though they shouldn't, so we might as well use them where we can. Stupid, really." He looked troubled, like he wanted to say something else.

"Go on, Sam," Isobel said, gently.

"Well, it was just that – at school, you know, some chaps weren't very pleasant to me. Because of how I looked. Which was ridiculous, of course, but there you are. That's why I got so good at hiding. That, and Dad always wanting me to look at sewers with him. But it's just funny, isn't it? That how you look can make such a difference?"

Isobel looked at him, and she looked at Lettie. She thought about it. She thought about whether either of them could look different at all, or whether it would be better if they did. Then she said, honestly, "I think you're both actually beautiful."

Sam blushed, a proper red blush right from his neck. "Stupid," he said, but she could see that he was pleased.

"I know," said Lettie, and Isobel threw a cushion at her, laughing. Lettie threw one back, which hit Sam, who threw one too, and for a few minutes the lifeboat rocked with feathers and upholstery, and they were all laughing so hard their sides hurt and they had to lie very still.

"So we need to get the keys from him, and then distract him while somebody else goes into his room and gets the Karamazova keys," said Isobel, when they had recovered themselves. "Double heist. Double distraction. Do you know what?" She looked thoughtful.

"What?"

"I think we need something else for this plan."

"Something else?"

"Well, we're both out. Yes?"

"Yes," said Sam.

215

"And this is a double heist and a double distraction. Yes?"

"Yes," said Sam.

"And we need him to be distracted twice, and not by either of us. Yes?"

"Yes," said Sam.

"If you say what I think you're going to say," Lettie said, "you're mad."

"I know," said Isobel. "But I'm right."

Lettie was nodding.

"We need—"

"We need Horace," said Isobel. "We need Horace."

"Horace?!" said Sam, horrified.

"Horace," said Lettie. "Horace."

It was not, Isobel thought, an especially *nice* plan. Which was surprising: it was surprising that she minded. Not enough to stop it; and not enough not to do it, but still, she had noticed that it wasn't an especially *kind* plan, and she did not like herself very much for doing it, and that too came as a surprise. She was used to being horrible. Somehow she had slipped out of it for a moment and it was a jolt to feel horrible again. It was truly astounding how many things a person could feel all at once.

There was almost nobody else in the dining room

when they went in; there never was after lunch. They all went for a lie-down in their cabins.

Horace was sitting at their usual table fiddling with a bit of stuff. It was gummy and blackish, and he was rolling it between his fingers into different shapes. His fingers were shiny and black, and he had obviously wiped them on the snowy-white tablecloth laid for dinner. The contents of his pockets had been tipped out, too: the good stamp, a pair of coins wrapped up in old newsprint, a bit of string, two brass fastenings that looked like they'd come off the porthole, and a small sugar mouse with no nose or ears. Everything was very black.

"What *is* that?" Lettie said, slipping into her chair beside him. Isobel hovered by the door. She did not really know how to talk to small boys and she did not want to ruin Lettie's plan. ("Leave it to me," Lettie had said.)

"Is that tar, Horace?"

"Boot black," said Horace, indistinctly. His mouth was full, as usual. "Shoe polish. It's gone all funny because it's colder here. Like wax. Like those sweeties. Look." He held out his gummy hands for Lettie to see.

"You've got it all over the table," said Lettie. "And what are you eating?"

"Turkish delight," said Horace. He opened his mouth to show her and Lettie recoiled.

"You really are monstrous," she said. "Stop cadging sweeties off people. Mummy would hate it."

"Mummy's asleep," said Horace. "And she can tell me to stop if she wants but you can't because you're a child as well."

"I'm much older than you," said Lettie. "And so is Isobel."

"Isobel is a snakey girl," he said, twisting round to fix his blue-button eyes on her. "So are you when you play with her."

"We must be kind to Isobel," said Lettie, sternly, and for a moment Isobel felt a flash of the old crossness. Don't be kind to me, she wanted to shout. Don't be kind to me just because everyone died. But you couldn't say that to people, and not to Lettie, who was only saying it to Horace because they needed Horace to play the game, to solve the crime.

Justice, she thought of Sam saying. Justice will be served. Get the keys to get the keys to find the empty room to show the captain to make him see that they had seen a murder: only five things, when you thought of it that way.

"Don't want to be kind to Isobel," said Horace. "Don't

want to be kind to anyone."

It reminded Isobel of something; and when she thought she found it reminded her of herself, a long time ago, on the docks at Calcutta. What a long, long time ago, she thought. What a long time ago they had left India, and soon they would be on the other side of Africa, and in Europe, and after that it would be the end. She felt quite sick when she thought about the end. She did not have enough imagination to be afraid of what it would be like, but the hazy, foggy blur that was England hung over her and in her lungs like thick yellow smoke, and she hated it all the same.

"Snakey girls," said Horace. "Always leaving me out. Couldn't find you *and* I didn't care."

"I'm here now," said Lettie.

"I can have secrets too," said Horace. "Wouldn't *you* like to know?"

Isobel saw Lettie press her lips together, frustrated. Lettie steeled herself and slid into the seat next to him

"Horace," she said. "Do you miss Daddy?"

Horace thought about it. "A bit," he said. "But we'll see him soon."

"Not for ages," said Lettie. "Not for ages and ages and ages. Didn't you know that? Daddy's going to be away for ages and ages and ages. So are we."

"For how long?" said Horace.

("He always cries about Daddy," Lettie had said. "Eventually anyway. You have to sort of remind him.")

"Maybe years," said Lettie.

"Why?" said Horace.

"That's the rules," said Lettie. Her voice was very sad, and it seemed to Isobel that perhaps she wasn't putting it on to make Horace cry.

"Why the rules?" said Horace. "The rules are stupid."

Isobel wondered whether Horace didn't have a point: the rules did seem stupid.

"Daddy has to stay in India, and we have to go to school," said Lettie.

"But why?" said Horace. He was sticking the bit of boot black to the underside of the table and peeling it off again. Isobel looked at her shoes.

"You miss Daddy, don't you, Horace?" said Lettie.

"Do you miss Daddy?"

Lettie said, like she was pushing something heavy up a hill, and there was just a little way left to go, "I miss Daddy *lots*."

Where was the purser? Surely, surely he must be coming soon? Isobel thought.

("He always goes to the dining room before dinner," Lettie had said, "to check everything is right.")

"Why can't Daddy come?" said Horace.

"He just can't," said Lettie, and her voice cracked, and Horace burst into noisy sobs. And Lettie was crying, too. Not the pretty tears that the plan required, but real, gulping sobs. Isobel watched as if she was in a different world, fascinated and horrified and very, very still.

"Miss Lettie! Master Horace? What on earth is the matter?"

Isobel jumped out of the way and stood like a ghost to one side.

Lettie flung her arms round the neck of the surprised – but pleased – purser.

"I miss my *daddy*," she wailed. "My *daddy* is far away! My daddy isn't coming to England!"

Then Horace started too, and ran into the purser's arms. He clung on to his arm. "My daddy is gone away," he sobbed.

Surely Lettie would not manage it now? Surely?

Fascinated, Isobel saw her hand steal into the purser's pocket, and then, quickly, into her own.

"Miss Lettie! Master Horace! What's all this? What's all this?" Horace was really crying now. Lettie detached herself.

("When he gets going," Lettie had said. "He keeps going for ages. So that will hold the purser in place, because nobody could leave Horace by himself when he was crying. He's so clingy. He sticks to people.")

"We just missed Daddy," she explained. "We just really missed Daddy."

"I'll go and get Mummy," she said, bravely, to the purser. "She's got a headache and she's lying down. Please look after Horace." Horace was still crying.

"Come, Isobel," she said quickly, imperiously, and Isobel came.

When they had reached the stairs and out of earshot of the purser, Lettie stopped. She dropped the keys into Isobel's outstretched hand and made a little curtsey. "I'm the queen of the heist," she said, very quietly and joyfully, the tears still on her face. "The queen of the heist!"

Then she ran on downstairs and Isobel followed, and when Lettie ducked into her mother's stateroom Isobel went on down to where the purser's room was, and to where Sam was waiting.

Chapter Seventeen: In The Purser's Rooms

Still Week 2, Day 6
Still the Red Sea

There were two keys to the purser's room. The top lock was easy, but the bottom lock was stiff, and for a moment Isobel wondered if they had made some mistake; got the wrong keys, gone wrong somehow. It seemed absurd that they could have done this right, and she frowned at Sam, who was concentrating on the door. Then there was a sturdier than usual clank, and it gave suddenly, and the door swung open.

The purser's room was a mess. There were papers everywhere, and a tall cupboard with more papers spilling from it, and a desk covered in papers and pens and charts.

"Success!" said Sam.

"Well, two bits of success," said Isobel. "Lettie got the keys. And we got in."

"Which is two bits more of success than we had before," said Sam. "Keep up. Play the game, Petty. We're moments from catching a murderer."

"Moments!" said Isobel.

"Moments," said Sam. "Mere moments. We get the keys, we open the door to their stateroom, we verify that Madam Karamazova really is missing, we verify that their handbooks are missing the pages used to write the notes, we take that evidence straight to the captain, who has to believe us this time because we have proof, they arrest Miss Natasha, Miss Olga and probably the maid too, we're hailed as heroes. It's simple."

"Simple!" said Isobel.

"Shut up," said Sam. "It's the simplest murder I've ever solved."

"It's the only murder you've ever solved," said Isobel, tartly. "And it's not even solved yet."

"Details," said Sam. "Mere details."

"I'll tell you what's not a detail," said Isobel. "The keys to the stateroom. Where are they?"

"Under these papers?" said Sam, hopefully, and Isobel scoffed.

"All the spares? No. He's quite an organised man," she said.

Sam looked at the paper chaos all around them. "You don't say," he said, sarcastically.

"No," said Isobel. "He really is. This looks like chaos to us because we don't understand it. But I think it's all in a kind of order. He'd have to be organised, or the ship would never work at all. And it's…" She hesitated. "I think it's a happy ship. Apart from the murder."

"Apart from the murder," said Sam. "Apart from that."

"Apart from that," said Isobel. She felt very suddenly very happy. She grinned at him. "If you were keys, where would you be?"

"In a cupboard," said Sam. "In a desk drawer. On a board. On a hook."

"We don't have very much time," said Isobel.

"Hardly any," said Sam, but neither of them seemed sad. It all felt quite exciting.

"In fact," said Isobel. "I'd be in that cupboard there." She pointed at the one with the papers spilling out of it.

Sam knelt down. He tried the door of the cupboard, and looked grim.

"Another locked door?!" said Isobel, disbelieving. "But wait!" She triumphantly held up the ring of keys Lettie had stolen. "Try one of these."

Sam did. Isobel held her breath; they fitted.

"Bingo," whispered Sam.

Inside were two dozen little hooks, and under each brass hook was a brass number, and under each brass number was a little plate into which you could slide a handwritten card, and each handwritten card bore the name of a person on board the ship. On each hook hung the key of the bedroom of that person, neatly matched up, and in order. Isobel took the keys from the Karamazova hooks, and Sam from Major Bourne's. As an afterthought she pocketed Diamonds Mrs D's, and Doktor Weiss's, too. "Just in case," she said to Sam, and Sam nodded. "We need to check everyone. We shan't get a chance for the keys like this again. They'll be careful next time."

They locked the door behind them.

"Drop the keys," Isobel said to Sam.

"What?"

"Drop the purser's keys. He'll think he dropped them. Drop the keys."

"That," said Sam, admiringly, "is devious. Very devious." He dropped the keys just in front of the purser's door. "Very nice, Petty. Well…" They looked at each other. Upstairs the bell for dinner was ringing.

"Well, well, well," said Sam. "Tomorrow?"

"Tomorrow," said Isobel. "When everyone's at breakfast, if we can, and lunch if we can't.

They nodded at each other and then Sam went back to his cabin, to his father, and Isobel to hers: to Lettie, and to hairbrushes, and clean pinafores.

Chapter Eighteen: The Lost Boys

Week 2, Day 7
The Gulf of Suez, Shaker Island, the Suez Canal

Isobel woke up before Lettie, and she woke up with a curious impulse to be alone. She got up carefully and quietly, put on her frock (with the usual difficulty) and went out into the corridor. It was very early. She thought with a strange detachment of the night of the murder. It had been like this, and yet not like this. *She* had been like this, and yet not like this.

The deck door was heavy, and when she pushed it open she saw there was someone on deck. She was not surprised, somehow, that it was Sam. He was standing at the telescope deck with his jacket over his pyjamas.

"Hullo," he said when he saw her, and he was not surprised, either. She went up and stood beside him, looking. The sea had narrowed overnight, and from the deck you could see land on both sides, and land ahead, quite close.

"I think that's Shaker Island," said Isobel, gesturing ahead of them, and she did not have to say any more.

The coast of Africa was coming ever closer, and they could see buildings now, on the shore. They looked very strange, after so long at sea: like houses for dolls, like pictures pasted on to cardboard and propped up to give the illusion of a place.

"Land ho," said Sam, softly.

The ship suddenly listed to one side. Sam slipped, and Isobel caught him by the arm before he fell down.

"Imagine if we were washed away," said Sam, idly.

"But we could take our lifeboat," said Isobel.

"No school for me. No Yorkshire for you. No uncle either. We could be gone forever, like the Lost Boys in *Peter Pan*. We could have new names."

"We could be completely different," said Isobel. "New lives."

"If Lettie were here, she'd tell you there's no such thing as a new life," said Sam.

Isobel wished he hadn't mentioned Lettie; she dropped his arm, but he caught hers again and tucked it through his. The linen of his jacket was scratchy against her bare arm. She thought, not for the first time, that boys must be so terribly hot in all their coats. They didn't wear petticoats, she supposed, which helped. His arm was warm against hers.

"Safety in numbers," he said.

They stood very quietly, looking as the land came closer, slowly, slowly. They looked together at the strange new coast of Egypt; the far-off redness of the earthworks where the canal had been dug before they were even born and that still had not completely settled; the small dark ant-shapes of moving things seen from far away; and the sunlight on the sea growing lighter and lighter from deep black to deep blue, and shading in front of them to pale jade green. The light caught it, and it was beautiful.

From the jetties of the port the small boats were putting up their sails, like little white triangles blotting out part of the town behind. Small boats always come to see what bigger boats are doing, like bridesmaids at a wedding, or flies around a fruit bowl; and they were coming to sell things and trade things and give the Suez mail. But neither Isobel nor Sam knew this; they just watched, and the light over all of it was reddish and clean and the air tasted thicker than before. Sam leaned against her, and she leaned against him, and the sky was very huge and distant, and there was a whole new land before her. It seemed to Isobel at that moment that there might be something more to the world than she had known before: some adventure, something worth having, something worth (she thought) playing for. She didn't want to write anything down: that was it. She didn't want to write any of this down at all.

Sam said, in a faraway voice, "I say, Petty?" and for a tiny moment she hated him for talking in her lovely moment.

"What?" she said, and she was surprised that she didn't sound cross.

"Do you think we really are in danger?"

"If we go into their rooms?"

"Well, whatever we do, we seem to have made a lot of enemies. Major Bourne, whether he's involved or not. Diamonds Mrs D. The German doctor and the Swede – something's going on there. The Karamazovas, of course. It's just – it has been an eventful kind of journey, don't you think?"

"I've never done a journey before," said Isobel. "They might all be like this."

"I don't think they are," said Sam, seriously. "This one seems to me to be fairly unique. But, Petty? If you did want to stop – if you didn't want to do it; if you decided that actually breaking into people's rooms was a bit much – I wouldn't—" He stopped. "I wouldn't think *less* of you."

"Do *you* want to stop it?"

She looked at him, and he looked at her.

"Well, Petty," he said, with something of his usual flair. "I'm afraid that as far as I am concerned it rather depends on… Well…"

"On what?"

"Well, on you, Holmes. I told you. I'll be Watson. You be Holmes, even though I've got the pipe. I wish I had my pipe, but it's in the lifeboat."

"On me?"

"I don't really fancy doing it alone," said Sam, airily. "I don't think it would be any fun. If you think it's too dangerous, I'll stop, and there it is."

"But I don't want to stop," Isobel said, amazed. "I want to know."

And she said it so fervently that Sam looked at her and laughed; and then they were both laughing, properly and really very much, while the boat tipped again and it rained little drops of salty seawater all around them.

"I think you're marvellous," he said, when they had got their breath. "I really do. I know I said I hadn't met many girls, but you're better than all the boys I knew at school for adventure. As it happens, I want to know, too. Golly! Imagine if I hadn't met you. What a terrible voyage that would have been. I haven't done many voyages, actually, but they were probably all worse than this. Hold on—"

The boat lurched again. It was slowing down and making a kind of zigzag motion towards the island, turning and turning on a complicated channel to avoid all the little boats that were going out fishing and selling and trading and just coming to see what was going on.

They held on, and the sea around them went from black to deepest blue.

"Breakfast?" said Sam, and Isobel found that she was hungry, very hungry.

"We'll do the search after," she said, and they ran up to breakfast together.

Lettie gave them a look as the door opened, but Isobel could tell she was bursting with her own news. "What is it?" she whispered, and Lettie whispered back, "The doctor is out!"

"Oh, well *done*," whispered Isobel, and she meant it. "How d'you know?"

"They've been sharing a room," she said. "The Swede's room, in Row B. I heard the steward, Edwards, talking about how much more difficult it was to change the sheets in a room with two beds – because you can't shake out the bedding properly. He was saying that he was always glad when it was just a single person in a room because they didn't have to worry about stepping on the other person's things while they were making up the first person's bed, and that he thought he'd been lucky on this voyage because he had the Swede and the German doctor, and how annoyed he was when they decided to share on the third night of the voyage. They're using the doctor's room as a sitting room now. But it's locked up at night to keep their work safe."

Isobel covered her face with her hands. "Lettie," she breathed. "He told us. When he warned us about Diamonds Mrs Drake. He told us that Herr Doktor would be in his cabin when Horace went to get the chocolate for him."

Lettie put her hand over her face. "Of course. And they sit together at all the meals," said Lettie. "I did notice that. But I thought it was because there weren't enough tables. But it wasn't that. They made friends on the voyage, and the German doctor hates to have a room that faces east—"

"Because it wakes him up in the morning," said Isobel. "I remember. That first few days he was so cross all the time because he was very tired because the sun

234

kept coming in. I even wrote it down."

"Yes. And our windows, on Row A, all are mostly east on the way to England. It's different on the way back home. Back to India, I mean," she corrected herself quickly.

"I remember," said Isobel. "He looked less tired that morning. And Edwards said he'd brought him his salt water in bed. Which was in Row B. So that's that done. Good work, Lettie."

She grinned at Lettie, and Mrs Colonel Hartington-Davis, paying no attention, thought that truly Isobel Petty was a different child when she smiled. And she was eating, for once! Letitia must be a good influence.

They met Sam on deck. Everyone was on deck, it seemed; everyone waiting to see Shaker Island, and to feel the solid steadiness of a moored ship after two weeks at sea. The ocean had gone from deepest blue to paler blue, and ahead it was green; green and silver where the clean light touched it. There was weed in the water that could be seen even from the deck; and there was a forest before them, made of the masts of ships, all spiking up in the sky. Between them their tiny ropes quivered like cobwebs. They were so bare and stark that Isobel felt almost sad when she looked at them.

There was a long, low blast from a horn, and suddenly

Isobel knew it was time. "Sam?" she said, and Sam nodded. "Lettie?" Lettie nodded too.

They stood and looked at each other for a moment and were silent, and then they went down the dark corridor to the doors that led to the staterooms, and stood before them, waiting.

"Well," said Sam at last, and slid the key into the lock of the door that bore the name of Madam Karamazova, and this time the handle turned all the way round.

There was nobody in the room, it seemed, and for a moment their hearts leapt.

"We were right," whispered Sam, and Isobel said, "We were right the very first time!"

And just then what they had taken to be a rumpled shawl and folded pillows moved, for in the bed was a tiny, tiny ancient woman, with a face as wrinkled as a walnut and eyes like a dormouse, like two tiny, tiny black beads sewn on – and when she saw them she stretched out a papery hand, with all the veins standing up very high and blue on the back of it, and caught Sam by the wrist, and screamed.

It was the loudest scream they had ever heard, and as it died away the door was flung open – and the Karamazova sisters and the missing maid burst into the room. The three of them stood there in amazement;

the three children stood equally amazed, and the ancient lady clung to Sam's wrist as if she would never let it go.

Miss Olga and the maid rushed to the bed. Miss Olga tucked the shawl (the thing, Isobel noticed, in a detached kind of way, that Miss Natasha had been knitting) around the woman's shoulders. But the ancient lady still did not release Sam. Her skin was the colour of parchment, and so thin you could almost see her bones.

"What," said Miss Natasha Karamazova, when she had recovered herself, "do you think you are doing in my mother's bedroom?" Her accent was very thick when she was angry.

"I—"

"We—"

"You run about on deck. You have no regard for your safety. You watch my sister and me as if we have done something to you. And now you come into this place! Now you come into our cabins to affright my mother!"

"Natasha," said Miss Olga. "I will speak, please."

The old lady was still gripping Sam's wrist. *She's alive*, Isobel thought, *she's alive. She's alive, and there is nobody missing, and perhaps we have all gone mad.*

"So," said Miss Olga. Her voice was soft, like it had

not been used very much and kept in a drawer, and very cold. "We have seen you watch us very much, on this boat," she said. "As my sister tells you, we have seen that you watch us. We see you watch us, and so, also, we watch you. We see you watch us like we are not wanted on boat, and why should we not be wanted? At first I think: they are only children. And then I wonder: what do these children want from us? And then my sister tells me she has tried to warn you for running about. You don't care to be warned, children?"

"I—" said Sam, but Miss Olga held up a hand to stop him.

"You are angry with us that my sister has told you to have regard for your safety," said Miss Olga. "So you have revenge by come to frighten our mother. That is what you have done here?"

"No," said Isobel quickly. "No, not that. We thought…"

"You think what?" said Miss Natasha, sternly. "You think what, to be in our staterooms, where you have no rights to be?"

Lettie looked at Isobel, who looked at Sam, who looked at Lettie. And then, collectively, as if they had said it out loud, they agreed: they would not tell Miss Natasha the truth. It made Isobel feel distinctly dizzy.

She did not lie; she did not like to lie; and she did not intend to make a habit of it.

"We were playing," said Sam. "The door was open and we thought it was empty."

"You thought it was empty?" said Miss Natasha.

"But you unlocked the door," said Miss Olga.

The keys were heavy in Isobel's pocket. She stood very still.

"Have you no manners, to play in our rooms, to disturb an old woman? Have you no shame, you children?"

"Have we not suffered enough?" said Miss Olga, and the children exchanged looks, for it had not seemed to them that the Karamazova sisters had suffered dreadfully on the voyage.

Then the woman in the bed said something in Russian, and Miss Olga bent towards her. Miss Natasha's face softened. "Mama?" said Miss Natasha.

It was strange to think of Miss Natasha and Miss Olga having a mother; it was strange to think they could be tender towards her. Isobel felt her heart contract and she reached out a hand automatically for Sam and found he was reaching out for her, too. She pressed her knuckles against his, and understood him completely. But Lettie was looking at them too, and while she did not reach out a hand – and Isobel was glad of that, for Lettie had a mother – Isobel saw that Lettie saw, and was glad of that too.

Then Miss Natasha nodded. In a gentler voice she said, "My mother, she says it is nice to see children. Children who play."

"We didn't mean to disturb her," said Isobel, and did not add: we thought she was dead.

"OK," said Miss Natasha. "OK. OK. Mama…" She said something to the old woman in Russian. But the woman still did not let go of Sam's wrist. "Mama?" But she did not let go, and she did not let go, and she did not let go.

Miss Natasha sighed. "My mother likes you," she said to Sam.

"Of course she does," said Sam.

"Why?" said Lettie.

"How do you know?" said Isobel.

Miss Natasha sighed again, and her face became very sad.

"We had, once, a brother," said Miss Natasha, heavily. "He went to sea a long time ago, as a sailor, and he was drowned. He was quite a young boy, really. He liked sweets, and the sea, and he died. And so, when I see you run about, I think: no more. Never again. So I try to tell you. And yet, I am angry with you. I am angry because you can run and my brother can run no longer. I am angry that my brother is gone. Do you understand?"

"I understand," said Lettie, gently. She put her hand on Miss Natasha's. "And we are sorry, truly we are. We were just—"

"Just playing," said Sam. He sighed.

"My mother likes to see young boys that make her think her son is still alive," said Miss Natasha, heavily. "And I do not like to see you run about the deck. Now, go away. We are all very tired by this, I think."

"Thank you for telling us," said Lettie suddenly. "Thank you. We'll be careful, we promise."

"Thank you," said Miss Natasha. The maid held the door open, and they filed out, along the corridor and up on deck, and they seemed to be alone, the three of them, in among all the people looking at the sea.

"It's fairly ghastly to be without your mother," Sam said at last. "But it must be just as ghastly to be without your boy."

"That's why they gave Horace sweeties," said Isobel. "He reminded them of their lost boy."

"Poor, poor Mrs Karamazova," said Lettie, and they stood in wonder of this strange adult thing that had touched them.

Chapter Nineteen: The Bourne Identity

Week 3, Day 1
The Suez Canal

"Tell you what else," said Sam, when the dust had settled. "We've been wrong all along."

It was the next day; the time after lunch when everybody was resting and the deck was empty but for themselves. There seemed to be no sun, and the sky was a uniform hot white. It seemed very heavy, the sky. On the banks of the canal was almost nothing: occasionally a house, occasionally a person. They had passed very few other ships, and few other ships had passed them, and the three of them were watching the horizon with dull indifference.

Lettie nodded. "There's nobody missing on this ship. They were right and we were wrong."

"No," said Isobel.

"Are you sure we saw everyone?"

"There's nobody missing, Petty," said Sam, and he sat down heavily. He leaned back against the railing, looking on to the deck. "Absolutely nobody. We've seen everyone. It's an impossible case, and I want to scream into the depths of the sea. This never happened to Holmes and Watson. A truly impossible case."

"It's not impossible," said Isobel. "We saw it and we saw everything and we will solve it."

"I don't know … well … if there's anything to actually solve," said Lettie, tactfully. "I mean, there's nobody missing. So we can't have seen it."

"Sam and I saw it," said Isobel firmly.

Sam looked at her, and then away into the distance. On the bank of the canal a man was fishing, and in a moment the wake of the ship was going to wash over his ankles. "Maybe I'm going mad," said Sam.

"Maybe we're all mad," said Lettie.

"We saw it happen," said Isobel.

"But there's nobody missing," said Sam.

"We saw it happen," said Isobel. "We both saw it. And Lettie saw the murderer."

"I don't know what I saw," said Lettie. She slid down on to the deck next to Sam, both of them looking up at Isobel.

"You saw the murderer," said Isobel.

"I saw somebody," said Lettie.

"We both saw it," said Isobel. She felt the old, familiar crossness rising in her. "We both saw it, Sam. We saw it, we saw it, we saw it."

"I don't know what we saw," said Sam, after a minute. He sounded very sad. He reached into his pocket for his pipe, but didn't take it out. He dropped his hands back down on to the deck as if they were made of stone.

Isobel looked at him in amazement. He was leaning on Lettie, and Lettie was leaning on him, and she thought they had both gone mad.

"You know what we saw!" said Isobel.

"We can't have seen what we thought we saw," said Sam. "We can't have seen it, because nobody is missing."

"We saw it," said Isobel. "We saw it, saw it, saw it."

"I thought I saw it," said Sam. "I thought I did. But…"

"But…" said Lettie. She leaned her head against Sam's shoulder. "Isobel, do admit that there is nobody missing."

"Somebody is," said Isobel, stubbornly. "Somebody is because we saw them get tipped overboard. We saw them get murdered." She felt as if the ship, slow and steady though it was, was tilting wildly; as if the

244

ground beneath her feet was less solid than it had ever been before.

"I don't invent things," said Isobel to Lettie and Sam. "I don't make things up. I haven't any imagination. I simply haven't. I can't pretend things. I can't imagine things like that. I didn't even want to see a murder. But I saw it." She held out her hands to them, like they might take them and stand up and start fighting, but they did not.

"Isobel," said Lettie, softly. "We haven't any proof." And Sam said, "But, Petty, who?" And for a moment she hated them both so passionately she couldn't speak.

"Do you think it's all a game?" said Isobel, when she had recovered herself. "Do you think it's all just play? Because I don't play, I told you. I told you right at the beginning."

"I don't think it's a game," said Sam, uncertainly. "I don't think it's a game. I didn't mean it to be a game. But it does look like we must have made a mistake."

"It does make sense that we made a mistake," said Lettie. "That's why no grown-up would care about it."

"Not the captain," said Sam. "Not that Swede either. Nobody thought it was real because it wasn't real."

"Wasn't real!" said Isobel. "Wasn't real!"

It was as if, somewhere between leaving the

Karamazova stateroom and coming on deck, they had been in conference, the pair of them; as if the two of them had decided something without ever consulting her at all. She had never felt so left out, and she felt nothing but blind rage at having wanted to play with either of them in the first place.

"It can't have been real," said Lettie, gently. "Or a grown-up would have cared. They do care about murder, you know."

"A grown-up! Why would anyone trust a grown-up?" said Isobel. She stamped her foot. Her hands were on her hips, and her face was quite pink instead of ordinary yellow. "Why do you think any grown-up would listen to anything you had to say?"

"My mummy—" began Lettie, and Isobel turned on her.

"Your mummy is an idiot!" Isobel snapped. "Your mummy is an idiot who doesn't care for anything except you and Horace! Your mummy never looks at anything except whether you've got a smudge of dirt on your frock! Your mummy wouldn't see a murder if it happened right in front of her! Because grown-ups never do!"

"That isn't very kind," Lettie started to say.

"Kind!" said Isobel. "I'll tell you about kind! I don't

care to be kind! I only care about looking at things and naming them! I only care about writing down the truth! And you—" She turned on Sam then. "You said that was the point of having a newspaper! And of being a detective! And you don't care about the truth at all! You just care about – about – about – you don't care!"

"I do care," he tried to say, but Isobel was still talking.

"This is the first thing I have ever cared about in all my life," she said, fiercely. "And you both want to give up on it. You both just want to go to school and forget this boat ever happened. You both just want to have ordinary friendships with ordinary boys and ordinary girls who invite you to parties and have tea with you and play – and play –" She struggled for the right word. "Outsidey games like cricket."

"I don't like cricket," said Lettie.

"I do," said Sam. "But that's not what's important. Petty, I don't want to give up. I just don't see what else we can do. There's nobody missing. We must have been mistaken."

"We weren't mistaken," said Isobel. "We weren't."

Suddenly the fight went out of her, and she sat down on the deck, next to the others. "We just weren't," she said, stubbornly. "We weren't, and if nobody is missing, we're not looking right."

"We've been through the passenger lists," said Lettie. She was looking at Isobel with a concerned sort of face. "We really have looked at everyone. And everything."

Then Isobel thought of something.

"But the notes," she said, desperately. "The notes. If we hadn't seen something, why would anyone bother sending the notes?"

"True," said Sam, unexpectedly. He looked up at her, and there was a spark in his eye again. "That is true."

"And the Swede said that Diamonds Mrs Drake was watching us," she said. "And the Swede has no reason to lie, because he's got an alibi."

"Go on, Petty," said Sam. "Go on, go on. You're saying something here."

"And Major Bourne was so angry with you, because of his note," said Isobel.

"Yes, Petty," said Sam, softly. "Yes. Keep talking." He was looking at her very intently, as if she was a crystal and he had a microscope.

"Nobody," said Isobel. "Nobody would be threatening us if we saw nothing. Major Bourne saw that we'd read the note, and he was furious. Diamonds Mrs Drake was watching us. Somebody is leaving us notes to warn us off."

"It was a love letter," said Lettie.

"What if it wasn't?" said Sam. He was still looking at Isobel as if under the microscope he had noticed that the crystal was a jewel all along. "What if it wasn't? Get it out, Petty, go on."

Isobel extracted the notebook from her knicker leg, and read out the contents of the letter.

"*We must talk about what happened*," Sam said. "What happened might be the murder. Perhaps they planned it together."

"Him and Diamonds Mrs Drake?"

"They're in it together," Sam said.

"But why would Major Bourne have the note?"

"He hadn't delivered it yet," said Isobel. "He was going to give it to Diamonds Mrs Drake but he dropped it and we picked it up."

"He wanted to talk to Diamonds Mrs Drake about something. Something he couldn't say out loud, even though they talk all the time. That's got to be a crime."

"They might just be in love," said Lettie, but they weren't listening. Then she said, "But, Sam." Sam looked at her. "There's still nobody missing. The problem is the exact same. There's still nobody missing. We saw everyone except Madam Karamazova yesterday, when they said about the cholera checks, and she's still alive."

"Say that again," said Isobel. "Say that again, say that

again, say that again."

"We saw everyone except Madam Karamazova when they said about the cholera checks," said Lettie, mystified.

"Sam!" said Isobel.

"Petty!"

"We saw everyone except Madam Karamazova – and the servants," said Isobel, importantly. "Remember? We didn't see Clara the maid."

"And the babies," said Sam. "The babies have been noisier than ever in the corridor. You can hear them crying in our room. Which they would, if nobody was looking after them."

"They tipped Clara the maid overboard," said Isobel, trying it out.

"Bourne tipped Clara the maid overboard," said Sam.

"Maybe she saw something bad," said Sam. "Maybe she knows that Major Bourne still has a wife. Maybe she knows something. Maybe she saw something she shouldn't."

"Just like us," said Lettie, and shuddered.

Then Isobel said, in a smaller voice, "But … we've seen her since. We have. We saw her that first morning, carrying the babies on deck."

"That's true," said Sam, deflated, but Lettie clutched

at his sleeve.

"Sam!" she said, urgently. "Isobel! What if she's in disguise?"

"In disguise?"

"Yes. Listen. What if … Clara is sometimes Diamonds Mrs Drake … and sometimes Clara?"

They were struck dumb.

Lettie went on nervously. "What if she sometimes puts on the turban, and sometimes that white hat that Clara wears? Because nobody really looks at servants," Lettie said, and blushed when the others looked at her. "Well, they don't. Not like they look at proper people."

Sam raised his eyebrows.

"You know what I mean, Sam."

"I do," said Sam, thoughtfully.

"Nobody really looks at their faces, because they don't think they count. We didn't think they counted, when we were counting people. And Clara always keeps her head down and carries at least one baby, and babies are very distracting."

"Lettie," said Isobel, after a moment. "Lettie, you're much cleverer than you look."

"I know," said Lettie, and beamed.

And then the door to the deck swung open, and Dr Khan strode out before them.

Chapter Twenty: A Frightening Man

Still Week 3, Day 1
Still the Suez Canal

He looked very tall, and very grave. He looked, Isobel thought, like Sam – if Sam wore glasses, and if Sam's hair had been tamed and held flat by some magic spell, and if Sam had been very old and very tired and very angry.

Sam leapt to his feet immediately.

"Sir," he said, and even though she was very worried, Isobel wondered at his saying "sir" to his own father. She, admittedly, had rarely spoken to her father. She could not picture his face now, but she was sure she had never called him "sir".

"Sameer," said Dr Khan. His voice was quiet with controlled crossness. He had the kind of accent that Isobel thought the queen of England herself might have: crisp, enunciated, with every vowel a little bit in the wrong place. "I thought I might find you here."

Lettie reached for Isobel's hand, and Isobel let her. Dr Khan, like so many adults, was a frightening man when he was angry.

"Sir, I—"

"I am speaking," said Dr Khan. His eyes were very shiny and his lips were pressed together tightly. "And I will not be interrupted. When I ask you a direct question, you may respond. Until then, and only then, you will listen. I will be heard."

Sam bowed his head and said nothing.

"I have been disturbed from my work, Sameer."

Sam bit his lip. Isobel could see that he was extremely unhappy.

"My work, Sameer, the most important I have ever done. I will save lives with this work, Sameer. I will save many lives, and improve many, many more. I believed you understood the deep and profound importance of my work. Do you not understand?"

"I understand, sir," said Sam swiftly.

"It has been said that my work is the most important work in the whole Empire," said Dr Khan. "It has been said that if I can have this legislation passed, we will revolutionise sewer systems throughout the world. No man is too good for sewers, Sameer, no man."

He likes to talk, Isobel thought. He likes to lecture. Like Sam.

"Tell me, Sameer, if you understand: why are sewers so important?"

Sam looked up. "Sir!" he said. He looked a little less unhappy. "If we have sewers, we have sanitation. If we have sanitation, we have health. If we have health, we have happiness." He rattled it off, and it was clear that he had learned it long ago.

"Sewers are happiness," said Dr Khan. "Sewers save lives. Sewers are my work. This is so?"

"It's so," said Sam.

"And so, when I am disturbed from my work, I cannot save those lives. That, too, is so?"

"It's – it's so," said Sam.

"When I am disturbed from my work, Sameer, by someone who wishes to speak to me about the conduct of my son…"

Sam gasped.

"You may gasp, Sameer. When I am disturbed from my work by someone who wishes to speak to me about the conduct of my son, by someone who believed I ought to know that my son – my only son – had let me down—"

"Who?" said Isobel.

Dr Khan stared at her as though he was surprised anyone else was there, and even more surprised that she had spoken.

"Who?" he said. "Who? Who are you?"

"Isobel Petty," said Isobel. She scrambled to her feet. "And Sam hasn't done anything wrong."

Dr Khan seemed even more surprised to be spoken back to. Sam shot her a worried glance.

"I will be the judge of that," said Dr Khan. "My son's behaviour is my concern, child. I will speak with him alone, please. Go and find your mother."

"My mother is dead," said Isobel, and Dr Khan looked a little taken aback. He swallowed, and again, Isobel thought, he looked exactly like an old, tired Sam.

"So is Sameer's," he said, more gently. "Who are you travelling with, child?"

"Mrs Colonel Hartington-Davis," she said.

He did not look very pleased to hear it. Isobel remembered the way Mrs Colonel Hartington-Davis had tried to befriend him at breakfast because he was important, and how rude she had been behind his back, and understood why Dr Khan was not pleased.

"My mother," said Lettie.

Dr Khan startled again. "Two girls!" he said. "Two girls! Yes," he said, thoughtfully. "Major Bourne did say you were running around with two little girls, Sameer."

"Major Bourne!" said Lettie.

Dr Khan shot her a glare.

"Yes, Major Bourne. Major Bourne, and, I might say, the American heiress Mrs Drake, have both been to see me – to disturb my work! – with a complaint about your behaviour, Sameer. Major Bourne has a very serious complaint about you. He says you have been reading his letters."

"No," said Sam, faintly.

"Only one," said Isobel, and shut her mouth quickly.

"Only one, she says, as if that is better!" said Dr Khan.

"We found it on the deck," said Isobel. "We didn't know it was his letter until we opened it."

"Is this," enquired Dr Khan, looking over his glasses, "supposed to endear me to your behaviour? Am I supposed to believe that this excuse makes things any better?"

Isobel shrugged. "I don't know," she said. "But it's true."

Dr Khan looked at her very carefully: just like Sam, like through a microscope. It was funny, Isobel thought, but he did not look at anything at all, until he wanted to look at something very small and up close. He had not noticed herself or Lettie until she spoke, but now he was looking at her she felt as if he saw everything she had ever thought.

"Do you frequently tell the truth?" he asked her. His voice seemed a little less stern.

"Always," Isobel said. "Absolutely always."

He looked as if he might believe her.

"Be that as it may," he said, eventually, and heavily.

Just like Sam! she thought. *Just like Sam!* She had had very little opportunity to examine families before. She, herself, was nothing like her mother (funny little thing, funny little thing) and Lettie seemed most unlike Mrs Colonel Hartington-Davis. She also seemed most unlike Horace. But Sam and his father were the same: one old, one young.

"Be that as it may," he said again. "Major Bourne also says that you, Sameer – and you, you little girls – have been running about and making a nuisance of yourselves. Mrs Drake says that you have been troubling the other passengers. They both say that they saw you disturb the elderly lady in her cabin after lunch yesterday, and heard her cry out, because you thought it was in any way acceptable to enter her bedroom for your own amusement."

"It was—"

"We were—"

"Sir—"

But Dr Khan held up his hand to stop them.

"Sameer will tell you girls: I do not care to be spoken to by strangers. I care even less to be spoken to by strange children. I care least of all to have my work disturbed. My work has been disturbed."

"I'm sorry," Lettie said, but Dr Khan held up his hand again.

"I do not care, either, for apologies. I care for ensuring it never happens again. I care to never be embarrassed by my son, or my son's—" He hesitated. "My son's friends. Therefore," he said, turning to Sam, "you will remain indoors with me for the rest of the voyage. We will take the air together. You will work. I will work. I have neglected you, and now I neglect my work for neglect of you."

"But—"

"Sameer, my mind is made up." He sighed, and now the crossness seemed to be gone, and he was only tired and sad.

"Sameer," he said, gently. "This is not the way. This is not how I have brought you up. This is not how your mother would have wished you to behave." He looked, inexplicably, at Isobel, and then back at Sam. "Without your mother, I have brought you up alone. I have brought you up to behave correctly. I have brought you up so that nobody can say you have missed manners by being brought up in India with me, rather than in England with your mother's family. Do you understand what is at stake here, Sameer?"

Sam nodded.

"It is my work, and it is you. I will not have you jeopardise either. Do you understand?"

"I understand, sir," said Sam, and Dr Khan reached out and put a hand on his son's shoulder.

"I know you do," he said, and Isobel wanted to cry and didn't know why.

"As for you two little girls," he said. "I think Major Bourne has seen your mother also, and I think she too is angry. As angry as I am. I think it would be best for everyone's sake if you went to find her now. Sameer and I will return to our cabin; and you must return to yours."

Chapter Twenty-One: The Space Where Things Aren't

Still Week 3, Day 1

Still the Suez Canal

Mrs Colonel Hartington-Davis was standing in the open doorway of Isobel and Lettie's bedroom, looking at the space where the girls weren't as if she didn't quite know what to do.

"Hullo, Mummy," said Lettie, and she spun round immediately to look at them. There was a frightful moment before she opened her mouth, and after that it was better.

"Never, Letitia!" She didn't say it. She shrieked it. "Never, never, never, Letitia! Never did I think you would behave in such a ghastly manner! Never in my life!" Her voice was extremely high and shrill.

"Mummy," said Lettie, but Mrs Colonel Hartington-Davis just wouldn't listen. Grown-ups never did, Isobel thought.

"To hear from a passenger – a major, Letitia! A major, no less, and one who knows your father! – that you have been running about with that nasty little Khan boy, reading people's letters!"

"We didn't," said Lettie.

"It was only one," said Isobel, again.

She had never been told off in her life, not once, not by her own mother or her own father, and it seemed rather a lot to be told off twice in ten minutes by two different people's fathers and mothers. It seemed rather a lot, in fact, to be told off for the same thing twice in ten minutes, and rather a lot more to have to say exactly the same responses in each argument. But Mrs Colonel Hartington-Davis was not Dr Khan, and she did not behave in the same way. She did not ask if Isobel was telling the truth. Instead she rounded on Isobel.

"You! As for you! How dare you? This is your doing, you nasty little girl!"

Isobel thought this was probably fair. She was quite nasty, and eleven was still a little girl. So she said nothing. But that only seemed to make Mrs Colonel Hartington-Davis angrier.

"You shabby little ... scrap!" she shrieked, and again Isobel said nothing, because she was shabby, and she was certainly scrappy.

"We take you in with us, out of the goodness of my heart, and this is how you repay us! That lawyer said you were a horrid piece of work, and you are!"

This hurt Isobel's feelings. She had rather liked the lawyer, or at least had not disliked him. He had been sensible, and she did not want him to think her horrid. She wondered if Mrs Colonel Hartington-Davis was telling the truth. She knew that Mrs Colonel Hartington-Davis lied, sometimes. She thought of how she had been to Dr Khan – charming to his face, and rude behind his back – and wondered if this was a lie like that.

She still said nothing, though. There did not seem to be any point. Mrs Colonel Hartington-Davis was still screeching.

"They said, the Petty girl? She's nothing like her lovely mother, don't think of that."

Funny little thing, thought Isobel with a pang.

"Goodness knows where she came from. Raised by servants, apparently, with manners like a servant too! They said that, but they didn't say you were trouble, and likely to lead my lovely little girl into trouble!"

"I didn't lead her anywhere," said Isobel. "She came of her own accord. I didn't even ask her to come."

"Truly, Mummy, she didn't," said Lettie.

It was really remarkable how little Mrs Colonel Hartington-Davis was listening to them. It was as if she was somewhere else: on a stage, with other actors saying words she already knew.

"You will go into your room," she said. "Now, at once, and you will remain there until dinner. At least. You're very fortunate I don't make you have supper in the stateroom, but I think it will be better for everyone to see you both clean. Yes, you, Miss Petty! You too!"

Isobel did not like it when Mrs Colonel Hartington-Davis called her Miss Petty. That was Sam's name for her, she thought, irrationally. That was what Sam called her and now they were all to be separated just as they had hit on the one solution to the whole horrible puzzle.

"But we're going to get to Port Said at the end of the canal," said Lettie. "Can't we even see that?"

"You can see it through your porthole," said Mrs Colonel Hartington-Davis. "I don't think it's suitable for little girls in any case. I have been very lax on this voyage. Goodness alone knows what your father would say. I have let him down. You weren't to know, Letitia. You're only a little girl. The fault is mine. Mine and my headaches."

She put a hand to her forehead. Just like she was

263

pretending, Isobel thought. Just like she was pretending to be ill on purpose for attention, but there was nobody there except Isobel and Lettie to see – and they already knew about the headaches.

"Could you not have had some concern for your poor mother, Letitia? Some gratitude for all I have tried to do? It isn't easy, bringing two children and a wayward ward across the world without a husband. Oh, dear." She passed her hand across her eyes again, with the palm facing them. Her hands were very soft and small and white. "Oh, thank goodness we shall be in England in a few days. Thank goodness we shall be in England soon."

"I want to see Port Said," said Isobel, stubbornly.

"You certainly will not see Port Said," said Mrs Colonel Hartington-Davis, as firmly as she could manage. "We shan't be stopping for long, anyway. Just enough to pick up the mail. And then it's on to Gibraltar, and then to London."

Mrs Colonel Hartington-Davis drew herself up to her full height, which was much less imposing than Dr Khan's. Isobel supposed she couldn't help it, but it would have been better if she were frightening. It was humiliating to be told off by someone so undignified.

"Go to your room, children. Lie on your beds. I

have left Horace in our room, resting. I should have insisted on a rest for both of you – for all of you. I should have done things very differently, but how was I to know? A poor woman travelling alone!" She wasn't poor, Isobel thought; she was quite rich. She looked at Lettie's expensive ribbons to check. Rich, rich, rich. And she wasn't alone, either. She had the three of them – and Lord Trimlingham.

As if he had been summoned by the thought, Lord Trimlingham appeared in the corridor. "Well, well!" he said. "What's all this? Trouble, is it?"

"The children have been running riot," said Mrs Colonel Hartington-Davis with a weak smile. "And it's hard for a lady on her own, you know."

"Deuced hard," said Lord Trimlingham. "You girls ought to be good to your mother, you know. You ought to rest when she tells you and be polite at table and all that sort of thing. Are you sending them to rest, Mrs Colonel?"

"I – yes," quavered Mrs Colonel Hartington-Davis. In the presence of Lord Trimlingham her voice had become even more high and fluty. She sounded very soft and vulnerable, thought Isobel. "They simply can't be trusted, Lord Trimlingham! They simply can't!"

"Gosh," said Lord Trimlingham, and for a moment

he sounded like a boy himself. "Can't be trusted! Well, girls! Do as your mother tells you!"

"She's not my mother," said Isobel.

"Well! Even more reason to do as she says," said Lord Trimlingham. He leaned over and took the door from Mrs Colonel Hartington-Davis. "In you go," he said. There did not seem to be any choice. They went in, and Lord Trimlingham smiled at them from the door. It was his ordinary smile, Isobel thought, but something about it wasn't quite right. He looked – he looked satisfied, she thought. He looked too pleased about it all.

"Let's lock this door, Mrs Colonel," he said, smiling at Mrs Colonel Hartington-Davis. "Since they can't be trusted. You stay in there until your mother comes to fetch you," he said, looking at Isobel and Lettie.

Isobel said again, "She's *not* my mother."

But this time Trimlingham didn't reply. He just kept smiling under his moustache, and the last thing they saw before the door shut and they heard the key turn in the lock was his pleased, pleased smile.

"He wanted to get your mother alone," said Isobel, viciously. "That's why we're locked in."

They were lying on their beds, not looking at each other.

"He didn't," said Lettie.

"He did. You believe that people fall in love all the time. Why not your mother and Lord Trimlingham? They dance together. They talk to each other."

"Mummy is in love with my *father*," said Lettie. "You wouldn't know about that, because you didn't even *know* your mummy and daddy."

"I didn't need to," said Isobel. "Not knowing mine doesn't mean I can't watch other people's. And I watched mine lots."

"Watched!" jeered Lettie. "You were brought up by servants, Mummy said so. I heard her."

"So?" said Isobel. "It doesn't make a difference." In her heart she thought it might make a difference, but she didn't want to say anything.

"It makes a difference," said Lettie. "If it didn't, you wouldn't say things about Mummy being in love with Lord Trimlingham. You would know that's not how mothers work. They love fathers, and that's all." She sat up and pulled the shade on the porthole down, so the room was dim and fady.

Against her will Isobel thought of her mother: the diamonds, the cloud of white taffeta, the cloud of dark hair above, whirling in the arms of the officers of the regiment. "You should have gone to the hills two weeks ago," she heard the officer tell her mother, and her mother reply, gasping, "I know! I only stayed to go to that stupid party!" and saw the officer's face of concern. He had loved her mother, she thought, and she had loved him enough to dance with him. That was the last time, she thought to herself. That was the last time, and after that it had been simply her and the snake, and the bitty, freckly dregs of the glasses of wine. And after that here. And then England. No. She said none of this to Lettie.

"He locked us in," said Isobel. "He locked us in so that he could talk to your mother alone."

"I don't believe you," said Lettie, but her voice was very small.

"Why else?" said Isobel.

"I actually don't like you very much," said Lettie.

"I don't like you either," said Isobel. She rolled over and looked at the wall, but when she rolled over she felt something – or rather the space where something wasn't.

The familiar pressure of the notebook was not there. There was nothing tucked into her knicker leg: no notebook. The pen was there, but the notebook was gone.

"Do you … have the notebook?" said Isobel to Lettie.

"What?" Lettie rolled over and looked at her. "Why would I have the notebook?"

"Does Sam have the notebook?" said Isobel frantically.

"Nobody touches it but you, Isobel, you know that," said Lettie. "You've always made that very clear. That's the rule."

"I can't … I can't find the notebook," said Isobel.

Lettie looked at her and fell back on her pillows.

"Well," she said, heavily. "Well. That's that then, isn't it. We've lost the notebook. We've lost the evidence, if we had any. There's nothing."

"It must have fallen out," said Isobel. She had never felt so sick in all her life. "It must have fallen out. I must have – or you must have – or Sam must have…"

"You lost it," said Lettie, dully. "You lost it, and I don't even care."

"Of course you care," said Isobel. Lettie seemed almost like a stranger.

"I don't," said Lettie. "Actually, I think it's better, probably, that we don't have the notebook any more. It's probably fallen overboard. Look, Isobel." She sighed like a grown-up. "It was a game and it went wrong and now Mummy is dreadfully angry with me."

"That doesn't matter," said Isobel. "Why should it matter that people are angry?"

269

"Mummy was never angry with me before you came," Lettie said.

"Nobody was angry with me before," said Isobel. "So it's your fault too."

"Nobody cared to be angry with *you*," said Lettie, and Isobel wished she would stop saying things like that. "Everything was much simpler before you came along."

"I didn't ask to come along," said Isobel, hotly.

"I just wish you'd stayed in India," said Lettie. "It was much easier before. Horace and I were always playing together nicely and I had nice friends who didn't like adventures and didn't mind about telling the truth all the time."

She sounded sad, but Isobel was cross now.

"*I* wish I'd stayed in India!" she snapped. "Everything was nicer there! I was by myself all the time!"

"You didn't like being by yourself!" Now Lettie was shouting, too, and then – somehow – Lettie was crying, and Isobel was saying all the worst things she could think of – and then the key turned in the lock, and it was Mrs Colonel Hartington-Davis, and she was hauling Isobel off by the collar of her dress.

"You will not make Letitia *cry*," she hissed at Isobel, and she thrust her into her own cabin and shut the door tight with the key.

Mrs Colonel Hartington-Davis's room was very tidy. The beds were both made, and the blinds were drawn, and the whole room was suffused with a kind of whitish light that made everything look fuzzy around the edges. Isobel threw herself on Horace's bed. She could tell it was Horace's, because Mrs Colonel Hartington-Davis had smelling salts and crochet on her bedside table. Horace had a paper bag of Turkish delight on his. She felt very hot behind the eyes, and her hands were curled up into little cross balls.

The door to the stateroom was very good at blocking out noise from the corridor, and it so was very quiet. She couldn't even hear the sea. She thought, for a while, of nothing. And then she thought of Major Bourne and Clara pushing Diamonds Mrs Drake into the sea, and how she had to stop them somehow, and how there must be some proof, somewhere, of what they had done. Perhaps she had written it down in the notebook, she thought. Perhaps if she just read it again, if she just wrote it all out again…

It hit her all over again that the notebook was missing, and she wanted to cry.

If I could just write it down, she thought. *Where can I write it down?*

The handbook! The handbook that they kept going

on and on about! The spare pages!

She opened the bedside drawer. More Turkish delight, she thought. More Turkish delight than one boy could eat. It rang a funny kind of bell, but she couldn't remember what, exactly. She took the handbook out – a little red leather book, with the name of the boat in gold on the front – and flipped through it. There were pictures, and maps, and lots of dull writing not even just in English. Where was the writing paper?

At the back, Lettie had said. She turned to the back of the book – and got a horrible shock.

The back pages had been ripped out with some force. Only the jagged margins remained, and the space where the pages should have been, and she thought of Horace's smudgy black hands, and the smudge of ink on the second horrible letter, and the writing that might have been done by a grown-up writing with their wrong hand, but might have been done…

"By a child," she breathed, to the empty room.

She thought of the scrawl, and of Horace saying, "I've got a secret" at dinner, and she knew that she was right.

If only the door wasn't locked! If only there was a way to talk to Sam, to talk to Lettie! If only Lettie was speaking to her! If only she hadn't lost the notebook! If only, she thought, briefly and bitterly, they hadn't seen the murder at all! But no. She shook herself. It was important. People should not be allowed to get away with bad things. There were rules for a reason; and since it seemed so important that people followed the rules (mystifying, she thought, absolutely mystifying) it was important that all people should be subject to them.

They could not be allowed to get away with this. They could not. She needed to find the notebook; find some proof; to go to the captain; something. Something. She needed to tell Lettie and Sam that it was Horace who had written the notes. And there was something else, too. Something cloying and clinging, like sugar melting in the sun, winding its sticky grasp around it all: something nagging at her that she couldn't quite place. She needed to talk to Sam. She needed to talk to Lettie, but Lettie wasn't talking to her. Everything was awful, and would never be fixed.

Chapter Twenty-Two: The Last Supper

Still Week 3, Day 1
The Levantine Sea

Perhaps she fell asleep, because she dreamed: she dreamed of sugar melting, of everything melting, and she woke when the key turned in the lock, and Port Said was behind them.

Mrs Colonel Hartington-Davis said, "Come, Isobel. It's supper time. Oh, dear!" She looked at Isobel closely. "You look disgracefully untidy, but there's no time to fix it." Isobel caught a glimpse of herself in the glass. Her eyes were even bigger than usual, and her face paler and more yellow, and her cheek all crumpled where she had been sleeping on it. Her hair was sticking out, strand by strand, as if it had been touched by static. "Oh, dear!" said Mrs Colonel Hartington-Davis, but marched her upstairs all the same.

Major Bourne was sitting alone, chewing thoughtfully.

He had his eyes fixed on her when she came in.

At least I'm out of the room, Isobel thought. *I can do something now, at least.*

But she didn't know what, and the notebook was missing, and the evidence was gone, and Horace, and the notes, and the something else…

Sam and his father weren't there at all, but Lettie was already at the table, starched and frilled, when Mrs Colonel Hartington-Davis marched Isobel in. Lettie didn't look up.

"Be nice," Mrs Colonel Hartington-Davis hissed at Isobel as they went in. "I expect you to be nice. Do you understand?"

She pushed Isobel into a chair, one away from her usual place. "*That's* my chair," said Isobel.

"If you made Letitia cry once," said Mrs Colonel Hartington-Davis, "you certainly shan't sit next to her to have the opportunity again."

"I didn't make her cry," said Isobel, stubbornly.

Surely Lettie will say something, she thought, but Lettie said nothing. She was eating her dinner with concentrated, steady small bites. Isobel wasn't hungry, and the smell of mutton rose up from the silver tureen in the centre of the table like a solid column. She looked at the mutton in the tureen, and the overboiled potatoes on her plate, and sighed.

"Be grateful," said Mrs Colonel Hartington-Davis. "Some children would be very pleased to be here, Isobel. Eat up."

It felt like the end of something: like the last time, the last supper.

"I don't like it," she said, finally.

"Not this again," said Mrs Colonel Hartington-Davis. "Honestly, Isobel, I am rather tired of your behaviour. After the day we've had, I expect you to behave as Letitia is: with some sense of contrition. Can't you learn from Lettie, Isobel?"

"Don't like it?" Lord Trimlingham loomed over her shoulder. "Let you out, did she? Let her out, did you, Mrs Colonel? And now she doesn't like her dinner. Dear, oh dear, what a trouble!"

He sat down in the vacant chair opposite and patted Mrs Colonel Hartington-Davis on the shoulder. Isobel tried to shoot Lettie a meaningful glance, but Lettie wasn't playing.

"Better eat up," he said to Isobel. He was still smiling. Why was the man always smiling?

Over his shoulder, Diamonds Mrs Drake was coming into the dining room. Her gown and turban were the deep blue of the night sky, and against it her diamonds shone like stars. She looked very beautiful, and rather sad, and Isobel tried to remember whether Clara the maid had been beautiful. Where are the babies? she wondered. If this was really Clara, the babies must be in their cabins, and she had not heard them crying on the way upstairs. Strange…

Diamonds Mrs Drake did not go to sit with Major Bourne; instead she ordered a cocktail and sat sipping it, looking out at the sea. When Isobel looked at her again she was scowling – at the French sisters, who were glaring at each other. *How very interesting*, thought Isobel, and wished for her notebook. That was just the kind of thing one ought to write down about a murderer, or an accomplice to a murder. It was just the kind of thing one ought to write down anyway; the kind of thing she had always written down. It was no good. She would have to get out after supper and try to find the notebook. She needed it – and besides, it would be awful if someone else found it. They would be no respecter of the words "PRIVATE PROPERTY: DETECTIVE WORK" written on the front page. Adults never had any regard for children's privacy, she knew, instinctively. Their own secrets they kept, but children's secrets were probably free to all. She must get out after supper. She must not be locked in. She must find that notebook. She must – above all – must talk to Sam.

"Eat up!" said Lord Trimlingham. "Go on!" He was eating with gusto. "Just like school food, this," he said to Horace. "You'll like school, I'll bet!"

Horace said, "I'm a very good writer, actually. I can write all kinds of things. And I know things already. I know lots of things." He didn't think Isobel was looking, and he shot her a meaningful glance.

"Do you, now?" said Trimlingham. "What a very clever boy you are! And you've eaten all your dinner! As I, myself, have finished mine. I shan't dance tonight, Mrs Colonel – a few bits of paperwork to sort. But, oh!" He stopped, and looked as though he had thought of something.

"P'raps I'll show you the stars later, Horace! They are very different here. We're due a grand storm in the early hours of the morning, so we shall only have this one evening to see them. Shall I show you the stars? Should you like that?"

"Maybe," said Horace, consideringly.

"Horace!" said Mrs Colonel Hartington-Davis. "He would love that, Lord Trimlingham. Wouldn't you, Horace?"

"If he brings me Turkish delight," said Horace, after

a few seconds. "I love Turkish delight."

"Horace!"

Lord Trimlingham gave a tight smile. "If you're good," he said to Horace.

"Maybe," said Horace again. "I might be good."

"You be good," said Lord Trimlingham. "All three of you be good, d'you hear? I'll see you on deck, Horace. Do your mother good to have a little rest, I expect. A little time with the girls, perhaps."

Just what we don't want, thought Isobel, and she was pleased in spite of herself that Lettie was looking at her with equal alarm.

"I'll take your boy and you can look after those two little reprobate girls," said Trimlingham, and he smiled again at Mrs Colonel Hartington-Davis, and it was the nicest smile in the world. Mrs Colonel Hartington-Davis smiled back at him.

It was clear, after dinner, that Mrs Colonel Hartington-Davis wasn't going to give Isobel any opportunity to make Lettie cry again. She whisked Lettie and Horace away to her room, and told Isobel to stay where she was until she came to fetch her. "I'm tired of managing you," she said. "I want my little boy and girl to get some gentle rest, and you can come along after. We'll write to Daddy," said Mrs Colonel

Hartington-Davis to Lettie and Horace. "And then we'll do some nice quiet game, like a jigsaw, in my room. Before that nice Lord Trimlingham shows you the stars, Horace."

"You can read a book," she said to Isobel. "Read a book, or something quiet."

"Isobel doesn't *read*," said Lettie, and she sounded so nearly normal that Isobel was a little bit relieved.

"Well, she can listen to the gramophone, or play Snap, or something. Come along, children," said Mrs Colonel Hartington-Davis, and she swept out.

There was dancing after supper, of course. Major Bourne danced with the French sisters; and then once with Diamonds Mrs Drake; and then with another French sister. Isobel watched him surreptitiously. The Snap cards were on the table in front of her, but it was impossible to play Snap with one person. Was he dancing with Diamonds Mrs Drake to pass on information? Was he trying to tell Diamonds Mrs Drake (or Clara) something secret? He didn't look like it. She tried to look for clues, but she was thinking so much about the notebook that it took up all her mind. She didn't dare leave until everyone was gone, and Major Bourne was dancing as if his life depended on it. He wasn't looking at her. He danced with each of the

French sisters in turn, and he tried to dance again with Diamonds Mrs Drake, but she shook her head, and held on to another pretty cocktail, and all the diamonds in her turban glittered.

It was quite dark before everyone was gone from the dining room. She scrambled to her feet. It was now or never, she supposed, because surely Mrs Colonel Hartington-Davis would soon return for her. Surely it was bedtime. Surely the letters and the jigsaw couldn't take up that much more time. She had to get the notebook, and she had to talk to Sam. Which? If she had only time for one…

The notebook, she thought, and made for the deck, but coming out of his room at the bottom of the stairs was Sam, and her heart leapt with gladness.

"Sam!" She couldn't, mustn't, shout. She whispered as loudly as she dared, and he turned and beamed, and he ran lightly up the stairs to her. He looked as if he wanted to hug her, but he didn't.

"Petty! I thought I'd never get to speak to you again. What's up? What's new that's up, I mean? You look –" he assessed her, and it made her wish she was tidier and prettier and had washed her face – "awful. Absolutely awful. What's up?"

"I lost the notebook," she said, flatly.

His face fell.

"Oh, Petty."

"I don't know how. We had it on deck. I think it might be in HQ, but it might not be. I don't know. And I found out – I found out that Horace was writing the notes. The pages were torn out of the handbook in his drawer."

"The notes? Horace?" She saw it dawn on him too, about the writing.

"OK," he said slowly. "OK. OK. That doesn't derail the investigation."

"Lettie doesn't care about it any more," she said.

"Lettie cares," said Sam. "She's just scared. This is all rather scary, you know. You might not be scared, but I am."

"I'm a bit scared," she said. "How did you get out, Sam? I thought you were locked in too."

"My father is working and eating a sandwich in our room. Like we did the first nights. I said I was still hungry and that there might be some real supper left in the dining room, and he said I might go if I promised I wouldn't go running about."

"You're a bit running about," said Isobel.

"Not really. But needs must," said Sam.

"You lied to your father," said Isobel.

"I know."

"I wish – I somehow wish you hadn't. He trusts you, I think."

Sam looked troubled. "I know. I often have to lie to him."

"You shouldn't," said Isobel, firmly. "I see why you do, but you shouldn't."

"That's why he likes you," said Sam, thoughtfully.

"He likes me?" said Isobel.

"He absolutely likes you," Sam said. "You remind him of my mother, I think. He has a face that he makes when he thinks about my mother, that's how I know. She was English, and he is Indian; you're sort-of English and I'm sort-of Indian."

"We're not getting *married*," said Isobel quickly.

"No! Goodness, no." Sam looked equally appalled.

Isobel stuck her tongue out at him. "Good."

"Well, of course good. It isn't like that. We're much too young to get married. But it makes him think of it all the same. But here I am, anyway."

"Here you are," said Isobel. She grinned at him. "Here we both are."

"Where's Lettie, then?" Sam said.

"In Mrs Colonel Hartington-Davis's room with her and Horace. They went to write letters to their father and do a jigsaw."

Sam made a face. "Jigsaws."

"Exactly. And letters. When we've got things to do. Listen, though," she said suddenly. "Lord Trimlingham is going to show Horace the stars on deck later. So I need to go up there now, before they get there, to try and find the notebook. We can't do a thing without that. Diamonds Mrs D – or Clara, I suppose – was crying at dinner again. It's them. It must be. We need that notebook so we can explain it all."

"Besides, it would be ghastly if someone else found it," said Sam. "The things you've noticed! The things we've seen! We're in enough trouble."

"Exactly," said Isobel. "Coming?"

"Of course I'm coming," said Sam. "Holmes and Watson, remember? We're in it together." He seized her hand. "Let's go."

They pushed open the door to the deck. From the stairs it looked deserted, and very dark. The moon was not yet risen, and the captain's lantern was not yet shining up on the brig, and it reminded Isobel forcefully of that other night, the one before, and it felt so long ago that she could hardly stand it. After the quiet of the canal, the sound of the sea was wild against the hull of the ship, and the rushing of the waves and the wind together sounded like many people on a road, going somewhere, all at once. There were dark clouds on the horizon, but the deck was lit dimly with starlight all the same, and the wind was high, and they stepped out on to the deck and it was then that someone grabbed them from behind.

Chapter Twenty-Three: Sugar In The Sun
Still Week 3, Day 1, but very late
The Levantine Sea and the Libyan Sea

Isobel almost screamed.

But there was a hand firmly over her mouth, a small hand, and someone whispered, "Sh!" into her ear, and it was Lettie.

She pulled them backwards, against the railing, where the shadows were deepest.

"You're not supposed to be here," she whispered, crossly, in the quietest, smallest possible voice, scarcely audible under the sound of the waves and the wind.

"Nor are you," whispered Isobel.

"I'm following Horace," said Lettie.

"Horace?"

"Yes. He came up here to be ready for Lord Trimlingham, and I spilled a bottle of scent on purpose because it gives Mummy headaches. She had to take a cachet, a sleeping tablet, to make it go away, and she's in our room to rest because there's no smell there, and I said I'd rest in hers, and get you to come to bed, and instead I followed Horace up here. His secret, you know. He was so squirrelly about it."

"I know," said Isobel.

"You know?"

"Yes. I know his secret. It's not a very good one, really. He made a secret up to get back at us. Horace has been writing the notes."

"What?"

"I know. The mysterious notes were from Horace. We came up here to get the notebook. Where is Horace now?"

"Round the corner," said Lettie. "Swinging on the ladder by the captain's cabin. Waiting for Trimlingham."

They sidled very carefully and quietly along the deck. Horace was swinging on the ladder. He looked very small, and his hair looked very golden in the light spilling from the captain's window.

"What are we waiting for?" said Isobel.

Lettie opened her mouth to speak but there was a noise from behind them.

"That's the door," whispered Sam, and without a word all three of them ducked down behind the lifeboat that had been their HQ for so long.

The door shut again, and there were footsteps, and a figure came into view round the corner.

In the half-light of the deck, with the sea wild at the hull, it was exactly like the night they had seen the murder; and the figure before them carried himself in the way the murderer had done, and his silhouette against the dark sea was the same shape.

Isobel felt like the ship was falling into the sea, down, down, deep down.

"Bourne!" Sam whispered, but Isobel dug her nails into his wrist and shook her head no.

"No," she whispered. "No."

"No?" Sam looked at her, and her face was white in the starlight, and then back at the figure.

"Oh, Petty," he whispered. "Oh, no. What's *this*?"

It was not Major Bourne. It was not even Diamonds Mrs Drake, or Clara, or whichever they had thought she was. It was Trimlingham's manservant.

His hair was very black, and his clothes were very white. He looked like a photograph, and in his hand he was holding a torn piece of paper.

"Isobel," said Lettie, and reached out for her, and they were all three holding hands.

He said, "Horace?"

Horace twisted round and dropped off the ladder. The wind must have changed direction, carrying their words away from him, and his words to them, because they heard him say very clearly, "Huh?"

"He looks confused," said Lettie. "Oh, he looks so confused. What—"

The valet strode forward and grabbed Horace by the collar. He was holding the note in one hand and Horace by the other.

"I KNOW YOUR SECRET," he read, scornfully, from the note. "Every word spelled wrong. I NO YORE SEKRIT. You silly little boy." Isobel wasn't sure she had ever heard him speak before, but his voice was somehow familiar to her: rich and English and expensive and boyish. It sounded like a voice she knew, and she hung on to this as he was speaking: who is it? *Who is it?* Something was wrong again; like a dream, like sugar in the sun, everything was melting into new shapes.

Horace said, helplessly, "I'm good at spelling!"

"That," said the man with a sneer, "is rather beside the point. You've been taking Turkish delight from me all this time, and I suppose you just wanted more. Greedy, greedy little boy."

"Turkish delight," whispered Sam, thoughtfully and

low into Isobel's ear. "Turkish delight?"

"I didn't," said Horace. "I didn't from *you*."

But the man wasn't listening. He held the note up and hissed close into Horace's face: "What's this?"

"That wasn't even for you," said Horace. "That was for—"

"Blackmail, is it?"

"I don't know what that is," said Horace. He tried to get away, but the man had both hands on his shoulders. "I don't know what any of that *means* actually."

"Blackmail, my boy, is when you attempt to extort money from me in exchange for keeping my secrets."

"I don't know what you mean," said Horace.

The man reached for something in his pocket. "Recognise this?" he said to Horace.

In their hiding place, Isobel and Lettie both gasped and clapped a hand to their mouths. Sam sat very still.

"I found this notebook on deck when I came up here just after supper," he said. "I haven't had time to read it properly, but rest assured, I will. I'll know exactly what you know soon, no note needed. No more sweeties, either. But I've looked at it. Oh, I've looked at it all right. Detective work, is it? I don't know much about children, and I would have thought you were too young to write this sort of rubbish, but since you're the person who left this note on the floor by my cabin…"

"I dropped it!" Horace said quickly. "It wasn't for you!"

"Damned right it wasn't for me," the man said. "Practise saying that, because I know it couldn't possibly have been for me. I have no secrets. Do you understand me? Whatever you think you saw, you saw nothing."

"I did see nothing!" said Horace.

"He's so frightened," whispered Lettie. "Can we just—"

"Wait," said Sam. "If it looks really awful we'll charge in, but he's very tall, and we're not."

"I heard you at dinner," said the man. "Maybe you'll be good. If I give you sweeties. All I've given you is sweeties. I've been very, very kind to you. Haven't I?"

"But I don't even *know* you!" said Horace, struggling. Then he paused and looked hard at the valet. "Do I? You look like… You look … funny…"

"No," said the man swiftly. "That's right. You don't. You don't know anything that you think you know. This notebook is full of rubbish. You know nothing. You saw nothing."

"I don't know nothing!" said Horace, feebly.

"Let me make it very clear to you, young man, that I have no idea what you're talking about. I don't know what you mean. I don't know what 'sekrit' you could possibly mean – and I suspect you don't, either. Do you understand?"

He shook Horace by the lapels, and Horace was as pale as a ghost. Then he lifted him off the ground, still by the collar of his coat. They heard Horace choke back a sob.

"He's trying to be brave," Lettie said, and her face was white too.

"Nobody will ever believe you," the man said to Horace. "Nobody. Will ever. Believe you. And do you know why?"

Dangling in the air, Horace tried to shake his head.

"Nobody will ever believe you, because if you try to tell them anything, you'll be at the bottom of the sea. Do you understand?"

Horace tried to nod.

"And do you know what else?"

Shake of the head.

"I should say, who else? Do you know who else? Your precious sister. Think of that, Master Hartington-Davis. Your lovely sister in the sea and I shall tell them you were both playing on deck. Everyone on this ship knows you children are menaces. An accident was bound to happen. This is a mail ship, did you know that? The safety barriers aren't nearly as high as on an ordinary passenger ship. What a very real tragedy: two children drowned. Better make a law against mail ships. I shall testify to that effect. If you say one single word of these lies to anyone else. Better safe, after all, than sorry.

"You keep your horrid mouth shut," he continued coldly. "You keep your horrid little mouth shut, and no harm will come to you. I've no wish to harm a child, but a blackmailer deserves what's coming to him. I suggest you go straight to bed and say nothing to anyone. Do you understand?"

Horace nodded.

And then he dropped Horace, hard, on to the floor and strode away, still holding the notebook, back across the deck, and back down into the belly of the ship.

Chapter Twenty-Four: What Horace Knew

Week 3, Day 2, extremely early
The Libyan Sea

They ran to him. He clung to Lettie like a little monkey, and between them they half carried, half dragged him into HQ.

"Snakey," said Horace. His voice was very shaky. "What is it under here?" He looked about him.

"It's our headquarters," said Sam. He looked at Isobel and Lettie. "We should let him in now. He's earned it. You've earned it," he said to Horace. "Have some condensed milk. It's good for shock."

He speared a can open and gave it to Horace. "Finger in, finger in mouth, repeat. Dip and lick. Be careful of the sharp edges. And welcome to our detective headquarters."

"Detective is what – what he said," said Horace, when he had eaten half the can. He was even stickier than before.

"What the valet said," said Sam. "Yes. Which means the valet is in league with Major Bourne."

Lettie and Isobel nodded, but Horace looked confused.

"Major Bourne?" said Horace. "He wasn't on deck."

"We're investigating a murder," said Isobel, before Lettie could stop her. "And Major Bourne did it. That's why he's been so cross; you must have seen—"

"No, it isn't," said Horace, briefly.

They looked at him in amazement.

"He's cross cos he hasn't got any more sweets," said Horace, and Lettie sighed.

"Grown-ups don't care about not having sweets," said Lettie.

"Not for *him*, silly," said Horace. "For *me*."

"For you?"

"I said he should buy me sweeties when we got into port," said Horace. "Or I would tell rude things I knew about him to everyone."

"What?!" said Lettie.

"What?!" said Isobel.

"What did you know?" said Sam.

"I saw him kissing a lady," said Horace.

"Diamonds Mrs Drake!" said Lettie.

Horace screwed up his face. "Not the *diamond* lady, silly. The other one."

"The maid!"

"Nooooo!" said Horace, as if they were being obtuse. "The Frenchie lady in the purple dress. But then the next day he was talking to a different purple Frenchie lady! And I said I would tell the other purple lady that I saw him being rude with the other purple lady. Or the diamonds lady."

"Oh, goodness," said Lettie. She put her head in her hands.

"So that's why he's cross," said Horace. "He kissed all the ladies and I said I would *tell* if he didn't get sweeties for me and he said he *would* get sweeties but then he never. So then I still wanted sweeties." He looked at them cunningly for a second. "What'll you give me if I keep telling you all the things I know?"

"Eat your condensed milk," said Sam. "We haven't got anything else. And this is important. What happened next?"

"I still wanted sweeties," said Horace, with an appraising look at Sam. "I still wanted sweeties, and I thought if it works with Major Bourne it will work with Trim, too. Trim is nice, and he has lots of sweets. He give me a whole bag earlier, cos I said I Will Tell If

You Don't, even though I didn't have anything to tell about. And he said Oh OK and I said More? And then he said When We Go On Deck Later. But then—"

Horace's face crumpled, but they weren't really looking at him. They were looking at each other.

"Go on," said Sam, in a strange, quiet voice. "Go on talking, Horace."

"But then," said Horace. "But then it wasn't Trim at all. It was his valet, and the valet said he give me Turkish delight earlier, but he never. And then he was horrible."

"He was horrible," said Isobel, in the same faraway voice as Sam. "He was horrible, and he said he gave you Turkish delight, and he said it in a voice I knew. And I've never heard Trim's valet – or the person I thought was Trim's valet – say anything."

It was all getting mixed up in Isobel's mind now: all the people, melting into one.

"We saw the valet coming in from the deck," said Isobel. "Then we saw Lord Trimlingham at breakfast. Have we ever seen them together? Since they came on board?"

"We've never seen them in one place," said Lettie.

"Because they're one person," said Isobel. "The valet and Trim. Trim and the valet. Trim killed his valet—"

"Or, more likely, the manservant killed Trim." Sam was sitting up now. "The Defenestration of the Discount Viscount!"

He was thinking in headlines, Isobel thought, and that was a good sign. Then he took out his pipe and tapped it on the floor, and so was that. Horace was watching him with interest. He yawned a big yawn, and tucked himself up at the end of the lifeboat. It was the quietest Isobel had ever seen him.

"What's defenestration?" Isobel was sitting now with her knees under her chin. She wished she had a notebook to write this down in.

Sam frowned. "It's actually means 'being thrown out of a window'. But I think you can use it for being thrown off a ship, don't you?"

Isobel shrugged. "It isn't accurate," she said. "But it doesn't matter. The manservant – Jamal – killed Trim and took his place. For the money. He threw him overboard and took his place."

But Lettie was shaking her head. "We would have noticed," she said. "More to the point, Mummy would have noticed." She looked quickly at Horace, who was asleep. She said, quietly, "Mummy is paying a lot of attention to Lord Trimlingham. She always pays attention to rich people, and she noticed him the minute we got on board. She simply would have noticed if he had changed into being a servant after the first week."

"Did you notice anything about Lord Trimlingham?" said Sam. "Anything different? Between – what was it? Day seven and day eight?"

They thought about it. "They didn't look alike at all," said Lettie.

"Didn't they?" said Isobel. "Listen!" They looked at her. "Listen. It's true that Trim's got a moustache, and all that fair hair like Lettie; and Jamal doesn't have a moustache and his hair is all sort of flat and black. Trim's got his glasses, so you can't see his eyes. And of course Jamal is Indian, and Trim is English. But they aren't really that *different*. Same height, I think. Same weight. You could—"

"You could fake a moustache," said Sam. "You could fake glasses. And I suppose the hair could be a wig."

"But a wig would have blown off," said Lettie. "You can *tell* a wig. In a way it would be easier to fake it the other way, from fair to dark—" She stopped suddenly and grabbed at Isobel's arm. "Isobel! There was something!"

"Something?"

"Between day seven and day eight. You saw it, you saw it too. We saw it together. He came into breakfast

– Trim, I mean – and there was something…"

"I don't think I saw it," said Isobel.

"You did, though," said Lettie. "You absolutely did. If I can just remember what it was, you'll remember it too. There was something—"

And suddenly, dimly, Isobel did remember. There was something there – something she had said to Lettie, or Lettie had said to her, like shapes in the mist, the morning after it happened, before they had been friends. (Were they friends now? Isobel thought to herself in surprise. Was that what they were?) But she had said – or Lettie had said – something? Something about the viscount? He had been different – or there had been something different about something about him…

"There *was* something," she muttered under her breath, and closed her eyes to try to remember. "There was, Lettie, you're right…"

"I know I'm right," said Lettie, but she didn't sound cross – only pleased Isobel had remembered too.

"I said something, or you did—"

"You said something, or I did—"

They were sitting very close to each other, like they were thinking with one mind.

"We got up—"

"You were horrible—"

"You were lazy, still in bed—"

"You'd been out on deck all night—"

"So had you—"

"Only for part of it, and only following you—"

"And then we were getting up and your mother came in to plait your hair—"

"Yes, and you were horrible about that too—"

"Well, nobody plaited my hair. Nobody does plait my hair."

"We know," said Lettie. "We can tell."

"Don't start," said Sam. They both turned and looked at him sharply, as if they had forgotten he was there, and he flushed. "Sorry. I didn't mean to interrupt."

"Thank you," said Isobel, and she meant it.

"So we went to breakfast," said Lettie.

"We went to breakfast and we saw Lord Trimlingham—"

"But if you saw Lord Trimlingham, he couldn't have been dead."

"No," said Lettie. "But—"

"But he *did* look—"

"He looked different," said Lettie.

"He *did* look different," said Isobel.

"Different like he was a different man?" said Sam.

301

They both shook their heads.

"It was definitely him," said Isobel, and Lettie added, "It was absolutely him."

"So he couldn't have been dead, so that rules him out."

Isobel's head was still leaning against Lettie's, and their hair was tumbling together, thin and dark and thick and fair. She felt suddenly very sleepy and sad, but in the middle of the sleepiness and sadness was something else: some spark.

"There was something to do with his hair," said Lettie. "Something about him not having shaved. And something – something black…"

"Something black *in his hair*," said Isobel, and Lettie said, "Horace's boot polish…"

"And the purser said someone was using all the hot water," said Isobel. "They were having to heat more water than usual because of one of the passengers."

"He was washing his hair," said Sam. "He was going from fair to dark, like Lettie said. He was using the boot polish to darken his hair and slick it down. Taking off his glasses to be Jamal – remember, how he was peering at the books? He couldn't see them without his glasses. And the moustache – the moustache must be fake too. Only that morning – we'd already seen Jamal,

302

remember? Going up on deck with the cushions. He must have had hardly any time. So he didn't get it all off properly."

"And I've never heard Jamal speak, really," said Isobel. "Only nodding."

"And nobody," said Lettie, "really looks at servants…"

"But why would he kill his servant?"

"Perhaps he saw something he shouldn't have," said Lettie. "Another murder. Or he saw him cheating at cards."

"He doesn't play cards," said Isobel. "He spends all his time thinking about space. He wants to go to the moon. He's crazy."

"Crazy people do murders," said Lettie. "All the time. Especially if they are crazy about something, like Hugo – I mean Lord Trimlingham – is about the moon."

It was the first time they had said his name since they had thought of it. It made the lifeboat feel very flimsy and small, and Isobel wished she hadn't.

"That's true," said Sam. He hesitated. "But besides … I don't know what either of you know about trials." They shook their heads. "Well, it's not always exactly fair. Sometimes English judges don't think English people can have done crimes."

"Lots of people go to prison," Lettie objected.

"Sometimes English judges don't think English people can have done crimes in India," said Sam, carefully. "Sometimes they don't think that English people should get blamed for it. And so. Well. What I mean is, why would Lord Trimlingham go to all this bother to murder Jamal in a secret way when he might well have got away with it anyway?"

"Surely if they saw him push him overboard they would arrest him," said Lettie.

"A murder murder, maybe," said Sam. "But he could have made it look like an accident. Nobody bothers much about servants who die. Do you even know the name of your servants who died, Petty?"

"What?"

"Your ayah. Your khitmutghar. Your dirzi, your dhobi. Your punkah wallah and panee wallah and chuprassi. Your boy who did your horses. Your man who did the washing-up." He fired these at her like accusations. "Nobody cares about the servants. You didn't."

Isobel felt very sick. "I'm sorry," she said, uselessly, and he shrugged.

"It's just how it is," he said. "One day it will be different. One day it won't be this unfair. You didn't notice. You didn't ask. People don't. It doesn't matter just now. But why, why do it like this?"

"Perhaps he wasn't a servant, then," said Lettie. "Perhaps—"

And then Isobel remembered: the scent of vanilla, thick and oppressive, and everyone talking at once, and out of the long-ago dinner-time babel she found the sentence she was looking for.

"Older brothers take precedence over younger brothers," she said, and they looked at her, bemused. "Older brothers sit closer to the viceroy than younger brothers. Older brothers inherit. I heard them talking about it at dinner: your mother and Trimlingham." She stumbled a little bit over the last word.

"The trouble with the will," said Lettie.

"The money trouble," said Isobel. "He needed money for space. And when they were talking about why he went to India, they were talking about brothers, and sisters, and who inherits estates, and an error."

"An error," said Sam, thoughtfully. "An error in the will. And the will was in the papers because of it."

"Did you see the will, Lettie?" he said, and Lettie screwed up her face, trying to remember. It was a thousand years ago, in Calcutta.

"Something about – about the only son," she said, and then, "No! The *oldest* son."

"But there was only one son," said Sam. "Trim's an only child, like me. He told me."

"What if he wasn't?" said Lettie. "What if there was a son in India? Older? What if—"

"Oh, no," said Sam. He looked crestfallen. "Are you seriously saying…"

"Yep," said Lettie.

"Yes," said Isobel. "Even me. Even I'm saying it."

"A long-lost mysterious brother?"

"A long-lost mysterious brother!" said Lettie, and she grinned at them like someone who has just worked out that all the stories are true, and not at all like someone unmasking a murderer. "A long-lost mysterious brother for real!"

Chapter Twenty-Five: Because That's What People Do
Still Week 3, Day 2, extremely early
Still the Libyan Sea

But Isobel thought of the wild joy in Hugo Trimlingham's eyes when he looked at the stars, and when he talked about the stars, and she was afraid again.

"He made a promise," she said. "He made a promise to help the man with the space vehicle. He wouldn't let anything stop him. He wouldn't let anything get in his way. That's why … that's why we have to stop him. I don't think he thinks he's even done something wrong. I don't think he'd mind doing it again. He made a promise."

"Remember? He *just had to go to India to solve the problem*," said Lettie, softly. "And the problem was his brother."

"If he'd just stayed in India," Sam said. "Surely

nobody would have known he was the brother."

"What if ... what if he knew he was the brother?" said Lettie. "What if the brother – Jamal – was in India, and he knew his father was in England? Like we know our father is in India. There's lots of people with fathers in different countries. That's just part of the problem of these modern times," she said. It came out rather pompously, and she looked embarrassed. "Well, you know what I mean."

"We know what you mean," said Sam.

"His brother knew he was the brother, and he knew his father was in England, and that his father died—"

"Because it was in all the papers," Isobel said. Lettie nodded.

"He knew his father died, and he was going to England to take the money," said Sam.

"And he couldn't let that happen, because of the stars, and the moon man, and the galactic vehicle," said Isobel.

"And the promise," said Lettie.

"And the promise," said Sam.

Isobel was thinking of something. "He was in the corridor talking to the captain," she said, dreamily.

"What?"

"He was in the corridor, looking for— Horace!" said Isobel.

Horace woke with a start.

"Looking for Horace?" said Lettie.

Isobel shook her head. She said, and her voice was shaky with excitement, "What's in your pockets, Horace?"

"All sorts," said Horace, sleepily. "Some good string. Some money I got. It all got a bit melty with my bit of boot polish."

"And a good stamp," said Isobel.

"An' a good stamp," said Horace. "I found that. You can't have it," he added quickly.

"Can we just look at it?"

"You can look at it," he said. "But you can't have it. I've got to soak it off the envelope. Mummy says there'll be a boy at school who can teach me. For my album."

"You've got the whole envelope?" said Isobel. Her cheeks were bright pink with excitement. "Most of it," said Horace. "It's quite black, but it's OK, I think."

"What good will an envelope do?" said Lettie.

"He went to ask the captain if it had been found," said Isobel. "Right at the beginning. When we were going to ask if anyone was missing."

"So it can't be just any envelope. Why would you ask the captain if he'd found just any envelope?" said Sam.

"The addresses," said Isobel. "You have to put the return address on the back when you post things from India to England. That's just what you have to do. You put where it's going to on one side, and where it's from on the other."

Horace was digging in his waistcoat pockets. He was dropping things – cogwheels, the sugar mouse (now missing both back legs and all its nose), the string, the coins in their twist of paper – on the deck of the boat. Isobel held her breath.

"Aha!" said Horace, and handed something white – smudged with black, but still readable – to Isobel.

It was a whole envelope, missing only one corner. It was addressed to Hugo Trimlingham of Trimlingham Hall.

"Turn it over," said Sam. "Turn it over carefully so the blasted boot black doesn't get on any more of it."

She turned it over, and there it was. "J. E. Trimlingham," she read aloud, and they stopped and stared at each other like they had never thought that any of this might be real at all.

"J. E. Trimlingham," said Sam, softly. "Jamal

Trimlingham. Two of them. A long-lost mysterious brother! Like in a real paper!"

"Who's a mysterious brother?" said Horace. "Is it me?"

"You're not mysterious," said Lettie swiftly.

"I wrote mysterious notes," said Horace.

"You did," said Sam. "And you gave us the final clue."

"Clue to what?" said Horace.

"Go back to sleep," said Lettie.

"Jamal Trimlingham, Trimlingham Accounting, 17 Curzon Street, Calcutta," read Isobel.

"Accounting!" said Sam. "Not a servant!"

"Not a servant," said Lettie. "Not a servant at all. A man coming to England to get what was left to him. So why did he get on the ship as a servant?"

"We won't find that out in a clue," said Sam, glumly. "That's motive. And we can't hope to find any more letters. He destroyed the letter and lost the envelope."

"And we can't ask Jamal, because Jamal is dead," said Lettie.

"But we can ask Trimlingham," said Isobel, as if it made perfect sense. "There's four of us, and one of him. We could go, now. We could make him confess."

They stared at her.

"Make him confess?" said Sam.

"But we couldn't," said Lettie.

"Oh, we could," said Isobel.

"Confess what?" said Horace. "And what's 'confess' anyway?"

"Confess means tell us what he did," said Isobel, carefully. "I think he'd tell us what he did."

"But why?" said Lettie.

Isobel thought about it. "He just will," she said. Then she said, "People like to talk. Trimlingham likes to talk. He told us all lots of things he didn't need to tell us, like about space, and he left a lot of things about like the Turkish delight and the envelope and the boot blacking, and he told Horace things."

"What things?"

"If he hadn't threatened Horace, we'd never have known for sure. We might have worked it out. We had the clues – some of them – but we would still be following Major Bourne about if he hadn't told Horace to meet him on deck. Our names are in the notebook – or mine is, anyway. He'll find me. He'll ask me what I know, tomorrow. I know that. He wants to talk about it," said Isobel. "People always do, somehow."

"How do you know?" said Lettie. "This is your first murder case. You can't possibly know."

Isobel thought about that, too.

"I know," she said, after a bit, "because that's what *people* do. And people aren't different when they do murders than they are at any other time. Not really. It's all the same set of things. They get cross, and they want things, and they need things, and they want to talk to each other. You can see it: it's like a pattern. It's like a dance, sort of, the way people are with each other. And – and I don't think like people, really. Not like most people anyway. I think in a different sort of way, and all the rules that people have don't really make sense to me, unless I try hard and write it all down. And that means I can sort of – sometimes – see what people are going to do, because people follow the rules, and I had to learn all the rules. It's not that I'm better, or that I'm worse. It's just different. I just think about things differently, I think. So I can see it. It's a bit difficult to explain."

"I think I understand," said Sam.

"I don't understand at all," said Lettie. She hesitated, and put her hand briefly on Isobel's arm. "But I do – I do trust you, Isobel."

"We all trust you, Petty," said Sam. "How extraordinarily lucky we are that you can see it all. Imagine! Imagine if we didn't have you."

"Do you – do you think we should go and ask him,

then?" said Isobel, and her heart was singing.

Sam nodded, and Lettie nodded, and Horace said, "You're not going to leave me out *again*?" in such a plaintive way that they all laughed.

"We had better leave a note or something," said Sam. "Just in case. That's what they do in the books."

"I haven't any paper," said Isobel. She thought with a pang of her notebook.

"I have," said Horace. He produced from his capacious pockets a piece of paper – torn from the handbook – and a blotchy pen. Isobel wrote, carefully, in her best handwriting:

To Whom It May Concern:

We have gone to confront the murderer Hugo Trimlingham. We saw him murder his brother Jamal Trimlingham, who came on board posing as his servant for

"Put 'for reasons currently unknown'," said Sam, and so she did.

reasons currently unknown. We saw H.T. push J.T. overboard in the Indian Ocean, on the night of 14th November 1892, at about midnight. We know it was H.T. who did it because he has been dressing up as J.T. every day since, and using boot blacking to make his hair shiny and washing it off (you can ask the purser about the person using up all the hot water). He cannot see very well without his glasses and he has to look closely at things. His moustache is a fake but his hair is real (you can tell because it does not blow off). Also he threatened Horace with being pushed overboard too (but that was a mistake because of complicated reasons). Also he always carries about Turkish delight and he dropped some that night (evidence eaten by Isobel Petty and Sameer Khan by accident). H.T. pushed J.T. overboard because J.T. knew that he (J.T.) was the oldest son of old Lord Trimlingham, who died and left all the money. H.T. wanted the money for himself so he went to India and somehow got J.T. to come with him and then he killed him. We don't know all the answers yet but that is why we are going to ask H.T. about these things but if you go to see a murderer it is important to tell someone where you have gone in case you get murdered too. Thank you. Sorry for being a nuisance, especially to Major Bourne, who just wanted to find a wife.

"Put 'yours faithfully' because we don't know who is reading this," said Lettie. "That's proper."

So Isobel wrote:

Yours faithfully, on the 23rd day of November 1892,

Horace Dignity Hartington-Davis
Letitia Lucrezia Hartington-Davis
Sameer John James Khan
&
Isobel Mary Petty

"Can I?" said Lettie, and Isobel passed her the pen. She signed it, and wrote – in surprisingly untidy handwriting:

P.S. Love to Mummy and Daddy. I didn't want to bring Horace but he got mixed up in it and I couldn't leave him out again, he would have minded.

Isobel and Sam both nodded. Then they signed it, and they gave the pen to Horace to sign too.

"We should have known that no grown-up could write that badly," said Lettie, surveying his writing. "Even with their wrong hand."

"Where shall we leave it?" said Lettie.

"On your mother's bed, I should think," said Isobel. "That's where she thinks we are. That's where she'll come and get us in the morning, when the cachet wears off."

"Well!" said Sam. "That's that."

"That's that," said Isobel.

And then they stood up – all four of them – and went into the dark to meet a murderer.

Chapter Twenty-Six: Like The Earth From The Moon
Week 3, Day 2
The Sea of Sicily

And Isobel was right.

It was one of the strangest things that had ever happened to her, until then, and it was something she never forgot for her whole life. It was the first time she had looked at the lines of a story, and followed it right to the end. It wasn't like an imagination. It was the opposite of an imagination. It was simply looking at things, and naming them, and knowing them for what they were. It was working out what was going to happen. It was looking at people properly; it was looking at everything properly; and it was like flying. It was like being among the stars, like walking on the moon, and looking at everything on the earth laid out before you, and she understood, when it happened to her, why Hugo Trimlingham had wanted it so much.

She understood that if you had thought of seeing the world from such a great distance, and seen the people from such a great distance, and seen their movements planned out as if you were outside time, you would do almost anything to have it; and more than that she understood that once you had dreamed of something like walking on the moon you could not leave it alone; and she knew then (and forever after) that she would not have been able to give it up for anything, either.

It made her gentler with him, this thought, than the others could understand, It was like the way that she and Sam had understood that Lettie could not grasp what it was like to not have a mother: there were some things too hard to teach, and which should not be taught.

And it was for this reason that it was Isobel who spoke first to the murderer Hugo Trimlingham, and perhaps it was for this reason that he spoke to her. Perhaps he saw that she understood him, in a strange sort of way. Perhaps he saw that here was a child of eleven who understood about the stars without ever having dreamed of the stars herself; and here was a child of eleven who understood that sometimes people do things that they themselves don't understand.

She felt very old just then, and very quiet, and very strange.

She knocked on the door of Hugo Trimlingham's stateroom.

He said "Hallo?" in a surprised way, and he sounded like Trimlingham: tanned and happy Trimlingham, who had danced with Mrs Colonel Hartington-Davis and promised to show them the stars. It was almost as if he was two different people: the man who had been so angry and so alarming on the deck, who had hurt Horace and threatened to hurt Lettie, who had pushed his own brother into the ocean – and this man. How could one person be so many people? How could all people be so many people? It was so strange, Isobel thought, so strange and so important to know.

She knocked again.

"Who the devil is it? I'm busy," and now he sounded a little more unnerved.

"It's Isobel Petty," she said, quietly, and then the door swung open, and there he was. He was wearing striped pyjamas, and his face was bare, with no moustache, and his hair wet and flopping over his glasses where he had washed out the boot polish and combed out the curl by accident. In one hand he held her notebook, and in the other he was holding a very nearly empty bottle of wine.

"I think you'd better come in," he said. "Oh, there's more of you. More children. More children. Wonderful. Wonderful. Just what I needed. I might be dreaming, you know."

"You might be," said Isobel.

"Don't lock the door," said Sam quickly. "There's more of us than there is of you, and although we're not uncommonly strong I think probably we could get out if we needed to."

"You're children," said Hugo Trimlingham. "What could you do?"

"I've got a penknife," said Sam. "You can't murder all four of us."

"A penknife! Well, goodness. I shan't lock the door. I've sunk pretty low, but I don't think murdering four children would help me much."

They came in, and he sat in the armchair by the porthole. The moustache was sitting on the arm of it, like a little animal. It had gum on one side of it, for sticking it on. He drank the end of the wine from the bottle and opened a second one with a great flourish. "None of you? You're all too young, even in a dream," he said.

Sam and Lettie, holding Horace tightly, stood by the door, but Isobel sat on the bed and looked at him. It was interesting, to look at a murderer.

"It's funny," he said, looking at Horace. "I really did think you were the one doing this detecting business. I should know more about children, shouldn't I? You're too young to have done this. Although I would have said the same about the rest of you, too. You, boy, maybe... I remember being twelve. Twelve? Eleven?"

"Eleven," said Sam, guardedly.

"Yes. I should have pegged you for the ringleader. For the – what d'you call him? Holmes."

"I'm Holmes," said Isobel quickly.

"You're Holmes!" And then the murderer started to laugh, and it was quite a nice laugh, really. It was only not a nice laugh because it was the kind of laugh that had killed someone, and threatened to kill two more of them – both of them in the room – and might threaten to do anything else at any time. "Of course you are. Of course you are, Isobel Petty, of the notebook fame. PRIVATE PROPERTY OF ISOBEL PETTY in very neat lettering on the back cover. I didn't see that until I looked at it properly. I was going to have to come and collar you after breakfast and find out what you knew, but you didn't seem to know enough to make a case."

"We didn't," said Isobel. "Not really. Not until we saw you threaten Horace. The note was meant for us, you know."

"I know," he said. "I knew that as soon as I'd looked at Horace on the deck. But I had to go through with it. I was sort of doing an impression of an old schoolmaster of mine. Frightfully horrid. But what could I do? I thought he knew. And, as it turns out, someone did know. But it was you, all along."

"That was what I was going to say," said Isobel. "It was you, all along."

Trimlingham shrugged, and for a moment she thought he might deny it. He took a big drink from his bottle of wine.

"You look quite a lot like your brother," said Isobel. "I am a noticing person, and I didn't notice you were only one person until tonight. It was the hair and the glasses. It makes people not notice."

"And the clothes," said Hugo Trimlingham, leaning forward. It felt like a strange spell had been cast on the room. "And the clothes. And the manner, and the running about, and the fact that nobody thinks that an Indian man and an Englishman could be brothers."

Isobel felt, rather than saw, Sam bristle. She did not have time; she could not break the spell by turning round. *Sorry, sorry, Sam*, she thought, and hoped he would hear it.

"But you were brothers," she said.

"So they say," said Hugo Trimlingham. "So he said. So my father said. He was married before, you know. Married before, in India, to an Indian lady who died. He came home, mad with grief, and married my mother. Awful fuss in the will. Awful. An elder son, when I was supposed to be an only child. I didn't know – imagine the shock."

"I can't," said Isobel, honestly.

"Then I thought nobody would notice, you know. Why would they go looking for another son? I said it was a mistake and everyone liked me so much. It helps to be handsome, you know. Well, you don't know. You're not handsome, are you? You've got bright little eyes but you're not pretty. It helps, I tell you." He was very drunk, Isobel thought, and that was good. That was good.

"I was handsome and charming and they all wanted it to be me," he said. "It was better that it was me. It was all going to be all right. I was going to make my promises come true. I promised them all the moon, you know. I promised them my fortune in exchange for the moon."

"I know," said Isobel, gently.

"And then he wrote to me. He said he knew. He said he knew I knew. He had a birth certificate – he sent me a copy of it. He had a marriage certificate. He sent me a copy of that too. He said things about what our father would have wanted. He didn't know – he didn't know anything. He said he would go to the papers if I didn't give him his money. He wrote a letter. Oh, a polite letter; a polite letter that crushed all my dreams. I knew then, you know," he said, staring at Isobel intently as if she would understand. He took another big gulp from his wine bottle and some splashed on to his pyjamas. It looked like blood.

"I know," said Isobel, again. "I know."

"So I went to his house," said Hugo Trimlingham. "His address was in the letter. He told me what I needed to know. I told him what I wanted him to know. I said that we could solve this in England. I said I had a passage booked in the name of my servant, and that if he came with me under this false name we could resolve this in England. I picked this boat for the observation deck. I knew nobody would wonder at my being out there at all hours, if I needed to. I came at this time of year, when the storms are high when they come. He looked just like my father," he said, suddenly. "Just like him. So do I. That made it harder, you know, but it had to be done."

"For the money?" said Isobel.

"Not the money," said Hugo Trimlingham scornfully.

He looked at her as if he was trying to explain something to her that he didn't know the words for, and for a moment she felt so sorry for him she couldn't breathe.

"I killed him for the stars," said Hugo Trimlingham, dreamily. "I killed him for the future. I killed him so that man could be like the gods."

"People shouldn't be gods," said Isobel. "Even if they want to be."

"No," said Hugo Trimlingham. "No. Perhaps not, Isobel Petty."

"Is this the end of it?" he said, and she saw that it had made him very tired, telling her this. It made him very tired to do it, and he was drunk.

"It could be an end of it," she said, carefully. "We can't not tell, and there's four of us. But you knew that, really. You knew that when you let us in."

"You were like things from a dream," he said. "You still are. Like little nightmare fragments. You aren't real people. You're some other kind of thing. Some kind of thing that sees. That's what I read in your notebook."

"I just like noticing things," she said.

"Noticing things! You see all the things, and you know what they are, and that's why you're a nightmare in my cabin now. That's why I let you in."

"Everyone can notice things," said Isobel. "It's just a matter of trying. That's all. Someone would have noticed in the end."

"In the end," he said. "If this is the end, you'd better do it. Go on. Get the captain, or whoever. Go now, before I change my mind."

He slumped back in his chair. He ran his hand across his forehead, and she saw with a shock there was a smudge of boot polish still at his hairline, and she thought of those hands tipping a person over the edge of a ship and into the sea in a storm, and she did not feel sorry for him then.

He closed his eyes.

She did not feel sorry for him at all, not then, and not later, when Lettie had gone, desperately and crying, out across the deck in the rain to fetch the captain with Horace in tow.

Not after that, when the captain had come, cross

and disbelieving, and they had told him all they knew; nor after that when she had seen Hugo Trimlingham carried off by the purser and the steward and the captain together to the German's old stateroom, cleared of papers.

She did not feel sorry for him when Mrs Colonel Hartington-Davis awoke from her sleeping tablet at the steward's knocking and the captain's explanations; she did not feel sorry for him when they sat in the captain's office, wrapped in blankets, explaining again; nor when Mrs Colonel Hartington-Davis, clutching the note they had left on the bed, fussed and worried and petted and cosseted; nor when Dr Khan, who had been working on a paper and had, in some very real ways, forgotten his son, came striding across the deck to the captain's cabin and swung Sam into his arms. She did not feel sorry for him when they were drinking the Swede's hot chocolate, and watching the sky lighten through the storm, and she did not feel sorry for him when the coastlines of Europe came into view, shifting and changing behind the clouds.

She did not feel sorry for him at all, and that was that, and that was all.

Epilogue

Week 3, Day 5
The English Channel

They were standing on the deck, the three of them. Lettie's arm was through Isobel's, and Sam's was over Lettie's shoulders. Everything was packed into trunks now, and the trunks stacked on the below deck, ready to disembark. On top of the stack of trunks you could see the six purple suitcases of the French sisters, with their gold monograms glinting. (The sisters had been very quiet after Major Bourne had announced his engagement to Diamonds Mrs Drake, and Mrs Drake had shone even more brightly than before.) The Swede's shabby little case had been packed into Doktor Weiss's enormous tin box, to make travel easier. Mrs Colonel Hartington-Davis had packed hers and Lettie's and Horace's things into one trunk, and Isobel's into another, and there had been nothing to say, so Isobel had said nothing, and without a word she and Lettie had suddenly run upstairs in their new coats to be completely by themselves with Sam.

"Aren't they white?" said Sam.

"Aren't they cold?" said Lettie.

The coast of England was made of chalk, Sam said. Chalk, and bones, and old things. It was all old, in England. "India is old," Isobel said, but Sam said it was different old.

"In books it is, anyway," he said, and they stood next to each other and looked at this strange, new, old, cold country before them. The sky over England was thick and grey, and they were wearing their coats. Isobel had never worn a coat this stiff before, and she felt safe in it. It was like armour, she thought. She could hardly bend her arms.

"But I liked him," said Lettie, suddenly. "He said girls could love stars." (They did not need to say who they were talking about. They knew.)

"I liked him too," said Sam. "He said he would show me the stars over Europe and how they were different to the stars in India."

"I don't think I liked him," said Isobel, suddenly. "I don't like most people. But I did understand him."

And she thought that perhaps that was better, in a way.

"You like us, though," said Lettie.

"You *absolutely* like us," Sam said. "You have to like us. We're an agency. We're a team. We're your people. We're – well, we're your friends."

"Well, *that's* true," said Isobel.

(And it was.)

Acknowledgements

I read many, many books and spoke to many people about the best way to write this story: too many to list, but I can tell you about them if you write to me. Thank you to all of them. Writing a book set in a really difficult, often distressing bit of history is much trickier than I first imagined, and I couldn't have done it without everyone's help. Special thanks to The National Maritime Museum for letting me look at the actual real handbooks.

I owe thanks at this point to many people, but first to Letitia Graham, for lending me her name; to Sameer Mohammed, for lending me his; to Alice (Olga) Cadwgan for hers and her love; and to Caroline O'Donoghue for hers, her love, and her constancy.

Thank you to Tash Hodgson, for lending her name, her strength, and her friends always.

(Thanks also to Adam Cléry, for being so willingly lent. I am pretty sure there is a reason I've written a book about two girls and a boy solving crimes next to the sea, and you two are it. (Any resemblance to persons living or dead is purely coincidental, &c. &c.))

Thank you to Tom Bonnick, who asked for this

book, and Daisy Parente, who read it first. Thank you particularly to my grandfather, Andy Maslen, who made this complicated book infinitely simpler by suggesting I set it on a mail ship (mail ship: thirty passengers; ordinary steam ship: three hundred) and to my mother, Nikki Risbridger, who put my first-ever copy of *The Secret Garden* into my sticky four-year-old hands.

This book is dedicated to two people I love with all my heart.

One of them is the aforementioned Lettie "Debo" Graham: Debo, this book is for you because you were my first try at having new friends in a long time. And this is (of course) really a book about how nice it is to have a friend. Thank you for being my friend when I needed one most.

The other one is my fairy goddaughter, Leila Abley. Ley, you have to share the official dedication with my friend Lettie (because I borrowed her name, so I owed her), but really we all know that I wrote this book for you. A lot of adults forget how important it is to be nine years old, and I am so grateful that with you around that would be impossible. What an interesting person you are, and how lucky we are to have you around. Thank you for always talking to me like there's a chance I'll understand.